Weddin

Wedding Bells at Villa Limoncello

DAISY JAMES

CANELO

First published in the United Kingdom in 2019 by Canelo

This edition published in the United Kingdom in 2022 by

Canelo Digital Publishing Limited
Third Floor, 20 Mortimer Street
London W1T 3JW
United Kingdom

A CIP catalogue record for this book is available from the British Library.

Print ISBN 978 1 80032 973 7
Ebook ISBN 978 1 78863 343 7

Look for more great books at www.canelo.co

Printed and bound in Great Britain by Clays Ltd, Elcograf S.p.A.

1

Chapter One

One Friday in Fulham
Colour: Magnolia

Izzie took a step back to cast a critical eye over the room she'd just finished styling. With the stark white walls of the newly-renovated property, and an employer who thought taupe was the ultimate in sophistication, she had done her best, but minimalism was an understatement! Her gaze fell on the beige linen curtains that matched the oatmeal cushions resting on the brown leather Chesterfield sofa and she cringed. Unfortunately, she'd forgotten to conceal her reaction from Jonti, her eagle-eyed colleague, who she could see was about to launch into another one of his eloquently crafted lectures.

'Darling, isn't it about time you chose your soft furnishings from a more vibrant part of the colour spectrum? I mean, ivory, chiffon and champagne maybe the go-to colours for a blissful wedding ceremony in St Paul's Cathedral, but this is Fulham! Now, I might not be a graduate of the Royal College of Art like you and Meghan, but don't you think a splash of Cambridge blue, or Venetian red, or my personal favourite, razzle dazzle rose, would spice up the ambience for potential buyers? Not to mention encourage them to fork out the exorbitant asking price our lord-and-master is demanding for this little piece of heavenly real estate.'

'I agree with Jonti,' declared Meghan, bursting through the front door with a tray of takeaway coffees and broadening the colour palette ten-fold. Izzie hadn't been expecting her best friend to arrive for at least another hour – Meghan always struggled to extract herself from the demands of her job as a window dresser at Harrods – and it was the first time in living memory she had been early for anything. She suspected foul play on Jonti's part. 'This place is snoring boring!'

'Snoring boring?'

'Yes! Dull, drab, characterless, bland…'

'Okay, okay, you've made your point,' laughed Izzie, reaching out to tweak a vase whose Chinese manufacturer had labelled 'frothy cappuccino' in the mistaken belief that an optimistic description would transform its basic shape into an upmarket work of art. 'However, I have to point out that this is Hambleton Homes' signature design.'

Of course, Jonti and Meghan were right to be disappointed with what she had created – the room was lacklustre by anyone's standards. Her professional eye told her that the beautifully apportioned property, with high ceilings, sculpted cornices, and chiselled ceiling roses that wouldn't have looked out of place in Versailles, was crying out for a magnificent crystal chandelier, and maybe even a bronze bust or marble statue or two.

'And Jonti and I have followed the brief to… the… letter!'

'That's because Darren Hambleton is a corporate dullard who wouldn't know taste if it rushed up and bit him on his Armani-clad buttocks. For God's sake, Izzie, have you forgotten that you used to own one of the most sought-after Interior Design studios in London with a client list the envy of Liberty's?'

'And what about that double-page spread in LuxeLife Magazine?' added Jonti, taking an experimental sip from his skinny latte before picking up the career-critique baton from Meghan. 'What did that feature writer with the movie-star good looks call you? You know, the one who fancied himself as the next Poldark? All tousled curls and rock-hard abs? It took all my self-control not to ask him where he'd left his scythe!'

'You mean Miles Carrington?' smirked Izzie.

'Ah, yes, Magnificent Miles. Now don't take this the wrong way, Izzie darling, but if he saw this dreary excuse for a living room he'd be forced to amend the effusive accolade he bestowed upon you from 'Isabella Jenkins, Queen of Colour' to 'Isabella Jenkins, Duchess of Dullness' otherwise he'd risk being sued for misrepresentation.'

Izzie shook her head. She'd heard Jonti and Meghan's complaints before – lots of times. But she had also learned that pleading the case for the defence would only prolong the discomfort currently swirling through her veins. There was no way she was about to admit that, uninspiring though it was, she actually preferred the predictability of Hambleton's design template because it cut down on the effort it took to be creative, something she was immensely grateful for. It was best to simply move the conversation on to the part where her friends shrugged their shoulders in resignation at another 'by-the-numbers' house staging so that they could launch into a blow-by-blow account of their forthcoming weekend shenanigans in the restaurants and nightclubs of Covent Garden.

Ignoring their raised eyebrows and exchanged glances, she began slotting the assorted accessories that made up the busy home-stager's armoury into her battered wheelie suitcase – industrial-sized scissors, Stanley knife, fishing wire, glue gun. Seeing everything returned to its allocated space helped to dissolve the anxiety that had been gnawing at her chest all afternoon. She snapped the lock shut, grabbed the handle, and made for the door, comforted by the fact that another job

3

had been completed on time, and that she had side-stepped another lecture on the merits of her personal development strategy.

Sadly, her relief was short-lived. Jonti took her hand, guided her towards the sofa and sat down, lacing his manicured fingers through hers whilst Meghan took a seat on the footstool in front of her, flicking her pink-tipped blonde hair over her shoulder and avoiding Izzie's eyes. Izzie's stomach dropped to her Sketchers like a penny down a well. Oh God!

'Guys, I know you mean well, but can we not do this right now? Come on, it's Friday night, let's wrap things up here and I'll buy you both a drink.'

'Sorry sweetie, Meghan and I have decided that enough is enough. Now, you know I love you, don't you? You guys are the best friends a man could ask for in this crazy metropolis we call home. But it's not just the décor that needs an injection of colour, Izzie. I'm no Marc Jacobs, but where *did* you get that sweater? Your grandmother? What colour is it supposed to be? Ecru? Khaki? Dishcloth? If you loiter for too long next to those curtains over there you'll disappear! I suppose that's the point, though, isn't it? Although, how you think you can possibly blend into the background with that delightful mane of Titian curls, I don't know!'

'Hey, I happen to like this jeans-and-jumper combo. It's warm, comfortable, practical...'

'What sort of words are they? Comfortable and practical? You sound like my great-aunt Marge – except even she has been known to flirt with the cosmetic geniuses of Yardley and Revlon every once in a while! I know you favour the pale and interesting look, and I totally get why you don't want to cover up that cute smattering of freckles with a mask of heavy foundation, but a little tinted moisturiser wouldn't go amiss occasionally!'

Izzie shook her head, her lips twitching at the corners. She felt like a naughty schoolgirl called into the headteacher's office to give an account of her sartorial sins. She adored Jonti – he was far more than a fellow purveyor of all-things fabric and sequin-related. With his quirky sense of fashion, from the orange winkle-pickers to the rainbow-framed glasses that enhanced his bright blue eyes and his signature bleached blonde quiff, he exuded a sense of style she'd long since discarded to the realms of a past life.

'Okay, okay, I promise to break out the scarlet lipstick and gold-flecked mascara when we partake in our usual pint of Guinness at the Hope & Anchor tomorrow night. Happy?'

'I'm not *un*happy.'

She made to get up from the sofa but was unceremoniously pulled back down. Clearly the lecture was not over yet. Now, it was Meghan's turn to assume the role of life coach.

'Unlike Jonti, I'm prepared to accept your new-found obsession with magnolia, your ever-lengthening 'to-do' lists, *and* your preference for hand-knitted garments that make you look like the Michelin Man, but when was the last time you ate a decent meal? Don't get me wrong, I love a round of buttered toast just as much as the next person, but not for every meal!'

'Meghan's right, darling. All that gluten is enough to make anyone's sparkle wither and die! My body is a temple and I just could not treat it with such disdain. How on earth do you manage to keep mind, body and soul together? I know you're not going to like me saying this, but I happen to think you've been looking a tiny bit peaky recently – like Eeyore's little sister at Winne-the-Pooh's going away party! I bet you're not sleeping properly either, are you?'

'I'm sleeping and eating just fine, thank you very much,' she lied, irritation beginning to poke its head above the parapet.

What did her diet have to do with anything? And so what if her sleep was frequently trampled on by the demons of the past? However, before she could express her indignation or make a humour-filled attempt to change the direction of their conversation to something less personal, Meghan was gearing up to launch her *coup de grâce*.

'And whilst we're on the subject of your love life…'

'My love life?' spluttered Izzie, feeling as though she'd just had a bucket of icy water tossed in her face.

'Yes, ever heard of it? When was the last time you had a date?'

'And don't try to fob us off with that old chestnut about still getting over Alex. It's been eighteen months since you guys split – you even like his new girlfriend, Perfect Penelope, whom I have to say is not a patch on you, darling. Did you see the cerise leopard-print heels she was wearing when we bumped into them at the Old Vic last month? So tacky! Although the same cannot be said for her delightfully fragrant brother Marcus – don't think I've seen biceps like that since I accidentally stumbled into the Fire Brigade's Boxing Club!'

'Jonti, off topic! Look, Izzie, all we're saying is why not take a leaf out of Alex's book and dip your toe into the shark-infested dating pool again? A little bit of romance is exactly what you need to unwrap that mantle of melancholy you insist on modelling whenever we go out!'

'Yes, sweetie, you need to break free of the past and get some music in your soul! Okay, lecture over, let's beat the post-work stampede and take a detour to that delightful little French bistro down the road and indulge in a bottle of fizz. My treat! I won't tell our slave driver of a boss if you don't?'

Jonti jumped up from the settee with a glint of schoolboy mischief lighting up his eyes.

6

'Best thing I've heard all day,' grinned Meghan, linking his arm as they made their way to the door. 'Come on, Izzie.'

Izzie heaved a sigh of relief that the sermon was over and was about to follow in their footsteps when her phone buzzed with an incoming text. She glanced at the screen and groaned. Was Darren psychic?

'Hang on – it's a text from Darren.'

'I thought he was showcasing his sporting prowess on the golf course this afternoon?'

Jonti's upper lip curled in disgust at another one of Darren's attempts to apply so-called 'progressive business practices' to Hambleton Homes' marketing strategy. Ever since Harry Hambleton, who had founded the business in the 1980s through sheer grit and determination, had given his son free reign to run the company, he'd been desperate to make his own mark. Unfortunately, dashing around town in his canary yellow Porsche, massaging egos and spouting corporate soundbites wasn't going down very well with many of their clients. Izzie knew that if Harry had any idea how Darren was conducting himself he would have ditched his extended sojourn in the Spanish sunshine and jumped on the next available flight back to London to remind his son that, in business, there was no substitution for hard work and integrity.

'He wants me to call him.'

'What now? It's five o'clock on a Friday!'

Jonti shook his head in irritation. He made no secret of his dislike of their new, fresh-from-business-school boss, although Izzie suspected it had more to do with Darren's enviable designer wardrobe and the fact that he smelled like a Parisian lady's boudoir than the new-style management techniques he had introduced to convince his father that the thousands of pounds he'd spent on his private education was money well spent.

'Why don't you and Meghan zip down to Pierre's and order the drinks. I'll catch you up in a few minutes.'

Unlike Jonti, Izzie did have some sympathy for Darren. It couldn't be easy stepping into Harry's shoes, not to mention coming to terms with his father's recent marriage to a woman the same age as Darren himself, especially after the death of his mother less than two years ago. She had personal experience of that kind of devastation and understood the impact it could have on anyone, no matter how privileged or comfortable their life was.

However, she also had a great deal of affection for Harry and was grateful to him for stepping into the breach with the offer of a position as a part-time house-stager when everything she knew and loved had crumbled around her ears. In another life, she had been commissioned by Darren's mother, Esme Hambleton, to completely refurbish their Knightsbridge townhouse after she'd read the feature in LuxeLife magazine. It was still one of the most enjoyable interior design projects she'd worked on and they had remained in touch until Esme had died suddenly, only six months later, which meant Izzie'd had two funerals to attend in the space of a few months.

'You go and grab a table, Jonti,' urged Meghan, pulling on the white denim jacket she'd hand-embroidered with crimson peacocks in preparation for the fifty-metre dash to the end of the street. 'Izzie and I will be right behind you. Shoo!'

Jonti rolled his eyes, planted noisy kisses on the two women's cheeks, and wriggled his fingertips. 'Later, peeps!' he said, as he set off down the street, a jaunty gait in his step. Izzie smiled, gratitude for his unwavering friendship encircling her heart as she turned back to Meghan.

'Okay, might as well get it over with.'

Izzie grimaced, eyeing her mobile as though it were a lethal weapon.

8

'Do not, under any circumstances, agree to work this weekend! I've got a hot date on Saturday night and I need you to help me with my buff-and-polish regime so that I sparkle like the diamond I am.'

'Who's the lucky man this time?' asked Izzie, knowing that Meghan fell in and out of love quicker than a Tigger does the Hokey-Kokey.

'He's a cameraman, worked on one of my brother's film shoots in the Caribbean last October. I met him again a couple of weeks ago at Suzie and Carlton's wedding – I'd forgotten he'd asked for my number. Oh, and don't get me started on the subject of my stupid, selfish brother! If Brad thinks I've got nothing else better to do than respond to his beck and call, then he's delusional as well as presumptuous!'

'What's he done this…'

'Anyway, whilst I've got you alone – you know what a huge gossip Jonti is – I've got another bit of amazing news. I only got the call this morning, and the whole thing is shrouded in absolute secrecy, but guess what? Giselle has broken her ankle and Martha, my department manager at work, has asked me to *compère* the Fenella Fratenelli fashion show next Monday night! It's a dream come true. Oh, not the ankle thing, obviously – I've started a collection to send Giselle a huge bouquet crammed with her favourite sunflowers – but I'm hoping to show Martha that there's more to my repertoire than dressing windows. God, Izzie, I'm just so excited. I adore Fenella's paisley jumpsuits, not to mention her pink shearling biker jackets!'

Izzie smiled, her heart ballooning with pride as she watched Meghan pogo on the spot like a toddler in need of the bathroom. It had been Meghan's dream for as long as she'd known her to make the move from creating stunning, if slightly avant-garde shop windows to staging cat-walk shows. This could be her big break.

'Oh, Meghan, I'm so thrilled for you. This calls for an extra-special celebration. Look, why don't you go and join Jonti. I'll finish up here, give Darren a quick call, and join you at Pierre's in ten minutes.'

'Okay.'

Meghan flung her arms around Izzie, then skipped out of the front door, her colourful hair flowing in her wake like a Medusa on steroids. Izzie shook her head as she selected Darren's number.

'Hi Darren.'

'Yo, Isabella!'

She grimaced at the familiar greeting and the mid-Atlantic drawl he affected, another trait at odds with his father. Harry Hambleton was proud of his Yorkshire roots and held no truck with people who put on airs and graces.

'What did you want to talk to me about?'

'Well… actually…' For the first time ever, Izzie heard Darren pause to inhale a deep breath before launching into his usual diatribe of corporate clichés. Looking back, she realised that his out-of-character hesitation should have set alarm bells ringing. 'I thought… well, there's no time like the present to bite the bullet. Your time is precious, my time is precious, so I'll just launch right in, shall I?'

A wriggle of unease tickled at her abdomen. 'What's going on, Darren?'

'So, as managing director of HH I've been doing a bit of blue sky thinking recently and it's time to raise the bar on everything we've been doing. I'm not sure if you've noticed but we're slap bang in the middle of an economic hurricane, so it's imperative that we push the envelope to come up with new and dynamic ways to eliminate waste and maximise profit. It's all about the bottom line, wouldn't you agree, Isabella?'

'Darren, what exactly…'

Her heartrate doubled as trepidation swirled through her body and the tight nugget of anxiety in her chest inflated. Whilst she had heard Darren's corporate sermons before, the fact that he was gabbling at a higher speed than usual meant she didn't have to be a contestant on Mastermind to realise he was building up to deliver bad news.

'We need to innovate to keep one step ahead of our competitors and so, moving forward, Hambleton's is ditching the sleek, clean lines of our current interior design template. Buyers don't need to be spoon-fed these arty-farty concepts. They need to know that they're not forking out for some pretentious Chelsea-type's vision and are bagging a bargain. That way it's a win-win. *I'm* not shelling out money on expensive paint and designer wallpaper and *they* know they're not being stung for useless tat that'll end up being tossed in the garbage can as soon as they get the keys. Who wants…'

Izzie could bear it no longer and a sudden surge of indignation gripped her body. She might have suffered a recent setback in her professional life, but she still believed in the positive impact good design principles brought to any building project. It was time to stand up to Darren and persuade him to consider an alternative future for Hambleton Homes. How was she to know that the director of fate had a thunderbolt tucked up her sleeve?

'Actually, Darren, I totally disagree. I've worked in interior design for over ten years now and research shows that a well-designed and presented property can increase the sale price by up to ten percent. Also, a high percentage of buyers appreciate the decorating suggestions – they might not have the time, or the vision, to make the most of a building's architectural attributes. I think…'

But Darren wasn't interested in listening to counter-arguments. He'd been repeating the words 'yes, yes, yes,' in an impatient monotone as he prepared to drop the bombshell on her already grenade-strewn world.

'So, it's nothing personal, you understand – hard decisions have to be made in business – but we've decided to dispense with your services. I'd like to take this opportunity to thank you for your invaluable contribution to…'

The force of the shock weakened Izzie's knees and she crumpled down onto the sofa. She gasped for breath as a concrete-heavy slab pressed the air from her lungs and a low buzzing sound reverberated in her ears, blocking out the finale of Darren's clearly rehearsed severance speech. However, as he continued with his diatribe of verbal misnomers, one thought did bob to the surface and a little of the old Izzie peered through the curtain of gloom.

'What about Jonti?'

Oh, God, she couldn't bear it if he lost his job too. Ever since he'd been kicked out of his parents' house in an affluent part of Cheshire, his father citing his choice of friends and unconventional lifestyle as justification, Jonti had been forced to couch-surf his way around the capital for months until he'd landed a part-time Christmas job at Harrods where he'd met Meghan. The two of them had clicked immediately and the rest was history. He'd moved into the spare room in the 1930s semi Meghan rented in Hammersmith and declared himself happier than he'd ever been, especially when Darren had offered him a few hours extra work to help Izzie whenever they needed to turn a place round quickly.

'I'll still use him on an ad hoc basis,' replied Darren rather too quickly.

Despite her own distress, Izzie experienced a surge of relief. She knew Jonti struggled to make his share of the rent. However, she wasn't completely stupid. She realised that the reason Darren was keen to retain Jonti's services had more to do with his generous sharing of his Harrods discount than his flair for interior design. Then something else occurred to her.

'Does Harry know about this?'

'I don't need my father's permission to make mundane personnel decisions!' snapped Darren, obviously offended by her question. 'Okay, must dash; things to do, people to bollock, if you get my drift. Your severance cheque's in the post. Ciao.'

An avalanche of emotions tumbled through Izzie's chest. Live cautiously was her motto; that way she would avoid getting hurt, but it was clear her strategy hadn't worked because once again life had conspired to toss another random grenade in her path.

Chapter Two

A tiny flat in Clapham
Colour: Raincloud Grey

Izzie had no idea how long she remained on that sofa in the sterile living room of what would be the last house she staged for Hambleton Homes, staring into oblivion like a gobsmacked goldfish – long enough for her bottom to turn numb, though. Eventually, she managed to pull herself together, lock the front door and drop the key through the letterbox, as per Darren's instructions, mentally crossing off the final box on her checklist.

As she tossed her suitcase into the boot of her sunshine-yellow Fiat 500, one of the few items she still owned from her previous life, she cast her eyes down the street towards the bright lights of the restaurants and bars welcoming in the exhausted office workers desperate for an injection of alcohol before braving the commute home. Despite growing up in the bucolic countryside of Cornwall, she was still able to appreciate the beauty of the capital's urban architecture, but that night its splendour went unnoticed because her head was spinning with a kaleidoscope of worries.

What was she going to do?

She decided that the last thing she wanted was to share her predicament with Jonti and Meghan. What had happened was not their fault and she didn't want her woes to spoil their

Friday night celebrations. She jumped into the driver's seat and joined the rush hour traffic, edging at a snail's pace towards the top-floor apartment she called home. Using the techniques that she'd learned when her business and relationship had failed, she managed to corral her emotions and resume control.

Control was good. Routine was good.

Only by adhering to a rigid routine, treading carefully, living as quietly and unobtrusively as she could, was she able to make it through to the end of each day. So, she got up at the same time every morning, dressed in the same Hambleton Homes T-shirt and hoodie, grabbed a flat white from the same coffee shop at the end of the road, and turned up at the designated property to stage another one of Hambleton Homes' clinical white boxes. Then, she would return home to her meticulously neat apartment – devoid of any personality or reminders of the past – and feast on a pile of buttered toast and another coffee, or, if she was feeling particularly indulgent, a bacon sandwich and a glass of inexpensive fizz, before pulling her duvet over her head and starting the whole process again the next day.

Over an hour later, Izzie arrived at her building feeling as if she'd just stepped from a ride on a rollercoaster – dazed, disorientated and a little nauseous. After the day she'd had, she wasn't surprised that there were no free parking bays and she spent another twenty minutes circling the streets until she spotted a miniscule space that took all her skill and concentration to reverse into. She wrestled her trunk from the boot, pulled on her hoodie, and began the lengthy walk back to her flat.

A splash of rain landed on the back of her hand, and, looking up at the heavily bruised sky, she received a generous dash of droplets for her trouble. Clearly the meteorological gods had had a bad day at the office, too, because they were in the process of gearing up to throw everything in their armoury at the already bedraggled Friday night commuters.

She began to jog, her head lowered against the sudden onslaught, her eyes smarting from the strength of the breeze slapping the rain against her cheeks and the toxic stench of the exhaust fumes from the stationery traffic. She raised her jog to a sprint, desperate to reach the sanctuary of her home where she could start to formulate a positive spin on the calamity that had befallen her before she called Meghan to explain why she hadn't turned up at Pierre's.

Could she brazen it out? Make up some excuse for not turning up at the wine bar?

Sadly, her guardian angel had packed her bags and flown off to sunnier climes because just as her glass front door came into view she saw her friend tumble from the back of a cab, shouting an energetic farewell to the taxi driver who gifted them both with a scowl despite the huge tip Meghan had pressed into his hands.

'Meghan, what are you doing here?'

'Well, Jonti and I were worried when you didn't turn up at the wine bar. We've been calling you and texting you, and when you didn't answer I volunteered to come over to make sure you were okay. Are you okay?'

'Let's get out of the rain first, eh?'

'No problem, you do look like a drowned rat! Hey, do you think that hunky Italian doorman with the come-to-bed eyes will be on duty tonight? I might just have to add him to my list of potential suitors. Don't you just love the way those guys exude a sexy Mediterranean vibe? Must be all the Chianti they drink!'

A sharp spasm of pain sliced through Izzie's chest at Meghan's casual reference to Italy. A crystal-clear image of a terracotta dome, a snippet of quick-fire Italian, and the

17

sharp tang of limoncello shot through her subconscious but she refused to allow her emotions to break free of their guy ropes and wreak havoc once again. Thankfully, she just had to laugh when she saw the disappointment flicker across her friend's face as the front door was whisked open by Albert – the building's septuagenarian doorman and metaphorical guard dog who was still going strong after forty years of dedicated service.

'Tea! I need tea!' announced Meghan, within seconds of stepping into Izzie's apartment. She dumped her turquoise satchel on the kitchen bench and set the kettle to boil before wrenching open the fridge door to look for the milk. 'Oh, my God! Does anyone actually live in this flat? There's nothing in here apart from… let me see; one, two, three, four, five bottles of prosecco and a tub of out-of-date butter! What do you eat?'

'Take-out,' Izzie muttered distractedly as she removed her clipboards from her duffle bag and slotted them, in order, into their allocated spaces on her floor-to-ceiling shelves.

'Take-out, my eye! You don't eat take-out! You hate take-out! You call it Devil's breakfast! Darling, there's nothing in the cupboards either!'

Meghan was now opening and shutting the kitchen drawers searching for a crumb to keep mind and body together at eight o'clock at night.

'There's a loaf of bread in the bread box over there.'

'Ergh, bread! Now that *is* a Devil's breakfast staple. So, black tea it is then.'

Watching Meghan clatter around her tiny kitchen alcove to prepare that universally acknowledged deliverer of solace, Izzie suddenly experienced the strangest of sensations; as though she were totally detached from her surroundings, floating high above a scene being played out below her. She surveyed her best friend from a neutral onlooker's perspective and decided that her choice of outfit matched her personality perfectly. White jeans that clung to her curves like a second skin, pixie-toed red suede boots, and a soft pink angora jumper that complemented that month's raspberry ripple hair-colour – another experiment by Jonti that hadn't turned out quite as expected but which Meghan had declared to be a fabulous success, choosing to wear a clashing satsuma kaftan for work the next day. Heaven knew what her boss Martha made of her sartorial craziness.

Izzie accepted a steaming mug of thick, dark tea and dropped onto the cream leather sofa, liberally scattered with Moroccan throws and sequined cushions – all of which had belonged to her past life when she had adored every colour in the rainbow. She hadn't been able to entertain anything so vibrant in her bedroom and so had relegated the hand-embroidered soft furnishings to the living room, along with the emerald silk curtains and the matching Persian floor rugs. Meghan joined her, curling her feet under her bottom and wrapping her fingers around her cup as she took a tentative sip, scrutinising Izzie from over the rim.

'Have you been crying?'

It was the sympathetic expression that did it for her every time. After two years, she could cope with most things except seeing the sadness her predicament instilled in others. That sympathetic look in the eyes, the head tilted to one side, the compassionate smile like the one that was currently scrawled across Meghan's face. Kindness; who would have thought that it was one of the toughest things to deal with?

'Izzie, what's going on? Is it to do with Darren? Come on, tell me before I spontaneously combust with curiosity!'

Izzie gulped in a lungful of air and garnered every ounce of courage she possessed. She knew that the sooner she pricked the expanding balloon of dread, the better she would feel.

'I've been fired.'

'Fired? Oh my God, is that what he wanted? And he did it over the phone? That man is an absolute moron! Does Harry know? There's no way he would fire you – Esme adored you.'

'Apparently hiring and firing is now Darren's domain.'

'What ridiculous garbage did he come out with this time? I bet the words *get-go* and *touch-base* came into it? He's a complete idiot, a walking cliché, a…' she stopped abruptly in her character assassination and softened her expression, a gesture that caused Izzie's heart to contract painfully. 'What are you going to do?'

'Look for another job, I suppose.' She shrugged, forced a smile on her face, and turned to face Meghan who she knew was hurting just as much as she was which caused another spasm of guilt to slice through her abdomen. She had to change the subject fast. 'Now tell me all about the fashion show. What are you planning for the…'

'Oh no, you're not getting away with that, madam. Have you forgotten that I know you better than you know yourself? That you're the Queen of Diversionary Tactics? Isabella Grace Jenkins, we've been best friends since art school and I can spot your shenanigans at twenty paces. We're going to talk this through until we've come up with a definite plan.'

Izzie groaned inwardly, chancing a quick glance at the door to her bedroom. She could almost hear the cool, calm sanctuary calling to her, and she experienced an overwhelming urge to escape into its orderly serenity. She just didn't have the energy to debate her future with Meghan at that moment. Then she recalled Jonti telling her that the best form of defence was attack, so she met Meghan's eyes and said, 'Well, if we're on the subject of avoidance…'

'You know, this could actually be a blessing in disguise,' interrupted Meghan, flicking her hair over her shoulder in a familiar gesture as she swivelled round to face Izzie.

'Really? Why?'

'You could use your redundancy money to take a break from the organised, over-scheduled, list-driven existence you call life and spend some time nurturing your emotional well-being. Why don't you go home to Cornwall for a few weeks? Relax, breathe in the sea air, indulge in some of that glorious seafood the county is famous for, catch up with a few friends?'

'You know I can't go home, Meg.'

She couldn't return to Cornwall, to stay in the bedroom she had shared with her twin sister, Anna, where they had taken the local High School by storm, their mischievous antics legendary with their friends for confusing the teachers, fooling them into believing that they were addressing the other sister when homework was late (always Anna's). No, despite the tentative steps she had taken towards acceptance of the way things were now, she wasn't ready to deal with her grief yet.

'Okay, well, if not Cornwall, then why don't you go up to Yorkshire? Mum would love to have you stay at the Stables. You could help Darcie and Fran with the horses.'

For the first time since Darren had dropped his bombshell, Izzie's lips curled at the corners at the look of abject disgust on her friend's face.

'Aren't we a pair of evasion junkies? Maybe we should both splurge a few pounds on a visit to that therapist your dad recommended?'

'It's my parents with the problem, not me! Why can't they just accept that not everyone's desperate to immerse themselves in an equine-filled lifestyle? Just because I grew up surrounded by the smelly, sweaty beasts does not mean I have to love them, or even like them! And anyway, Brad's the eldest

– it should be him who's fending off all the parental pressure, not me. Just because he's this 'award-winning' film director and I'm a lowly window dresser! It's so unfair! I love my career just as much as he does! Why would I want to live in a crusty old Barbour jacket and a pair of green Wellies and when I can float around in an array of wonderful designer clothes?'

'But how can they be expected to understand your phobia unless you talk to them about it?'

'I will, I will.'

'When?'

'Soon.'

Izzie couldn't blame Meghan for dodging the problem. After all, she had a gold medal in the sport herself. Jack and Claire Knowles had hoped Meghan would join them at Hollybrook, one of the best stud farms in North Yorkshire, so that they could pass on the techniques of breeding race horses and eventually hand over the business reins to her when they retired. They were devastated about their daughter's rejection of what had been in the family's blood for generations; to them it was a fantastic opportunity, and they were baffled at her attitude. Without an explanation of the reasons behind her actions, they were also angry, which had pushed Meghan even further away, resulting in a self-perpetuating dilemma for both parties.

If Izzie had learned one thing from what had happened two years ago, it was that communication was the most important aspect of any relationship, and choosing not to confide in her family was at the root of Meghan's estrangement; that as soon as she explained her problem to them, they would understand what had caused her to choose a different path, and why she only visited them at Christmas. However, Izzie had no desire to offer her opinion on someone else's family feuds. She had her own issues to deal with, which to others might seem miniscule compared to what they were going through, but everything was relative.

'Meghan…'

Izzie paused, watching her friend scroll distractedly through her messages until she stopped to reread one of them, her eyes igniting with delight.

'Oh my God! I have the perfect solution!'

'You do? For confessing to your family the reasons why you've swapped muddy Wellies for sequinned sandals?'

'Not for me, for you!'

Izzie's stomach contracted around what felt like a particularly large pineapple as she saw the gleam of excitement in Meghan's sea-green eyes. Oh no, what had she cooked up now! She braced herself for another of her outrageous suggestions – like the time she'd proposed a weekend on an outward-bound expedition which involved wild camping and scavenging for food because the course leader bore more than passing resemblance to Bear Grylls. There was no way Meghan could have survived even one night without the use of her hair straighteners, let alone exist on a diet of wild berries and foraged leaves.

A more pleasurable excursion, for Izzie at least, had been the time they'd taken advantage of the VIP tickets Meghan had scored from her parents for the Cheltenham Gold Cup in March and it was testament to their friendship that Meghan had stoically endured the whole episode with a smile on her face, despite her aversion to all things horse-related. On the journey back to London on a packed train, Izzie had confided that the trip had nudged her another step in the right direction on the journey to resume her place in normality at last.

'So, promise you'll hear me out before you refuse?'

'Oh, Meghan, I'm not really…'

'Promise?'

23

Izzie rolled her eyes and signalled her agreement by gesturing a zipping action across her lips.

'Okay. Remember I told you my brother rang this morning in a complete panic? What's new I hear you say! Well, apparently Lucy, his incredibly efficient PA, went to visit her family in Dublin at the weekend and after a trip to the local oyster-fest, has gone down with a bad case of food poisoning, poor girl.'

Izzie had met Meghan's brother Brad Knowles, a charismatic and award-winning film director/producer, on a few occasions over the years. Each time he'd been chasing around like a headless chicken trying to rectify some kind of calamity. She had no idea how such a talented director could be so disorganised and get anything done. Meghan had even confided in her that when he and his wife Rachel had returned from their honeymoon in the Maldives, he'd forgotten where he'd parked his brand-new Range Rover and it had taken three days to locate it because he couldn't remember the registration number.

Surely Meghan wasn't about to suggest that she step into the sensible heels of his super-efficient Girl Friday who was probably the only reason he ever got to say the words 'it's a wrap!'? She could feel her heart start to beat a little faster and the anxiety demons raised their enquiring eyes above the parapet. Meghan, however, misinterpreted her concern.

'Oh, don't worry, she's out of hospital now, but the medics have advised her to take it easy for a week or two, so she's staying on in Ireland so that her parents can pamper her until she recovers completely. Anyway, would you believe my dear delusional brother had the audacity to ask me to use the last few days of my annual leave to help him out with a wedding shoot in Italy! The cheek! Obviously he's conveniently forgotten the fiasco last October when I agreed to take a precious week's holiday to join him and his crew in Tobago for that perfume commercial and we ended up getting stuck there during one of the worst hurricanes ever. Remember?'

'Meghan, if you are about to suggest what I think you're about to suggest...'

'And anyway, I can't possibly miss the catwalk show on Monday, can I?'

'No, no you can't...'

'It's the perfect opportunity for you to forget about Dastardly Darren and decide where you want to go from here. Brad assured me that Lucy has everything organised and it's just a matter of overseeing the last few tweaks for a very short wedding ceremony – it'll be a doddle with your love of lists and organising. In fact, getting involved in such a lovely occasion might just reignite your creative streak whilst you soak up a bit of Italian sunshine, sample the food and wine, and who knows, you might meet a sexy, passionate Italian stallion who'll sweep you off your feet and show you what you've been missing!'

Meghan wiggled her eyebrows suggestively.

'Meg, I don't know the first thing about staging a film shoot!'

'How hard can it be? Knowing Lucy, everything will be sorted. Hang on, I'll just call Brad and ask him for a few more details. Oh God, I hope he's got his phone switched on – that's if he even has his phone with him!'

Meghan was right to be sceptical because her call went straight to voicemail.

'Oh well, never mind. He's probably found someone else to step into the breach,' said Izzie, struggling to disguise the relief in her voice.

'I'll give Rachel a quick ring. She doesn't get much further than the school run these days. Only three weeks left to go until I get a new niece or nephew. Squeee, how exciting is that!'

Izzie's heart gave a nip of pleasure at the joy spreading across her friend's face as she dialled her sister-in-law's number. Meghan had talked of little else since Brad and Rachel had announced they were to become parents for the second time and she had already amassed a trunk full of baby clothes in white, lemon and pistachio from Harrods' nursery department, along with a cute red tricycle that Jonti had declared the most darling thing he'd ever seen.

'Hey! Rachel, it's Meghan. I don't suppose Brad's with you, is he? He's got his phone switched off again.'

'That's because he's probably half way up a volcano in Bali. Didn't he mention that when he spoke to you this morning?'

'No, he did not!'

'Of course, he's left his wallet behind again, so I hope his crew are feeling in a generous mood. I'm sorry he's dumped this wedding gig on you, Meggie. I'm just booking your flight tickets now and I'll email over the details to you along with the notes Lucy's sent through.'

'Booking my tickets? What do you mean? I told Brad I couldn't do it because of the fashion show on Monday!'

'Well, that isn't what he told me, darling.'

'Bloody typical! My brother is a complete and utter...'

Izzie watched Meghan pause, then meet her eyes with a look reminiscent of the one Charlie, her childhood pet spaniel, used to give her whenever she was eating a piece of her mother's famous lemon drizzle cake. She sighed and nodded her head. After all, Meghan had come to *her* rescue many times over the last two years, offering her a listening ear and her unquestioning support – not to mention her insight into the dating scene – and it was time to repay her friendship.

'Okay, Rachel, send over the emails and change the flight into Izzie's name. She's just agreed to come to my brother's rescue – so he owes her big time. I'll ask for a couple of days off work after the show and fly out on Thursday to help with the finishing touches, although I'm confident that Izzie will be able to pull this off with one hand tied behind her back and her eyes closed.'

Meghan tossed her phone onto the coffee table and padded to the huge silver SMEG refrigerator to grab one of the bottles of prosecco and a couple of glasses.

'Thanks for doing this, Izzie. You've just saved my brother's ass.'

'So, do you have any idea who any of the actors are?'

'None…'

'Or whereabouts in Italy the wedding is taking place?'

A tickle of trepidation agitated in her chest when she said the word 'Italy' but she ignored it. It was a huge country and fate couldn't be so cruel.

'All Brad said was that it's in this amazing farmhouse with a vineyard and an olive grove and a tennis court! Hang on while I take a look at what Rachel's sent through. Ah, look, here it is. I told you it would be okay. Lucy is a whizz at stuff like this. Here's an email with a list of things that need to be done. Oh, and you don't need to worry about the catering because she's arranged for someone called Carlotta who lives in the local village to sort that out, so there's just overseeing the location. What could be easier?'

'Just because I can stage a room doesn't mean I know anything about staging a wedding for a film shoot! It's a whole different ball-game, and one which you only get one chance at getting right! Any mistakes will be captured on camera for all eternity!'

Izzie pulled a face and Meghan's expression softened.

'Look, Izzie, you'll be amazing – you have all the right skills – and if I can do it, so can you! It'll be good for you to go somewhere where no one knows you or your history. And weren't you learning to speak Italian before… well, just… before. Oh, I can't wait to join you. I've never dated an Italian guy. Remember that French waiter I literally bumped into when we went over to Paris after we graduated? And what about Dimitri and Andreas we met in Cephalonia? I swear they must have been the descendants of Greek gods…'

But Izzie wasn't listening. She had seen the location of the farmhouse where the filming was due to take place in a weeks' time. Tuscany. And not just any old village hidden in the rolling Tuscan hills, but one that had Florence in its address. Her fingertips fizzed with mounting panic and anxiety gnawed at her gut. She couldn't go to Florence.

'I can't do it, Meghan,' she whispered. 'I can't go to Florence. You know why.'

Meghan squinted at the sentence in the email Izzie was pointing to.

'Oh my God, I'm so sorry, Izzie. I swear I had no idea. Yes, yes, of course, I understand. I'll call Rachel back straight away and tell her to find someone else. There's bound to be some kind of agency in the area that can organise a wedding on short notice – we don't have to tell them it's for a film shoot.' And Meghan began scrolling through her contacts for Rachel's number again.

Later that night, when Izzie was stretched out on her bed, listening to the pigeons dance a final fandango on the roof tiles, and the traffic on the street below morph from shrill cacophony to a low, gentle hum, she still had no idea what made her change her mind and say 'No, don't. I'll go.' The words had flown from her lips before she'd had a chance to engage her brain and when she saw the way Meghan's eyes lit

28

up, she didn't have the heart to renege on her spontaneous loss of sanity. Also, as they'd chatted about the adventure that lay ahead, her spirits *had* edged up a notch and she experienced a tiny tickle of excitement, mingled with a dose of trepidation, deep in the crevices of her befuddled mind.

She was going to Italy! To Florence, a place she had wanted to visit since school. It wasn't how she had planned it, of course, and she knew the trip would be filled with painful 'what ifs' as well as sunshine and cannoli, but she had to admit that Meghan was right. It was time she jumped back onto the carousel of normality, time to stitch her grief into the tapestry of her life and create a new picture – and finalising the arrangements for a short film shoot could be exactly what she needed to do that.

Ideas had already started to flood her brain. There hadn't been a photograph of the Tuscan farmhouse that would be her home for the next week, but the name of the place evoked a sensation of better times ahead.

Villa Limoncello!

Chapter Three

San Vivaldo, Tuscany
Colour: Olive green

'Stupid, stupid car!' cursed Izzie as she struggled to slot the Citroën 2CV's dashboard gearstick into the right groove to ease the climb up the vertiginous slope in front of her. Why hadn't Rachel been able to hire her a decent car, like a cute Fiat Cinquecento, the colour of the cloudless sky overhead, or a zippy Alpha Romeo?

But her irritation with Rachel's taste in Italian transport, and the weird mechanics of the oversized bluebottle that had the audacity to masquerade as a motor vehicle, melted from her mind when the next bend in the road revealed the terracotta-roofed village of San Vivaldo nestling in a crease of the verdant Tuscan hillside. Despite her reluctance to visit Tuscany, she had to admit the scenery was every bit as impressive as she had expected. With the sun bleaching through the windscreen, the aroma of baked earth floating on the breeze, and the bobbing battalions of sunflowers in the endless fields, she could feel the place starting to work its magic on the knots in her neck already.

Had she been living a monochrome existence – physically and emotionally – for so long that she'd forgotten the power of a simple ray of sunshine? It was as if someone had flicked a switch and she had entered a world of technicolor brilliance.

Could Meghan have been right? Would a break from the humdrum treadmill her life had become be enough to thaw her frozen emotions and set her on the path towards coming to terms with what had happened?

Izzie slammed her foot onto the accelerator to coax one final splutter from the ancient engine before it finally surrendered its grip on life, and the entrance to Villa Limoncello hove into view, its black wrought-iron gates spread wide in a gesture of welcome. With its honey-coloured façade crumbling gracefully, and its paint-blistered shutters closed against the late afternoon heat, the two-hundred-year-old farmhouse gave the impression of an aged duchess taking a well-earned siesta amidst the olive groves and the vines.

She parked the car, leapt from the driver's seat, and crunched down the dusty driveway on foot, marvelling at the cypress tree guard-of-honour, until she arrived at the impressive front door flanked by a pair of huge terracotta pots containing lemon trees, their pendulous yellow fruit hanging like quirky Christmas tree baubles. Apart from the eternal backing track of the cicadas and croaking frogs, only the faint clang of a distant church bell and the buzz of a speeding Vespa broke the silence and she took a moment to appreciate the tranquillity after the cacophonous journey from Florence airport.

Now, where had Lucy said she would find the key?

She made her way around the side of the villa, past a pretty pergola festooned with a headdress of pink and white honeysuckle, to the stone terrace at the rear where she was gifted with a magnificent view of the whole valley, its slopes bedecked with row upon row of emerald green vines. The gardens encircling the terrace had been equally well mani-cured, showcasing winding pathways lined with neat box hedges, and an abundance of smooth terracotta pots filled with

32

lavender and geraniums, their scarlet petals dancing in the light breeze. There was also a contingent of naked marble statues, an old fountain, currently devoid of water, and, if she stood on her tip-toes, she could just about see a somewhat dilapidated tennis court, its net sagging like a widow's stockings.

When her eyes snagged on the whitewashed dome of a columned gazebo poking out from a crowd of magnolia trees, she sighed with delight; this was obviously where the filming was going to take place. She was about to make her way through the fragrant foliage to take a closer look when an even more impressive sight materialised; a huge glasshouse attached to the south gable of the villa – it was the *limonaia* that had given the villa its name! Ah, if she closed her eyes she could almost taste the acidic tang of crushed lemons, the very essence of summer, but the sensation vanished as her phone buzzed in her pocket. She smiled when she saw the name flash up on the screen.

'Hi Meghan.'

'Hi, darling, how's Tuscany? Is it teeming with deliciously scented Italian guys, clad in Armani, and piloting their Alfa Romeos with the speedy abandon of a Formula One racing driver? What's the villa like?'

'I've literally just arrived so I haven't been inside yet. It looks a bit shabby around the edges to be honest, but the gardens are amazing. There's a vineyard, and an olive grove, and there's even an old tennis court that looks like it hasn't been used for decades. Oh, and you should see the gazebo – it's gorgeous – and the view is just stunning!'

'Argh, why did Fenella have to organise her fashion show this week? I want you to promise me that you'll channel your inner Annie Leibovitz and post lots of photographs on your Facebook page!'

'Sorry, Meghan, I'd love to, but I don't think I'm allowed.'

'What do you mean?'

'Well, I read the paperwork on the flight over here... oh, and by the way, this is not just a twist-and-a-tweak job, Meghan, it's a complete, from-scratch location staging for a wedding scene! You have no idea how much work there is to do!'

Whilst Izzie had been waiting at Heathrow for her flight to be called, she had decided to use her time to scrutinise the email and attachments Lucy had hurriedly sent through to her. The more she read, the more she realised that she had inadvertently agreed to assume the role of full-blown film location manager, and if she hadn't been sitting in the departure lounge, she would have turned on her heels and high-tailed it back to London.

Leaving aside her issues with all-things wedding related, she was daunted by the prospect of being personally respons- ible for organising every aspect of the location brief. Not only were there drawings, diagrams and charts illustrating the correct layout of the chairs for the ceremony and exactly where to display the numerous floral arrangements, but there were instructions on how she should lay the tables and fold the napkins! Then there was the food; a five-course menu showcasing everything you would expect to find at an Italian wedding – including photographs and recipe cards to guide the chef on how the finished dishes should look!

Of course, when she had tried to call Brad on the number Rachel had given her, the call had gone to voicemail, and she didn't want to disturb Lucy with complaints about something she handled every day of her working life, especially whilst she was still recovering from her bout of food-poisoning. So, she had scoured the paperwork, and, in true Isabella Jenkins fashion, set about making her own detailed, daily itineraries and colour-coded lists of tasks she needed to do to pull off her very first staging for a film shoot.

'From what I've been able to glean from the Lucy's scribbled notes, there're two areas that need staging; the wedding gazebo for the ceremony and the courtyard where the reception will be filmed. Would you believe one of the stipulations is that the red carpet should be exactly ten metres long – not nine, not eleven, but ten! And whoever drew up the shopping list has even ordered rosebud-printed toilet rolls! Anyway, sorry, moan over, there'll be no photos because there's apparently a social media embargo, so, no Instagram, no Facebook posts, no tweets, no photographs on blogs.'

'But that's ridiculous! Why?'

'Well, I did think it could be because the actors playing the bride and groom are some kind of Italian celebrities. Maybe Brad's keen to avoid unwanted attention whilst the filming is taking place? Can't blame him, can you? Who wants a pugnacious paparazzo training their long lens on your stars' faces whilst they rehearse or deliver their lines?'

'Wow, I wonder who they are? Trust my brother not to mention that part of the gig! Maybe I *would* have dropped everything if I'd known real-life Italian film stars were going to be there! Oh well, don't worry about the photos…'

Izzie heard Meghan pause to inhale a breath and she knew immediately that her friend was preparing to change the subject to something less neutral. Her heart gave a nip of apprehension – she had been determined not to go there, not for one moment to relive the whirlwind of excitement that had accompanied the lead up to the previous, real-life wedding she'd been involved in, nor dwell on the hen weekend that had never happened. It had been the most agonising time of her life, and the only reason she'd agreed to come to

Brad's rescue was because of her appreciation of Meghan's unwavering support.

'How are you coping? You know, with being in Florence?'

'Actually, I managed to avoid the city altogether. Just picked up this ridiculous little rust bucket of a car at the airport and headed straight for the Tuscan hills!'

'Maybe if you visited a few of the places you and Anna…'

'You know, I don't think I'll have much free time to go sightseeing. Every single hour between now and Friday has been filled with a kaleidoscope of tasks. And it's not just the staging I have to worry about; there's visits to the florist and the *pasticceria* in San Vivaldo, and the whole five course menu has to be taste-tested too…'

Even Izzie could hear the self-justifying tone her voice had acquired, and it was testament to their enduring friendship that Meghan chose not to argue with her, or to chastise her for her lack of courage, but Izzie could tell her friend was disappointed.

'Okay, must dash, things to do, places to be, people to dazzle with my brilliance! See you on Thursday, darling. Don't worry about coming out to meet me at the airport, I'll catch a cab! *Ciao, Bella!*'

Izzie returned her phone to her pocket, guilt spreading through her like a warm shower, augmenting the stress headache that had been threatening to overwhelm her since she'd disembarked at Florence airport. In the distance, the sun was slowly descending towards the horizon, sending flashes of apricot and salmon-pink through the sky and bathing the scene in a rich golden glow and she decided that exploring the *limonaia* could wait. It was more important to get settled in and have an early night before the madness started the following morning.

She returned to the terrace and had just turned the heavy iron key in the back door when she heard a gruff voice hailing her from the driveway. She strode back around to the front of the villa, a smile on her lips, ready to experiment with her first Italian greeting, but before she could utter a syllable, her visitor launched in with a tirade of irritated invective, his arms flaying the air like an out-of-control windmill.

'*Cosa diavolo pensi di fare?*'

Izzie stared at the man whose stature was impressive, if a little daunting. Probably in his late forties, his unruly salt-and-pepper curls sported a generous sprinkle of dust and his biceps bulged through the sleeves of his plaster-splattered denim shirt. Judging from the slash of paint on his cheek and the hammer protruding from his jeans pocket, he was clearly in the middle of some sort of building project, yet that conclusion jarred with the presence of an incongruously ostentatious gold Rolex at his wrist. She had been so busy scrutinising his appearance that she hadn't realised he'd paused in his vociferous reprimand, his forehead creased at her lack of instantaneous response before rolling his eyes in realisation.

'English?'

Izzie bristled. Who was this person? And why was he shouting at her? Oh, God, could he be the owner of Villa Limoncello? If so, this wasn't the arrival she had anticipated, but it certainly explained his attire.

'Yes, I'm…'

'Thought so. Bloody tourists!'

'Oh, I'm not a tourist. I'm…'

'Come!'

And without waiting for her to explain, he strode off down the driveway, the heels of his work boots scattering gravel in his wake, until he came to a stop next to Izzie's hire car.

'Does this roller-skate belong to you?'

If she hadn't been so disgruntled at the man's abrupt attitude she would have agreed with his assessment of her transport – and would probably have also noticed that he spoke English without the whiff of an accent. As it was, her feathers were ruffled. She tilted her chin, squared her shoulders, and confirmed with as much dignity as she could that the car was indeed hers.

'Move it!'

'I beg…'

'You're blocking my access.'

That threw her. 'Your access?'

'Yes.'

The man pointed to an almost-concealed wooden gate across whose path Izzie had parked the 2CV, then indicated the rust-blistered truck that was wedged between the gate posts unable to continue its journey to the main road.

'Oh, right, sorry. I didn't notice the gate. I'll just…'

The man stood there, arms folded across his chest, tapping his foot, totally disinterested in her apology or explanation. What was the matter with him? Why did he have to be so rude? Maybe if he smiled he would be quite handsome, thought Izzie, before she noticed that mingled with the irritation there was a haunting sadness buried in his dark eyes that no amount of false jollity could erase. She grabbed her keys from the pocket of her jeans and drove the last twenty metres down the driveway to park outside the villa's front door. When she got out of the car, her grumpy neighbour had secured the gate behind him and disappeared in the direction of the village.

Well, that was not the best of starts to her sojourn in the Tuscan countryside.

Izzie wondered whether she should take the opportunity of her neighbour's absence to find out what lay at the other side of the gate – just so that she could avoid the place at all costs.

However, dusk was now beginning to tickle the treetops and a surge of tiredness grabbed at her bones. So, she shoved their unsettling encounter to the back of her mind, liberated her suitcase from the back seat of the Citroën, and sauntered back to the terrace, pausing once again to appreciate the patch-work of fields that stretched as far as the eyes could see; olive green and emerald, shamrock and jade, all stitched together by rambling hedges and dotted with triangles of terracotta and sandstone.

She sighed and made her way into the house, pausing briefly in the dingy hallway, unsure whether to investigate the rooms downstairs or to just climb the stairs and fall into bed. It was clear that the place hadn't welcomed guests, or any kind of visitor, for some time; the air was stale and smelled of dust, cobwebs and nostalgia for a bygone era. She suspected that she wouldn't like what she found in the kitchen and decided to postpone that particular treat until the next morning when she was in a more receptive frame of mind after a good night's sleep.

She made her way upstairs and opened the first door she came to, barely noticing the riot of sunflowers that covered all four walls as well as the front of the wardrobe and the vanity unit. She sunk down onto the bed – its hand-made throw also embroidered with the ubiquitous blooms – and closed her eyes. The emotions she had kept tightly corralled since leaving London burst through their restraints and threatened to overwhelm her. Two years ago, almost to the day, she had hoped to visit this most magical of places with her best friend, her beloved sister Anna, but fate had other ideas.

And yet, whilst she was sad that she was taking the trip they had both dreamed of for years alone, she had the strangest feeling that she was meant to be there, at Villa Limoncello, and was hopeful that its serene ambience would help to plaster over the cracks in her heart.

Chapter Four

Izzie squinted at the clock on her bedside table. Six thirty! A full two hours before the first delivery was due to arrive. Yet there was no way she was going back to sleep. Sunlight streamed through the slats in the dilapidated shutters, providing spotlights for the dust bunnies dancing their morning jig, and the dawn chorus was already busily chirping its second verse, accompanied by a much less melodic backing track of... what was that noise?

Ergh, she knew exactly what it was *and* who was responsible for it.

She leapt from her bed, shoved open the windows, and for a moment the early morning concerto of hammering and drilling receded and all she could think about was the magnificent panorama spread out in front of her. It was picture postcard perfect. The sky was a translucent aquamarine and a scant veil of mist lingered on the emerald flanks of the hills giving them a magical Tolkienesque quality. Who needed five-star luxury when there was a view like that to feast your eyes on before breakfast?

She inhaled a deep invigorating breath, savouring the aroma of damp soil and a hint of something she recognised only too well – dried lavender – which conjured up a place she tried not to visit too regularly. She decided to take Meghan's advice on what to do when sadness poked its nose into your business. Keep busy! For all her exuberant, happy-go-lucky attitude, and flamboyant approach to sartorial glamour, Meghan too had her demons to slay.

Reluctantly, Izzie dragged her eyes away from the view and turned back to survey the room she had chosen as her home for the next week. She had been so exhausted the previous night that she'd fallen asleep as soon as her head hit the pillow and so now, for the first time, she could see that the interior décor would not be featuring in a glossy Italian Homes & Gardens magazine shoot any time soon. Did the owner have some kind of sunflower fixation?

She unzipped her suitcase, grabbed a handful of toiletries, and subjected herself to the torture of a shower that alternated between scalding hot and ice-cold; not the perfect prescription to kickstart her first full day in Tuscany. She piled her unruly curls, more bird's nest than Sunday Best, onto the top of her head, pulled on a pair of skinny jeans and a long-sleeved Breton top, and padded down the stairs to the kitchen in search of a caffeine injection. In a world filled with chaos, if there was one thing she was certain of it was that the day couldn't start without a decent cup of coffee.

When her eyes grew accustomed to the gloom in the kitchen, her heart gave a sharp stab of surprise. Instead of the orderliness she had expected of a venue preparing to host a film crew in less than a week's time, she saw a room that had *previously* been a kitchen but was now masquerading as the local jumble sale. Everywhere she looked there was an assortment of culinary paraphernalia: glossy Italian cookery books, menu cards, shopping lists, photographs of wedding cakes and desserts, all liberally sprinkled with a scattering of recipes scribbled on scraps of paper. Someone was clearly excited about catering the forthcoming shoot!

But it wasn't just the untidiness that concerned her – she'd have the place ship-shape in no time. It was the careworn condition of the furniture and appliances; the fact that the cupboard doors were off their hinges, the shelves were leaning against the wall instead of hanging from it, and two of the chairs at the huge battered table in the middle of the room didn't have seats – although even those issues could be sorted out with a hammer and a few nails. No, what was worrying Izzie the most was the fact that the sink was covered in a thick layer of grime and the oven looked like something out of the dark ages – how could an *upmarket* Italian wedding feast, fit for immortalising on celluloid, be prepared using that? Her spirits sank as she anticipated what the rest of the downstairs was going to look like.

However, she needed a coffee before she attempted that expedition, not to mention make a visit to her cantankerous neighbour to ascertain the low-down on his renovation project and to make sure that he wouldn't be engaging in a bout of frenzied cement mixing or jackhammering on Friday when they were in the middle of filming the bride and groom exchanging their vows!

She filled the kettle, wondering why the villa was in such a state of distress when the gardens, the vineyard and the olive groves were so immaculate. Once again, a spasm of self-doubt meandered through her thoughts. Why on earth had she agreed to do this? She was an interior designer, not a film set designer – they were completely different skills sets! What had made her so presumptuous as to think that she could step into Lucy's shoes, irrespective of the itemised checklists she had prepared on the plane that wouldn't have looked out of place in a nuclear power plant manual?

In the hope of lifting her spirits, Izzie raised her gaze to the kitchen window to be met by a pair of kind pewter eyes staring back at her.

'Argh!'

She leapt backwards, clutching her chest as her heart hammered out an aria of terror. Eventually, when her brain took over, she realised who her visitor was, and relief swept through her veins as she rushed to the door to welcome her in.

'Hi, you must be Carlotta? I'm Isabella Jenkins, but please, call me Izzie.'

'Ah, *buongiorno*, Izzie, *buongiorno!*'

Carlotta leaned forward to deposit the regulation kisses on Izzie's cheeks, before enveloping her in a fragrant hug. She was the same height as Izzie, but that was where the similarities ended. From the crinkles across her forehead and around her lips, Izzie estimated she was probably in her early sixties, but she exuded more verve and vitality than Izzie could muster up on any day of the week.

'*Benvenuta a Villa dei Limoni! Benvenuta nella nostra bella cucina!*'

'*Grazie, Carlotta. È bello essere qui!*' and with that Izzie's recall of conversational Italian was almost depleted. '*Erm, parli inglese?*'

'*Sì, nessun problema*,' smiled Carlotta before she switched to English laced with an almost musical Italian accent. 'Okay, so first we shall have coffee – and I picked up a selection of breakfast pastries from *Pasticceria Da Oriana* on the way over.'

Izzie felt Carlotta's eyes linger on her slender frame and she groaned inwardly. She knew she had lost weight since her split from Alex, but she just hadn't been interested in rustling up a nutritious home-cooked meal for one – even answering emails from Darren had to come higher up the 'must do' list

44

than peeling a vegetable or whipping up a batch of cupcakes. However, as Carlotta was responsible for the catering, Izzie suspected she probably greeted everyone with similar scrutiny before pressing another helping of *torta della Nonna* on them.

The aroma of warm buttery croissants floated through the air, along with the freshly ground coffee she had been in the process of making, and, surprisingly for a woman who never ate breakfast, her stomach rumbled in anticipation. She broke off the corner of a croissant and popped it into her mouth so as not to offend – or invite enquiries about her aversion to breakfast – nodding in appreciation of its sweet buttery taste. She couldn't remember the last time she had eaten something so moreish, which wasn't surprising given her staple diet was toasted white bread.

'*Mmmm, delizioso!*'

'I'm pleased to hear it. Oriana is in charge of creating the magnificent seven-tier wedding cake!' said Carlotta, laughing as she handed Izzie a tiny cup of espresso that was strong enough to revive the dead.

'I'm really looking forward to meeting her. I've got an appointment to see her tomorrow to go over the final details. Tell me, Carlotta, do all Italian weddings have such extravagant cakes? And is it really necessary to prepare a full five-course meal for the reception?'

Carlotta's eyes widened in astonishment at the question. 'Of course, it is! We Italians love food; it goes way beyond simple nourishment for us. We love talking about it, shopping for it, preparing it, and eating it. We also have our own rules that must never, ever be breached; what kind of cheese we use to top a particular pasta dish, what cake we eat on which saint's day, which wine to serve with which meat. Would you believe that my grandmother did not speak to her neighbours for many years after she found out they put parsley in their minestrone?'

'Really?'

'Italian cuisine is a serious business. Most of our recipes have been handed down through generations, and the thought of experimenting with something new is as absurd as sitting in front of the television to eat dinner from a tray. And don't forget, the wedding breakfast is the most important meal in a couple's life! So, shall we go through the menus and make sure everything is in order?'

'Absolutely!'

Izzie reached into her duffle bag to remove the checklists and itineraries she'd prepared the previous day, when her gaze fell on the kaleidoscope of clutter that covered every available inch of the kitchen surfaces. The whole room looked like a hurricane had passed through.

'Why don't we take our coffees out to the terrace and use the table under the pergola? You can tell me what's already been done and what still needs our attention, and then I'll edit my daily countdown schedule and allocate...'

'*Aspetta un minuto,*' interrupted Carlotta, disappearing through the back door and returning seconds later with her beloved chihuahua in her arms, a smile lighting up her face. The dog gave a yap of welcome. 'Izzie, allow me to introduce you to Tino.'

'*Buongiorno*, Tino,' smiled Izzie, giving the little dog a rub between the ears before taking a seat next to Carlotta beneath the fragrant white honeysuckle of the pergola. 'He's so cute. I'd love to have a dog, but pets aren't allowed in the building I live in in London.'

'How very unkind of the owners,' pronounced Carlotta, her expression filled with real sadness for Izzie's predicament. 'I firmly believe that animals enhance our lives and improve our emotional well-being. Unlike some humans, their love is always given unconditionally – and it is good to know we are loved, don't you think?'

Once again, Izzie experienced the unsettling sensation that her very soul was being scoured. Discomfort prickled at her forearms, so she did what she always did whenever someone challenged her on the issues of love, life and loss – she reverted to the safety and predictability of her lists. She opened her purple folder and removed the sheet headed 'Monday', but not before she had seen Carlotta flash her a glance filled with curiosity.

'So, it seems the staging for the ceremony is straightforward, thank goodness…'

'The reason the wedding is being held at *Villa dei Limoni* is because of that!' Carlotta cast her hand at the hills in the distance, their flanks swathed in striped green velvet, their peeks crowned by medieval villages. 'There's nothing you or I can do here that could possibly enhance the spectacular panorama; no amount of white voile floating on the breeze, or ivory gardenias climbing around those Romanesque columns, or garlands of fairy lights entwined around the trees will divert the onlooker's attention from the wonderfulness of our Tuscan landscape.'

'You're right, Carlotta, it is absolutely amazing, and it makes my job so much easier, too. I confess to being a little out of my comfort zone here. I'm actually an interior designer by profession, so staging an al fresco wedding is outside my realm of expertise, but as long as we stick to the lists I've made, I'm sure everything will be okay. Do you know if anyone has considered the health-and-safety aspects of the venue? Should I conduct a proper survey of the gardens for tripping hazards like that loose step over there, not to mention those stray electrical wires I noticed hanging from the lampposts at the entrance – what if someone gets electrocuted, or garrotted? And, what about toilets? Will people be needing access to the bathroom in the villa?'

Izzie looked up from the list she had been scrutinising, her pen poised to tick off the next item when Carlotta confirmed it was in hand. But instead, Carlotta tossed her hand in the air and up-ended her lips in irritation.

'Pphh, the health and safety! This villa has been hosting weddings, christenings, fiestas, every kind of wonderful celebration for over two hundred years. And I've never heard of anyone being garrotted! Isabella, this is Tuscany – we do things differently here. All these niggles you refer to add character to the very essence of our lives; life is not a carefully constructed set of lists to be rigidly adhered to. It's a random set of events, some pleasurable, some tragic, all of which we must embrace as part of our journey. Relax. Things don't have to be perfect! They have to be beautiful!'

'Yes, that's true…'

A hard kernel of anxiety settled in Izzie's stomach. She respected Carlotta's viewpoint, but the only way she could deliver Brad's vision within the very short timescale was to adhere to the itinerary and the lists that she had prepared. It was the way she had worked for the last two years whilst at Hamilton Homes and it was how she had kept a rein on her emotions.

Control meant coping.

She couldn't embrace the laid-back approach to anything because it meant giving up control – and if she did that her whole, carefully-constructed world would fall apart. So, whether it be one of Darren's minimalist interior design projects, Jonti's thirtieth birthday celebrations, or a film shoot of an Italian wedding, she intended to deliver exactly what she had been asked to deliver, just like a professional events planner would. Hadn't she promised Meghan – and Rachel – that that was what she would do?

She made a mental note to delegate the cooking side of things to Carlotta and to handle everything else herself – including overseeing the safety issues. She glanced back to the sheet of paper in front of her to see that the next item on the agenda was setting out the chairs in front of the gazebo, a task which had a whole paragraph of instructions detailing their precise positioning, including how many centimetres should be between each chair. Whoever had drawn up these instructions was a person after her own heart, she thought with a wry smile, before checking her watch. Where was the delivery van with the furniture?

'So, according to the brief,' Izzie tapped her clipboard with the end of her pen, 'the chairs, along with the glassware, the crockery, the cutlery, and all the linen should have been delivered this morning at eight a.m. which makes it... almost two hours late. Do you know anything about the suppliers?'

'Ah, yes, I saw the van parked outside Antonio's Trattoria on my way over here. It should be with us sometime today.'

'Oh, right, erm...'

It was no good. Her control demons surged out of their cave and all the techniques in her armoury to manufacture nonchalance couldn't quash her need to ensure things ran according to schedule. She couldn't just sit there, drinking coffee, waiting for the delivery driver to turn up when it suited him. It was like an itch in her chest that she couldn't scratch. Anyway, if they had any hope of meeting the deadline of Friday morning, every hour was precious. If she had the chairs, she could make a start on attaching the white satin rosettes Brad had asked for, and if she had the muslin she could design the flounces to wrap around the columns on the gazebo.

'Well, I think I'll just pop over to Antonio's to see what's holding him up.'

Carlotta shook her head, the sides of her elegant silver bob swishing at her cheeks, but Izzie took no notice. If there was one thing that irked her it was lateness. In her view, people who turned up to appointments late had no respect for other people's time. She grabbed her duffle bag, slung it over her shoulder and trotted to the front of the villa where she'd left the 2CV, her anxiety melting with every step of purposeful endeavour. She plonked down in the driver's seat, turned the ignition key, and her ears were met with a short splutter followed by silence. She tried again but the car refused to budge from its comfortable retreat in the shade of a magnolia tree.

She slammed her hand on the steering wheel in frustration, and, refusing to be diverted from her mission, she jumped out of the car, only just managing to rein in the urge to give it a sharp kick, à la John Cleese. Spotting Carlotta's bicycle, complete with wicker shopping basket, she decided to ask if she could borrow it, but had taken only a few steps back towards the kitchen when she caught sight of a wheel protruding from the open door of an outhouse next to the *limonaia* and curiosity forced her to investigate.

To her complete surprise, nestled amongst the rusty detritus of ancient garden implements, half-used paint tins and what looked like a medieval poisoner's idea of apothecarial heaven, was a shiny, sugar-pink Vespa! In a moment of complete madness, she seized the handle bars and wheeled the iconic machine from its lair. She was surprised to see that it was brand new – unlike every other item at Villa Limoncello – its silver chrome glinting in the early morning sun.

Who did it belong to? Not the villa's owner, that was for sure! It was more the sort of thing Barbie would use on a weekend jaunt to visit her unicorn!

Out of interest she twisted the key and the engine thrummed into life immediately. Could she? She kicked her leg over the seat, plonked her bag at her feet, and wobbled down the driveway towards the main road, her confidence edging up a notch with every yard she added to the milometer. A sense of complete liberation tumbled through her body as every twist in the serpentine road revealed yet another field of sunflowers, their smiling faces bobbing like a crowd at a pop concert; every turn another crumbling Tuscan farmhouse with its green shutters sealed to ward off the ferocity of the midday sun.

As she got the hang of the controls, she increased her speed and a whoosh of exhilaration rushed through her chest when the oncoming breeze flicked her unruly curls high into the air like a mermaid on steroids. She was surprised to find she was actually humming a tune! She inhaled a deep satisfying breath, revelling in the intoxicating fragrances that tickled at her nostrils. Maybe Carlotta was right. Maybe if she could just relax, free herself from the self-imposed obsession with ever-expanding lists, perhaps her ferocious need to oversee every detail that bubbled constantly beneath the surface would diminish. But that meant she would have to use the extra time and space that gave her to face up to her demons, and no amount of fresh air and pretty countryside could persuade her to do that.

She was just about to navigate a particularly vicious bend when the sudden blast of a car horn sent her senses scrambling and a scarlet Alfa Romeo Spider Convertible shot past her, music blaring, engine revving, as it swung into her path with inches to spare before accelerating towards the red-roofed village of San Vivaldo on the brow of the hill.

'Moron!' she screamed.

She let go of the handlebars to shake her fist at the driver only to lose control, exit the road to her right through a gap in the hedge, and end up on her bottom in a field of potatoes under the watchful gaze of a bemused donkey who stared at her with nonchalant disgust for interrupting his lunch. Her heart flayed at her ribcage as she waited for her fear to subside. When she caught her breath, she inspected her grazed elbow, picked a few blades of dried grass from her hair, and pushed herself shakily back to her feet, patting the dust from her black skinny jeans that were now scuffed at the knees.

Oh God, how could she expect the tardy delivery driver to take her seriously when she looked like Worzel Gummidge's sister!

Chapter Five

Antonio's Trattoria, San Vivaldo
Colour: Chocolate Brown

After the incident with the Alfa Romeo the remainder of the journey to San Vivaldo was incident-free. She even had cause to send up a missive of gratitude to her mischievous guardian angel because her switch in transport from four wheels to two meant she was able to navigate the narrow streets and cobbled alleyways with ease and not spend hours searching for an elusive parking space.

The town was exactly as Izzie had imagined it would be, with its slanted terracotta roofs, honeyed façades, and ubiquitous green shutters. Shadowy archways led to sunny courtyards resplendent with hand-painted ceramic pots filled to bursting with scarlet, crimson and pink blooms, and every nook and crevice oozed a fairy-tale aura, promising stories of mediaeval feuds, battling dragons and fallen dynasties.

She made her way towards the central piazza where a myriad of shops, bars and cafés catered to a visitor's every need, all under the watchful benevolence of the church's bell tower. Her gaze was drawn immediately to *Pasticceria Da Oriana*, its window a riot of colourful sugary treats all lined up with military precision. Now that she was here, she wondered whether Oriana would mind bringing forward their appointment to discuss the wedding cake. However, she had only travelled a few yards when her eye caught on a large white van parked at an incongruous angle next to a raised wooden veranda, and when she investigated further, a hand-painted sign confirmed she'd found Antonio's Trattoria.

She briefly wondered what the delivery driver had been thinking. Okay, stop for a quick coffee, she didn't begrudge him that, but for three hours?

She parked the Vespa, removed her helmet, and ran her fingers through her hair hoping that she didn't look like she'd just suffered an electric shock. Moments later, she felt a splat land on her head. She glanced upwards, expecting to see a bank of bruised clouds to add to the catalogue of exasperating incidents that had befallen her so far that day, but only a wisp of cloud floated across the wide expanse of cerulean blue. Then her gaze fell on the self-satisfied pigeon and her stomach lurched when she realised what had happened.

'Ergh!' she groaned, searching in her bag for a tissue whilst trying not to retch.

Having done what she could to make herself presentable, she squeezed past the van, rounded the veranda and came face-to-face with the scarlet Alfa Romeo that had run her off the road earlier. She quickened her step, her mood heightened after the pigeon fiasco, intent not only on giving the delivery driver a lecture on the importance of sticking to a schedule, but also the racing driver a piece of her mind on road safety.

She could have been killed! What if that donkey – who in all fairness could have challenged Eeyore for first place on the melancholy monitor – had been an angry stallion who had taken umbrage at the disturbance of his mid-morning snack?

She squared her shoulders, but the surge of righteous indignation seeped from her bones when she saw that the restaurant was completely deserted, not to mention the fact that she didn't possess the language skills to politely berate the two

54

drivers in Italian. Instead, she plonked herself down in one of the cushioned chairs and decided to order a cappuccino to calm her nerves. What would stressing achieve?

After several minutes of waiting, she realised that no one was anxious to take her order. She pushed herself up from her seat, intending to go off in search of a waiter when she noticed the door that led through to the kitchen was slightly ajar, giving her an uninterrupted view of a tall, dark-haired man, decked out in pristine chef's whites, busily preparing the ingredients for that day's menu. She watched him finish chopping a plump, ripe mango before selecting a lemon, raise it to his nose and inhale, his eyes closing slightly as he did so.

A surprise ripple of attraction raced through Izzie's veins and she dropped slowly back into her chair, mesmerised by the way his large hands caressed the fruit, as if thanking it for its bounty, before placing it on the chopping board and slicing it at speed. She couldn't drag her eyes away, fascinated at the choreographed performance of food preparation, yet it wasn't a rehearsed routine, more a freestyle culinary ballet. Izzie could feel her taste buds tingle as he scooped up the lemon slices and set them to one side.

Next, the chef took a large silver bowl, poured in a generous slug of fresh cream and began whisking, his biceps straining against the sleeves of his white jacket as he focused completely on the task in hand. When he paused to dip his finger into the whipped cream, placing its tip in his mouth, then running his tongue along his lower lip to catch any lingering remnants, Izzie gulped as a hot frisson of desire scorched through her body.

What was going on?

She felt like she was the only audience member at a very intimate show, one that had been put on for her sole enjoyment, with Antonio Banderas's younger brother playing the lead role in her personal culinary performance. She almost drooled when he scraped every last molecule of the cream into a pastry case he'd prepared earlier and sprinkled the top with a handful of flaked almonds.

Wow, desserts weren't usually her thing, but she could happily dig into a slice of that pie!

From her vantage point, she feasted her eyes on his profile; how his mahogany hair curled over the back of his collar, his strong muscular forearms rippled with dark hairs, the way he dragged his palm across the stubble on his jawline as he contemplated which task deserved his attention next. Suddenly, a crystal-clear image of those same hands running the length of her glistening body, his long fingers slotted through her hair at the back of her neck as he pulled her lips towards his, appeared in her mind and she let out an involuntary gasp.

Had he heard her exclamation, or perhaps he'd sensed her scrutiny?

In any event, he looked up from the ball of pizza dough he had started to knead and met her eyes. Her cheeks flooded with heat when she saw his mouth curl into a knowing smirk. He wiped his hands, those wonderfully expressive hands, on a tea towel, flicked it over his shoulder, and sauntered out to the veranda.

Oh God, she groaned inwardly, why did she have to look like she'd been dragged behind one of those tractors she'd seen ploughing the fields? Why couldn't she be relaxing at the café's table looking effortlessly glamorous – admittedly something she had always struggled with due to her wayward profusion of copper curls. A nip of astonishment snapped at her chest – it had been a long while since she'd worried about her appearance when approached by a man. However, before she could analyse that revelation further she met a pair of the softest brown eyes she had come across.

'*Cosa le posso portare?*'

'Oh, I'm… yes, please, I'd like… could I have a coffee?'

Her words came out like a garbled mess and her cheeks coloured again. Thankfully, the chef thought it was because she didn't speak Italian and switched to fluent English.

'Sorry, have you been waiting long? I didn't see you arrive. What can I get you?'

The cadence of his voice, the sexily accented English, the way he held her eyes as he smiled, the scent of his citrusy cologne, his unsettling proximity, all melded together to send spasms of heat from her chest southwards like red hot pokers. Oh, for God's sake, get a grip, Isabella! She was reacting like a love-struck schoolgirl – but then she had never been faced with such masculine magnificence.

'Can I get you some breakfast?'

'Oh, no thanks. I don't usually eat breakfast. Actually, I'm just here to…'

'You don't eat breakfast?'

To her surprise, the chef pulled up a chair and sat down next to her, shaking his head, tutting at her answer as though she was the craziest person he'd ever met.

'You do know that breakfast is the best meal of the day, don't you? Well, after lunch, and dinner, of course. Oh, and maybe the midnight snack… and let's not forget brunch!' He laughed, the cute dimples appearing at the corners of his lips doing nothing to dampen Izzie's interest. 'In fact, in my humble opinion, every meal is important and should be treated with the respect it deserves.'

'Well, you would say that, wouldn't you? As a chef, I mean!'

Izzie smiled, suddenly feeling completely at ease in this man's company, as though she'd just met up with an old friend for a chat about the meaning of life – except for the inconvenient fact that her heart was galloping way ahead of her brain, riding on a wave of romance and hot, steamy passionate embraces.

'Of course! But I adore food! It's so much more than a means of keeping body and soul together. It's art, it's science, it's passion! What is your favourite dish?'

'Oh…' Taken by surprise, she was unable to invent something quickly enough, so she decided to go with honesty. 'Actually, I'm not really interested in food. Give me a plate of buttered toast and a cup of coffee and I'm happy. I never seem to have the time, or the inclination, to labour over a mountain of ingredients. I live by myself, so what's the point?'

Oh God! Had she just managed to drop into the conversation the fact she was single!

'You don't enjoy cooking? Everyone loves cooking! For an Italian – life revolves around the pursuit of culinary excellence; from sourcing the raw ingredients, to their preparation and devouring with gusto and the right wine. Food is part of the fabric of life – without it the journey would be dull, don't you think? If you spent even a little time in my kitchen you would change your mind like that!' He clicked his fingers to demonstrate his point. 'In fact, you must taste my tiramisu. I will bring a slice with your coffee. I'm Luca Castelotti, by the way. I am the owner of this little slice of Tuscan paradise.'

'Pleased to meet you, Luca. I'm Isabella.'

She held out her hand, but he leaned forwards and for a moment she thought he was going to kiss her. The air between them crackled with attraction and she even found herself lowering her eyelids in preparation for that particular dose of ecstasy, but sadly she was mistaken because instead of placing his lips on hers, he reached up to remove a stray leaf from her hair. The intimacy of his gesture sent her emotions

58

into a maelstrom of confusion, so she croaked out the reason she was sitting on his veranda in the first place.

'Erm, before you go, do you happen to know where the driver of that van is? He's supposed to be delivering the contents to us this morning and he's already three hours late!'

'Alberto?' Luca rolled his eyes in exasperation. 'Yes, he's here – almost drank the place dry celebrating his birthday last night. He's upstairs sleeping off his hangover. I had to tell him that he wasn't fit to get behind the wheel and I promised to deliver his cargo myself. Sorry for the delay, as you can see, I have the lunchtime preparations. Does that mean you are staying at the *Villa dei Limoni*?'

'Yes, I am.'

'Are you involved in the wedding?'

'Yes, well, actually, it seems I'm responsible for organising the whole thing.'

'What happened to Lucy Harwood?'

'Oh, you know her? Well, unfortunately she's suffering from a bout of food poisoning and, crazily, I agreed to step into her shoes and help out at the last minute. I don't want to let anyone down, but there's so much to do if everything's going to be ready on time, so...'

'Okay, give me a couple of minutes while I fetch the keys.'

Izzie watched Luca stride back into the restaurant, lean over the bar – gifting her with a fabulous view of his taut, muscular buttocks – and hook his finger through a bunch of keys. He returned to the veranda, smiling as though he'd just stepped from a toothpaste ad. In fact, thought Izzie as he removed his chef's jacket to reveal a black T-shirt that hugged his torso like a second skin, Luca could give a professional model a run for their money.

She leaped from her seat and followed Luca back down the steps of the veranda. However, to her surprise, instead of turning left towards where the van was parked, he turned right and leaned through the open window of the Spider to remove the keys from the ignition.

'Oh my God! Is that your car?'

'Yes,' beamed Luca misinterpreting her expression for that of awe. 'Magnificent, isn't it?'

'The car is, the driver is a lunatic who shouldn't be allowed on the roads,' she blurted before swivelling on her heels and striding towards where she'd left the Vespa, leaving Luca gaping in her wake, his forehead creased, clearly regretting his encounter with the crazy Englishwoman with hair like a rust-coloured bird's nest and a sharp line in driving etiquette.

Chapter Six

The garden at Villa Limoncello
Colour: Sherbet lemon

'A pigeon? Oh, God, Izzie that could only happen to you!'

'And don't get me started on my encounter with the donkey!'

'I thought you were organising a film shoot for a wedding scene not opening a zoo?' giggled Meghan, then softening her tone. 'Look, I'm sorry, Izzie. I should have been more sensitive before I stuck my oar in and asked you to do this. I just thought you needed a break from the tedious treadmill that your life seems to have become over the last few months. You can't continue to go on like that or your health is going to suffer and, as your best friend, I won't let that happen! Please promise me that you'll use this chance to work through your feelings?'

'Okay, I promise,' she muttered, before swiftly changing the subject. 'So, I don't suppose Jonti has any news from Darren?' She was embarrassed by the hopeful note in her voice, but the thought of starting the search for a new job filled her with gloom.

'No, nothing, sorry darling. It's early days, though, isn't it? Now, tell me more about Villa Limoncello? It's such an amazing name! I can almost smell the lemons ripening on the

61

trees, although I much prefer them cut into slices with a few ice cubes and a slosh of gin!'

'The interiors are a bit threadbare, to be honest, but the place is completely private which is probably why Brad chose it. Did you manage to get in touch with him to ask why we're all sworn to secrecy? I've tried to ring him a few times, but his phone always goes to voicemail and there's nothing about who the actors are on the file – which is surprising given the detail in the rest of the brief.'

'I'm sure Brad'll ring you when he can, but I wouldn't bank on it. You know what he's like, and with Lucy still laid up I'd be surprised if he manages to catch the right flight home! So, what is there left to do?'

'Well, the main thing is dressing the area where the ceremony is going to be filmed – this gorgeous white gazebo in the gardens, complete with marble flooring and roman columns. Everything was supposed to be delivered this morning, but apparently the delivery guy is still sleeping off his drunken stupor!'

'Drunken stupor?' laughed Meghan.

'Apparently it was his birthday yesterday.'

'Must have been one hell of a party!'

'Talking of parties, how was your date with the cameraman?'

Since the demise of her relationship with Alex, Izzie had loved living vicariously through Meghan's romantic exploits, giggling over a bottle of prosecco at the dates that didn't work out because she'd decided that their reading preferences were too prosaic, or their avid interest in on-line gaming was dull beyond belief. Despite these setbacks, her enthusiasm for exploring the dating landscape never seemed to diminish and Meghan remained optimistic that her soulmate was out there, somewhere, waiting for her to tumble into his lap. Her favourite mantra, which she quoted frequently to Izzie and Jonti, was that if you dated enough frogs you were, by the process of elimination, bound to find your prince at some point, but in the meantime, you might as well enjoy diving into the pond.

'Oh, it was okay, I suppose. I'd don't think there'll be a second one, though.'

'Why not?'

'He wore Birkenstock sandals with his cords!'

'So?'

'Not sure you'd be saying that if you'd seen his toenails.'

'Ergh!'

'Exactly. I think it was the director of destiny stepping in to tell me to wait until I get to Tuscany where there'll be an Italian hunk waiting to whisk me off my feet! So, what else is on your list?'

'There's the floral arrangements and the wedding cake to check up on – although apparently Francesca and Oriana are floristry and confectionary maestros – and I really need to do something with the inside of the house. Would you believe that the villa hasn't been lived in for two years?'

'Who does it belong to?'

'I have no idea – there's no mention of the owner in Lucy's notes.'

'So, who else is helping you? I remember Brad mentioning someone from the village?'

'Yes, that's Carlotta. Actually, she's just left on a mission to stock up on all the non-perishable items on the menu cards. As there's going to be five courses, I think she could be some time! She's a culinary wizard, though, so I'm leaving the catering side of things in her capable hands.'

'Phew, thank God for that,' spluttered Meghan, her voice filled with laughter. 'I'm not sure Brad's vision of an elegant

Italian wedding scene includes the wedding party celebrating their nuptials with a banquet of buttered toast and black coffee. Anyone else?'

'There's a guy, Gianni, I think Carlotta said his name was, who looks after the gardens and the vineyard. At least *they* haven't been neglected like the house. Oh, you should see the view from the terrace, Meghan. It's perfect – exactly how you imagine a Tuscan landscape to be, all pointy cypress trees, rolling green countryside and gorgeous hilltop villages with terracotta roofs and church bell towers.'

But Meghan wasn't listening to Izzie's critique of the splendour of the Italian countryside.

'Mmm, Gianni, you say? What's he like?'

'I haven't met him yet. Why?'

'Well, I'll need something to do when I get over there!'

'Oh my God, Meghan, there will be plenty to do! There's the pond to cover up, the cute wishing well to paint, the tennis court to sweep, the honeysuckle and wisteria on the pergola to trim, the...'

'Fab! So, speaking of Gianni, do you think you could take a sneaky photo and text it to me? I need something to help soothe my nerves – I'm commentating for Fabulous Fenella's fashion show tonight!'

'I'll try,' laughed Izzie, rolling her eyes at her incorrigible friend.

'Great. Okay, so, got to dash; places to go, people to see. Can't wait to see you on Thursday, darling!'

'Me too! *Ciao!*'

'*Ciao, Bella!*'

With a smile still tweaking her lips, Izzie meandered to the back door and was surprised to see it was raining. Not just a gentle sprinkling but ramming down in vicious stair rods that bounced on the glass roof of the *limonaia* with a vengeance.

She lingered for a while, sipping her coffee, watching the meteorological gods do their worst, yet the rain did nothing to detract from the beauty of the landscape. In fact, if it were possible, a glaze of precipitation enhanced its appeal and the sharp staccato of the raindrops on the flagstones provided a much more musical backing track than the repetitive thump of a jack-hammer from the house next door!

She glanced over her shoulder at the culinary miscellany still scattered across every surface in the kitchen, now amplified by the neat piles of checklists she'd prepared for her own use and attached to her faithful colour-coded clipboards that went everywhere with her. She sighed and was alarmed to find that she had been invaded by a surprise squirm of reluctance to get started.

What was the matter with her? She loved the challenge of a list! There was nothing that pleased her more than ticking off each item and moving on to the next, filled with a sense of satisfaction at a successfully completed task, which meant she was edging nearer her goal. But, for the first time she could remember, she felt drawn to embark on an impromptu diversion from the schedule.

Why shouldn't she play hooky for an hour or so?

The fact that she had even had that thought shocked her to the core! Safety in predictability had always been her motto. But the concrete-heavy block she had been carrying around with her for the last two years had eased under the Tuscan sun, and the pull of the checklists simmering on the heavily scarred kitchen table had diminished. Smiling to herself, she slipped her feet into a pair of old green espadrilles lurking in a basket by the back door and paused on the threshold to survey the sky.

The dark bulbous rainclouds had performed their finale and moved off northwards allowing the sun to resume its starring role. Izzie closed her eyes and listened. All around her, nature was speaking its appreciation for the rejuvenation the storm had brought and its welcome to the returning warmth – the crackle of the drying leaves in the borders, the cicadas tuning up to deliver their second sonata of the day.

Maybe it was time she too emerged from the mantle of melancholy the clouds of grief had brought and turned her face to greet the sunshine?

With a burst of renewed energy, she stepped onto the terrace. Where should she explore first – the olive groves at the far end of the garden where the leaves shimmered like silver glitter, the gorgeously fragrant glasshouse at the side of the villa, or perhaps a quick recce of her neighbour's property whilst the rain had stopped play? There was really no competition. It had to be the *limonaia*.

She lingered on the threshold of the old glasshouse, savouring the warmth and the ambient calm of the place that had given the villa its name. When she stepped inside it was as though someone had pressed the pause button on the background music as silence enveloped her with a blanket of tranquillity. Everywhere she looked, clusters of heavy terracotta pots lined the gravelled walkways or huddled on the white-washed stone shelves that ran the length of the gable wall. Each pot housed a single lemon tree, its trunk gnarled and twisted, but displaying an array of bright yellow fruit.

What surprised her most was the variety on show; some lemons she recognised as those she and Meghan enjoyed sliced in their gin and tonics, but there were others sporting wide green stripes or skin the texture of lumpy porridge. She marvelled at the intensity of the colours, the juxtaposition of the hard terracotta pots, the soft shingle under foot, the smooth glass of the windows, the golden light streaming into the room, the vivid yellow of the fruit. She sighed, contentment swirling around her body. She could spend all day in there, safe from the world and her demons, just lounging in the old rattan chair in the corner with a good book.

Okay, playtime was over, it was time to tackle those lists!

She decided to make a jug of home-made lemonade to share with Carlotta, and whoever was driving the delivery van – if they actually deigned to show their face at all that afternoon! Taking care not to damage the stem, she removed a couple of the lemons, smiling as she sniffed the skin just as Luca had, appreciating the sharp zing the fragrance sent to her taste buds.

With a spring in her step, she had just emerged from the *limonaia* when a gust of wind caught the awning above her and sent a barrage of rainwater over her head. She gasped, spluttering from the shock of the ice-cold dousing, sending her precious cargo bouncing across the terrace.

'I prefer to shower in the bathroom myself.'

She glared at Luca, standing before her, barely containing his mirth, those cute dimples bracketing his full, sensual lips. As she took in the figure-hugging black jeans, the way the cuffs of his baby pink shirt had been rolled back to reveal his muscular forearms rippling with golden hairs, her stomach gave an uncomfortable lurch and a smouldering ember of desire thrummed in her chest. Oh god, why did he have to be so handsome? Yet, despite the effect his proximity was having on her emotions, a sudden whoosh of irritation blasted through her veins.

'You do know that you ran me off the road this morning, don't you?'

'Yes, I do, but if you let me explain…'

'Explain what? That you're secretly training as Italy's next great Formula One driver? I could have been killed! And another thing – if a friend made a promise to another friend

67

that he would step into his shoes to make a very important delivery then the least that friend could do is be on time. You are, let me see, over seven hours late! Seven hours! Do you know how much there is to do here before Friday?'

'Actually, I know exactly what there is to do because…'

'Well, in that case I can only assume that you have no interest whatsoever in ensuring everything runs smoothly!'

The amusement reflected in Luca's dark, sensual eyes riled her even further. She watched his lips part, ready to pursue the case for the defence, but then he must have thought better of it because he simply shrugged his shoulders, thrust his hands into his pockets and strode away from her, straight across the terrace, and back to the front of the villa.

Izzie shook herself, her thoughts colliding. What was the matter with her? She barely knew Luca and yet the mere sight of him had ignited emotions that had lain dormant for years. She quickly smoothed her palms over her hair to calm her wayward curls and followed in his wake, an apology forming on her lips. As she rounded the corner, she was just in time to witness the white van reversing at speed towards her, tossing a generous confetti of pebbles in her face, before accelerating away down the driveway.

'What the…'

But then her gaze fell on a higgledy-piggledy pile of white wooden chairs, a thick roll of red carpet, and several tall columns of cardboard boxes with the words *posate*, *vasellame* and *cristalleria* scrawled on the sides in black marker pen.

That'll teach her to react before engaging her brain!

Chapter Seven

The Wedding Gazebo, Villa Limoncello
Colour: Chianti Red

Izzie was still trying to work out which task to tackle first when
her eye caught on a cloud of dust moving slowly through the
vines and heading in her direction. Clearly the director of her
fate, and keeper of her sanity, had taken pity on her because
within minutes George Clooney's younger brother had drawn
to a halt in front of her, jumped from the seat of his decrepit
quad bike, and offered her his palm. She had never been so
pleased to see anyone, despite the fact that he was wearing only
the skimpiest of T-shirts and the shortest denim shorts she'd
seen since a Nineteen-Eighties fancy dress party Meghan had
dragged her to.

'*Ciao!*' declared the Adonis, before launching into a stream
of complicated Italian until he saw the look of bewilderment
on her face and switched to English. 'Hey, you must be
Isabella?'

The way her name tripped from his tongue sent sparkles of
delight through her veins and when she reached out to shake
his hand, her stomach performed a somersault of interest.
What was the matter with her! First Luca, now…

'I'm Gianni Lombardo. Carlotta told me you would be here
today.'

'Hi Gianni, it's great to meet you. Yes, yes, I arrived last night,' she said, unable to wipe the stupid grin from her face. 'Fancy a coffee?'

Ignoring the mountain of furniture piled in a topsy-turvy mess on the terrace for the time being, she led Gianni into the kitchen and poured them both a coffee from the percolator. She swallowed a mouthful of the fragrant brew, pausing to allow its revitalising properties to seep into her veins before sliding into a seat opposite Gianni at the scrubbed kitchen table, pushing a stack of magazines and recipes to one side to make space for her cup. For some reason, Gianni's presence in the kitchen made the room look even more chaotic!

'Now, Isabella, what can I do to you?'

'Pardon?' spluttered Izzie, wiping a dribble of coffee from her lips.

Gianni waggled his eyebrows suggestively, his eyes resting on hers for a beat longer than necessary, and for the first time Izzie understood Meghan's reference to 'come-to-bed eyes'. With a mop of liquorice curls that he flicked from his forehead at regular intervals, and long spidery lashes, he oozed Italian sexuality. His muscular biceps and torso stretched the fabric of his snow-white T-shirt, and yet Gianni didn't look to Izzie like the sort of person who spent hours in the gym honing his body to perfection. He did, however, frequent the local perfumery because an aroma of spicy cologne hung in the air like a nuclear fallout cloud. A perfectly formed image of a drooling Meghan floated across her vision and she smiled.

'I think you mean what can you do *for* me? Actually, I'm glad you asked because…'

'Did Carlotta tell you that it is I who am responsible for the whole of the *Villa dei Limoni* estate? The olive trees, the vineyard, the gardens, the plants in the *limonaia*? Everything blooms as a result of my own hands!' declared Gianni, a mixture of pride and love suffusing his face. 'Come on. I'll give you a tour!'

Without waiting for her to reply, Gianni scraped back his chair, tossed his cup in the sink and strode from the kitchen, motioning for her to follow in his wake. She didn't have the heart to refuse, so she swallowed her last mouthful of coffee and galloped after him, keen to discover what hidden secrets the villa's land would reveal in the company of its guardian.

Over the next hour, Izzie was introduced to a menagerie of insects, frogs and birds as well as being treated to an enthusiastic monologue on every aspect of Italian viticulture, horticulture, and the management of olives groves. As they strolled through the kitchen garden, soft leaves caressing her naked shins, she was urged to inhale the intoxicating perfume of the aromatic rosemary and basil, to taste the plump ripe tomatoes, the asparagus and the chard, before coming to a halt at the end of a row of vines that hugged the south facing slope to her right.

'What are these plants here?'

'They are *carciofi*, artichokes.'

Izzie glanced at Gianni, wondering if he was teasing her. 'Artichokes?'

'Yes, and these are roses. They're often planted around the perimeter of a vineyard as a sort of early-warning system against disease. Roses are much more susceptible to mildew than vines, so if they are showing signs of distress we can treat the vines immediately to prevent infection.'

'Is that what's happened to these vines?' she asked, fingering the brittle brown leaves that crumbled when she touched them.

'No, that's something else,' said Gianni, his forehead furrowing with concern. 'I don't know what it is. The same thing happened last year to a couple dozen grapevines in the

71

bottom field and I thought my heart would break, and this year it looks like the problem has spread up here.'

Gianni paused to caress a healthy vine leaf as though it were the silky ear of his pet spaniel. 'I love these vines more than life itself! The grapes are *sangiovese* and the wine they produce this year will be my gift to the world! I want this vineyard to be my legacy to the valley, but it looks like I might lose another twenty vines this season. I'm *devastato*.'

Izzie didn't know what to say after such an impassioned speech about viticulture. She wasn't sure, but she thought she saw tears collecting at the corners of Gianni's eyes. At home in Cornwall, her parents loved tending their garden, even more so now as a way of soothing the intensity of their grief, but horticulture had never interested her, nor Anna. She and Gianni walked in silence back towards the house, each dwelling on their respective troubles, until they arrived at the handsome stone wishing well.

'Is this ornamental or an actual working well?'

'Oh, it's a real well. Until twenty years ago it was the villa's only source of water. Now the house is connected to the mains, but I prefer to use the well for the garden and the vines, and the plants in the glasshouse. This water comes straight from the hills, so there's none of the harsh chemicals you'll find in tap water, and it's what makes my grapes the best in the area!'

'Well, it's really charming. I think I might clean it up a bit, give it a lick of paint.'

She saw Gianni roll his eyes, but she ignored him, her mind scooting to the possibility of throwing a coin into its depths and making a wish. If she invested in three coins, did that mean she would return to Villa Limoncello? Was that something she wanted?

She and Gianni continued towards the house and came to a stop next to the raised dais that housed the white-domed gazebo where Brad intended to film the ceremony. Izzie could easily envision the six columns entwined with white muslin, interspersed with fresh white roses and finished with ribbons floating in the breeze like angel's wings. In her mind's eye she could see the white-painted chairs in rows on either side of the red carpet with posies attached just as the brief had stipulated. It really was an idyllic place and it was a perfect choice to showcase an authentic Italian wedding – if you angled the lens away from the dilapidation of the villa's façade.

'So, I can see that nature is your passion. I feel the same way about interior design.'

Or she had, she thought, until the director of fate stepped in and numbed her creativity.

'Oh, yes, I love working on the land, watching the seasons change, appreciating the fruits of my labours, but my true passion is music. My dream is to become an opera singer!'

And without skipping a beat, Gianni launched into an ear-splitting rendition of *O Sole Mio* as if to prove his talent. As the shock and urge to giggle subsided, Izzie realised he was actually very good.

'Maybe I will sing at the wedding? Maybe my talent will be discovered and I will be asked to perform at La Scala!'

'Maybe, maybe... So, is everything outside in hand?'

Izzie glanced at the tennis court, wondering why it had been left to fall into such disrepair. It was the only area of the grounds that let the side down, but that wasn't a problem. She would think of something she could use to hide its scruffiness from straying eyes and lenses.

'*Certo che sì!* The rest is for you to worry about.'

'Yes, worry being the operative word! I've only ever staged an interior before. I have to confess that it's all a bit daunting.'

'Ah, but with Carlotta on board you'll have nothing to worry about! Oh, apart from one thing!' Gianni shoved his hands into the front pockets of his shorts, his lips curling into a mischievous grin that caused his eyes to sparkle like a naughty schoolboy.

Despite having just met him, Izzie felt like she had known him for ever. Some people, no matter where or when your paths crossed, were just on the same wavelength as you. Yet, despite her initial reaction, although he was extremely hand-some, friendship was the overriding emotion that bubbled inside her, not sexual attraction. However, she knew for certain that Meghan would go weak at the knees at first glance.

'What's that?'

'Well, Carlotta is famous in San Vivaldo for two things. First, she is a fantastic cook, with an armoury of recipes handed down from her mother and grandmother and, if you are not careful, she will feed you until you burst! A visit to her home can often stretch into a ten-course banquet and an extended waistband.'

'I think I've already experienced some of this. What's the second thing?'

Gianni's dark eyes widened and his lips stretched into a beaming smile.

'What?'

'You had better watch out, Izzie.'

'What do you mean?'

Her stomach gave a lurch of alarm. Oh God, just when she thought a slice of culinary luck had been handed to her on a silver platter! Why did there always have to be a 'but'?

'Gianni!'

His eyes twinkled, and she relaxed a little. Clearly Gianni enjoyed winding up the gullible.

'Carlotta is our village's unofficial matchmaker.'

'Matchmaker?' That had been the last thing she had expected him to say.

'Sì. She possesses an instinctive understanding of a person's character, of their hopes, their desires, and their flaws too, and then she matches them to their perfect partner. One way or another, she has been involved in introducing many couples and, to her credit, every one of their partnerships have lasted. You don't have to take my word for it. Ask Paolo and Carina – their third child is due next month, there's Alessandro and Camilla who got married just six weeks ago, and Flavio and Elisabetta who have just announced their engagement. So, if you don't watch out, Izzie, you will have a ring on your finger before you board your plane back to London.'

With a splash of unease, Izzie recalled Carlotta's scrutiny of her that morning when she thought she was analysing her slender silhouette. Could she have, instead, been flicking through her Rolodex of available men within a fifty-kilometre radius of San Vivaldo for a potential introduction to the new arrival? God, she hoped not!

'Oh, don't worry about me, Gianni. I'm definitely not here to dabble in any romantic dalliances. I don't have the time, or the inclination, for love at the moment. I prefer to spend every spare second I have sourcing new fabrics, tracking down accessories and...'

She paused when she saw Gianni twist his face at her well-rehearsed dismissal of love in favour of work commitments, and his reaction reminded her of the way Meghan also rolled her eyes when she refused to double-date. She'd uttered the same rendition of 'no time for dating' so many times over recent months that it trotted off her tongue easily. However, for some reason this time, standing there in front of Gianni, she heard her words more clearly than she had before. How sad she sounded, how cheerless, how boring! Why had she allowed her life to become devoid of romance? But she knew the answer to that question only too well.

'Anyway, Carlotta won't have time to sprinkle me with her magic potion, or whatever it is she does to cause people to fall in love, because as soon as the words "it's a wrap" have been declared, I'll be flying back to London.'

Gianni scrunched up his nose in confusion and Izzie decided to head him off before he travelled any further down the road of the ups and downs of the dating game in Tuscany.

'What about you, Gianni. Have you succumbed to Carlotta's matchmaking skills?'

To Izzie's surprise, Gianni's expression morphed into one of despondency and she chastised herself for forgetting that external appearances could be deceptive and that everyone, no matter how jolly and chirpy on the outside, had something gnawing at their heart and she resolved to offer Gianni a listening ear.

'Oh, Gianni, I'm sorry. That was rude of me. I…'

'So, the delivery has arrived at last!' exclaimed Gianni, striding away from her, keen to move onto a different subject. 'Why didn't Luca stay to help set everything up? Need a hand?'

'Thanks, Gianni. That's the best offer I've had all day!'

'Where do you want to start?'

'If we could take these boxes, and those packages over there containing the table linen, into the kitchen, I'll check everything against the inventory later. I think we should make a start on setting out the chairs over by the gazebo.'

'Sure, no problem. I'll move the quad bike and be with you in a minute.'

'*Grazie*, Gianni.'

Izzie exhaled a long sigh, and, not trusting Gianni – who had just crashed his quad bike into the outhouse door so forcefully that the door was now hanging from its hinges – she carried the box containing the crystal into the kitchen herself. When her eyes fell on her faithful colour-coded clipboards, she experienced a welcome resurgence of her craving for an orderly approach to the tasks in hand. She grabbed the sheaf of paperwork that included the illustrations of the seating plan and made her way to the gazebo where Gianni was waiting for her, surrounded by a battalion of white chairs and wreaths of coiled fairy lights.

'Right, I'll make a start on dressing the columns with this muslin, if you wouldn't mind setting out the chairs – five rows of four on either side of the carpet, each chair must be ten centimetres apart. Here's the ruler.'

'The ruler?'

'Don't look at me like that.' Izzie giggled at the comedic disbelief on Gianni's face, grateful that this time the anally-retentive specification had originated from Brad and not her. 'Sorry, that's what the brief stipulates. Look!'

Izzie pointed to the drawings that looked like they'd been crafted by a professional architect. However, she had no intention of confessing to Gianni that it was her addiction to order and precision that had resulted in the added detail of placing sticky tape on the floor of the dais where the bride, the groom, the best man and the two bridesmaids would stand when the vows were being exchanged.

Gianni rolled his eyes at her but set to work without complaint whilst she studied the photographs and step-by-step directions on how to drape the fabric around the columns, create and attach the rosettes to the chairs, and where to hang the fairy lights. On occasion she was tempted to divert from the brief, to introduce her own touches of bridal embellishments, and whilst the upsurge in creativity gave her a warm feeling in her heart, she decided to adhere to the instructions.

'Where do you think Carlotta is, Gianni? I thought she would be back at the villa by now?'

'Ah, but it's Monday.'

'Ye…es?'

'It's market day. She and Vincenzo usually grab a fortifying coffee before embarking on a frenzy of extreme haggling. You should see them together – the stallholders have no chance!'

'Vincenzo? Is that her husband?'

'No, not her husband. Carlotta's husband died over thirty years ago just two years after they were married.'

'Oh, that's so sad. Poor Carlotta, to lose her husband so young. I assume they didn't have children? She hasn't mentioned a family.'

'No children, but she's been an amazing sister, aunt, friend and confidante to almost everyone in the village. She is universally adored, as is Vincenzo who is a maestro forager and grows the most amazing organic produce that Carlotta uses to create delicious banquets for visiting holidaymakers in the area. Can you keep a secret?'

'Of course!'

'Well, everyone is hoping that one day Carlotta will apply her legendary matchmaking skills to her own situation. It's like everyone knows they are in love with each other apart from them! Now, if they did decide to get together that's a party I would definitely not want to miss.' Gianni ran his fingers through his mop of curls and laughed. 'Enough of the village gossip – and not a word to Carlotta or Vincenzo, okay?'

'Sure!'

'So, what's next?'

'The paintwork on that chair is chipped,' said Izzie, indicating the chair at the centre back of the line-up. 'I think I saw a pot of white paint in the outhouse, do you think you could touch it up whilst I finish off the sweeping up the leaves, and then we'll call it a day?'

'Sure,' smiled Gianni, strolling down the red carpet with an exaggerated swagger.

Working in tandem, they managed to transform an already handsome garden gazebo into a fairy-tale venue which conformed exactly to the vision in the brief. Izzie decided to take a few photographs to email to Brad to reassure him that things were on schedule – despite the lateness of the delivery. She took her time, keen to get the best shot, until Gianni came into view, an open paint pot dangling nonchalantly from his index finger looking like a young Michelangelo. Perfect, thought Izzie, remembering her promise to Meghan.

'Hey, Gianni, smile!'

She raised her phone and waited for him to swivel on his heels and attempt to strike an impressive 'strong man' pose to show off his bulging biceps for the camera, completely forgetting that he was still holding the paint tin and sloshing a generous splash onto the red carpet.

'Argh!'

Izzie shot forwards, relieved Gianni of the paint, and began to pat the carpet with an off-cut of the white muslin she'd been using to the decorate the gazebo.

'*Spiacente!*'

'It's okay, don't worry. Look, if we just cut off the last metre of carpet and have a nine-metre aisle instead of a ten-metre aisle, I'm sure no one will be any the wiser.'

She hoped, crossing her fingers behind her back.

'*Buona idea!*' beamed Gianni, producing a lethal looking pen knife.

'No! Hang on, I'll get the scissors. It'll make a cleaner line.'

When they'd washed away the final dribbles of the paint and covered the area in a few pebbles, Izzie decided it was time to call it a day before any more accidents happened. Anyway, it was almost seven o'clock and streamers of violet and peach stretched across the sky and the swallows were busy rehearsing for the overture of their evening symphony.

'Thanks for your help today, Gianni. I couldn't have done any of this without you. You are an absolute star. See you tomorrow.'

'*Prego*, Izzie. *Ciao!*'

Chapter Eight

Trattoria Antonio, San Vivaldo
Colour: Blush Pink

From her vantage point on the terrace, Izzie watched Gianni mount his quad bike and trundle away through his beloved vines, the hum of the engine blending seamlessly into the cadence of the evening's music. As darkness enveloped the valley, she returned to the kitchen to grab another coffee and make a start on unpacking the myriad cardboard boxes. She wanted to submerge every plate, dish, cup and wine glass in a bowl of soapy water and polish the cutlery until it sparkled.

She discovered a pair of ancient yellow Marigolds in a bucket next to the back door and an hour later perspiration was bubbling at her temples, her shoulder blades were screaming their objection to the unexpected exertion, and she was desperately in need of a shower. She hung the rubber gloves on the swan-necked tap, folded the tea towel into neat quarters, and padded out of the kitchen, relishing the feel of the cool terracotta tiles beneath her feet.

As she climbed the threadbare stairs, steeling herself to brave the psychedelic effect of her bedroom's quaint decor, she wondered why no one was living in villa at the moment. Who was the owner and where were they? Okay, so the place was a little frayed around the edges, its cornices draped with cobwebs, its furniture and appliances throwbacks from the nineteen sixties, but a glimpse beneath the surface told you that Villa Limoncello had soul. She knew it was the interior designer in her poking its head above the parapet, but with a little imagination and a gallon of white paint, the place could be amazing. Not Darren Hamilton amazing, but Isabella Jenkins amazing!

She paused at the door to the bathroom, running her professional eye over the paint-blistered window frames, the purple flowered wallpaper peeling from the eaves, the old-fashioned sink complete with pleated fabric skirt in matching lavender. Yet despite all this, the house seemed to envelope her in a warm, comforting hug, letting her know that if she wanted to talk, then it would listen.

But was she ready to relieve herself of the burden she had carried for two years? And was this really the place for her to do it? Tuscany, the place she had hoped to explore with her beloved twin sister by her side, the place they had researched and researched and researched until they knew everything there was to know about its culture, its history, its food, its art, its architecture and museums. Everything!

She wasn't sure, but one thing she *was* sure of was that she needed a shower!

She switched on the radio, something she rarely did in London, thinking to herself that any country that could produce music like that was surely a place she wanted to spend more time in. With an upbeat tune spinning through her head, she stepped under a stream of luxurious hot water. Washing away the dirt of the day was pure bliss. She even ran a dollop of coconut oil through her wayward curls to tame them into something manageable – a trick that her Aunt Cath, who had similar tussles with her own hair, had taught her.

She glanced in the mirror and for a fleeting moment she didn't recognise the face staring back at her. Smooth hair, the colour of a fox's tail, sparkling eyes, a hint of colour in her cheeks from spending the afternoon in the sun, and a generous smattering of freckles scattered across the bridge of her nose.

But what really threw her was the fact that the reflection sported a wide smile. Wasn't it wonderful what a few hours of physical exercise could do for a person more used to curling up on a sofa in front of the TV. She had expected to be exhausted, to crave nothing more than to fall into her bed and sleep for twelve hours straight, just like she had the previous night when she had arrived, but instead, energy zinged through her veins and she knew that if she crawled under her duvet now she wouldn't sleep.

With a start, she realised that apart from the croissant she had nibbled on to please Carlotta at breakfast, she hadn't eaten all day and she was starving. She made her way back down the stairs to check the fridge, but apart from several bottles of mineral water it was empty. There was nothing in any of the drawers either, and whilst she didn't hold out much hope of finding anything in the cupboard under the porcelain sink, she decided to investigate anyway. Maybe that was where the owner had hidden their stash of gin! She opened the door, bent down to peer inside, and recoiled at such speed that she knocked over a chair.

What the...?

Recovering her equilibrium, she squinted into the gloom where a rotund black-and-white cat had made her home amongst the dishcloths and bleach, looking very disgruntled at having her snooze disturbed. She shut the door, her heart rate slowly returning to normal, only to have her stomach growl at her. The London Izzie would have given up and gone to bed, but the Italian Izzie wasn't having any of it. She needed food and if that meant she had to jump on the Vespa to see if there was somewhere open in the village, then so be it.

She snatched up the keys and zipped off down the driveway, her mouth watering as she dreamed of all the delicious aromas Tuscany was famous for. Mmm, she would start with a simple bruschetta topped with tomatoes, basil and a drizzle of extra virgin olive oil, move on to a plate of *spaghetti aglio e olio*, then round it all off with a scoop of saffron gelato, all washed down with a glass of pinot grigio.

This time her journey to San Vivaldo was trouble-free and she pulled up outside a café she had passed earlier that day. However, when she peered through the open door she saw that Café Pani was filled to bursting with elderly men watching a rerun of the previous day's hotly-contested football game, shaking their fists in the air and shouting at the screen, at the waiters, and at each other.

No grazie!

So, if she didn't want to go to sleep on an empty stomach, she had no other option than to try Antonio's Trattoria. Maybe it would be Luca's night off? But it seemed that once again her guardian angel was missing-in-action because as soon as she stepped onto the veranda she spotted him, looking amazingly attractive in his chef's jacket. She quickly scanned the restaurant, hoping she could perhaps blend in with a throng of lingering diners, but it was late and, apart from a couple of middle-aged guys sitting on the bar stools staring into their beer glasses as if expecting to stumble across the Holy Grail, the place was empty. Monday night probably wasn't the busiest night of the week for a village trattoria.

She couldn't face another spat that day, so, feeling like she was in some kind of Italian farce, she swivelled on her toes and picked her way, slowly, silently, cautiously back to where she'd parked the Vespa.

'Izzie? Are you… are you actually *tiptoeing*?'

She hated the light tone of mockery in his voice.

'No, of course not. I was actually hoping to get something to eat, but as it looks like you're finishing up for the night I'll just leave you to it and...'

She wished Luca wouldn't look at her like that, his dark espresso eyes scouring her soul for her deepest darkest secrets whilst at the same time his lips curled with amusement at her crazy antics. He was still wearing the jeans she had seen him in that afternoon and despite her attempt to appear unaffected by the powerful sensuality radiating from his pores, a shiver of desire ran the length of her spine.

'Please. Stay. You can help me tidy up and afterwards I'll cook you the best omelette you have ever tasted.'

She wanted to refuse, but her stomach was having none of it and forced her brain to say, 'That sounds great. Thank you.' And after a pause she continued, 'Actually, I also came to apologise for my outburst at the villa earlier. I've been under a lot of pressure lately, with my job and now with the villa and the wedding to sort out. And, well, it's not your fault the delivery was late, and if you hadn't stepped into the breach, then who knows when the stuff might have turned up.'

'No problem. Believe me I understand about the stress of event organising, even more so when you step in at the last minute. Do you think you'll be able to get everything done in time?'

She had followed Luca into the kitchen, grateful that he had accepted her apology so graciously, and slid into a seat at the huge pine table not dissimilar to the one at Villa Limoncello. It looked like it belonged there, at the centre of the cooking universe, just like in every Tuscan kitchen. Apart from that, the rest of the room couldn't be more different to the kitchen at the farmhouse. Everywhere she looked there were state-of-the-art stainless-steel appliances, shiny copper saucepans, a variety of unidentifiable silver cooking utensils, and a set of lethal-looking kitchen knives that wouldn't have looked out of place in a hospital operating theatre. The whole room was immaculate, everything in its allocated place, ready for the next day's preparations.

'So, does the woman who hates cooking know how to make an omelette?'

'Sure, I do.'

'Have you actually ever made one?'

Oh, God! How did he do that? It was as though he could read her mind. How could he have her sussed after only meeting her that morning?

'How hard can it be?' she laughed to disguise her lack of culinary know-how. 'Whisk a couple of eggs, put them in a pan, and *ecco!*'

Luca rolled his eyes at her false bravado. He took a step towards her, his lips mere inches from hers, and stretched out his hand. She gasped as a pleasurable squirm began to meander through her abdomen – until she realised he was only reaching for an apron that was dangling from the hook on the door behind her. Warmth flooded her cheeks as he flicked the hoop round her neck and smirked.

'I see you've ditched the scarecrow accessories you were wearing this morning?'

'Yes, well, if you…'

Again, she experienced a surge of heat-filled emotion. However, this time she managed to rein in her indignation over the reasons for her dishevelment. Hadn't she snapped at him enough that day?

'So how many eggs?'

'Three.'

She watched Luca crack the eggs into a stainless-steel bowl and was surprised when he handed her the whisk.

'You want me to do this?'

86

'Need me to show you how?'

Before she could reply, Luca had positioned himself behind her, drawing her body so close to his that she could feel his breath on her cheek. When he snaked his hands around her waist to guide her hands in a rotary movement, her heartbeat kicked up a gear and she was grateful she had her back to him so he couldn't see the effect his proximity was having on her. As it was, perspiration was already prickling at her temples and beneath her breasts.

'Okay, so this is the consistency and colour we're aiming for, now for the cooking part.'

Oh, God, thought Izzie. The temperature in the room was already climbing!

In one, smooth, well-practiced move, Luca selected the perfect pan, placed it on the burner, added a dash of olive oil and poured in the mixture, gentling easing the eggy edges into the middle with a spatula. When the omelette was almost ready, he sprinkled on a handful of fragrant goat's cheese and a garnish of chopped chives, then slid it onto a wide white china plate and handed it to her, his eyebrows raised, his dark eyes holding hers as he waited for her verdict.

The whole thing had taken less than five minutes and Izzie didn't think she'd seen a performance so sensual in the kitchen in her life. She had heard people say that food and passion were intrinsically linked but she hadn't believed them until that moment – her emotions had certainly ratchetted up from semi-thawed to almost sizzling!

'Taste it,' murmured Luca, running the tip of his tongue slowly along his lower lip.

Izzie couldn't tear her eyes away from his, from the way his dark lashes brushed his cheeks when he blinked, the way his dimples framed his wildly seductive mouth, the cute way his fringe fell across his forehead in the heat of the kitchen, the jaunty angle of the collar of his chef's jacket. Everything about him screamed sex appeal and her body was ordering her brain to enjoy the sensations that were cascading through her veins. This was what life was about!

She lifted the fork to her mouth and wrapped her tongue around a morsel of omelette, allowing the flavours to crash through her taste buds; the savoury richness of the eggs, the creaminess of the cheese, the zing of the freshly snipped chives, all melded together to produce what she thought was perfection.

'It's absolutely amazing – definitely knocks buttered toast from my culinary top spot!'

'Good to hear.'

Luca had taken a step nearer and only the empty plate separated them. He removed it from her hand, placed it safely on the counter and tucked a stray coil of her hair behind her ear.

'Izzie, I...'

But she would never know what he had been about to say or what would have happened next because the strange buzzing sensation on her thigh was his phone ringing and he shrugged, stepped away from her, and flicked his finger across the screen.

'*Ciao, Stefano.*'

The expression on his face told Izzie that it was time to make her way back to the villa.

Chapter Nine

Pasticceria Da Oriana, San Vivaldo
Colour: Luscious Lime

The next day dawned with a clear blue sky and a surprising nip in the air. Izzie skipped down the stairs, eager to launch into a full day of list-tackling and determined to make Villa Limoncello the most picturesque wedding venue for a movie shoot that part of Tuscany had ever seen.

Well, she could try.

She poured herself a coffee and padded out to the terrace. If anything, the view was even more impressive that morning and she took a moment to savour the rustic charm before the crazy whirl of chores began. She loved the verdant beauty of the landscape, the stone façades of the farm buildings sporting a patina of a bygone era, the lone campanile on the horizon striving for eternity, but what made her heart sing was the warm golden glow that suffused the whole valley and everything in it.

A feeling of complete serenity descended, something she had not experienced for a long time. Why had she thought that reducing her life to a minimal set of ordered tasks to be achieved before she could claim the oblivion of sleep was the answer to her problems? She had railed so hard against including any extraneous clutter to her daily agenda that she had eradicated any chance of stumbling upon a random moment of pleasure, of happiness. She had refused to spend even a second reflecting on what life had thrown in her direction because that wasn't one of the items on her carefully crafted list. Maybe if she had allowed herself just a little leeway, she would be further down the road of recovery than she was now.

Better late than never! whispered Meghan's cheerful voice in her ear.

However, today was not the day to contemplate reducing her reliance of her faithful friend the list. There were the tables to organise in the shaded courtyard, the silver candelabras to polish, not to mention the dreaded task of folding the napkins into the shapes Brad had requested. She understood the need for attention to detail, but Brad had never seemed like the kind of guy who held such firm views on the presentation of his table linen.

Whilst she'd waited in Departures at Heathrow airport, in order to distract herself from thinking too much about her impending visit to Florence, she had watched a couple of YouTube videos that offered a step-by-step guide on how to achieve the correct shape. Complicated wasn't the word!

Where was Jonti when she needed him? She knew he'd breeze through the challenge!

Well, when there was a difficult task to complete, the only thing to do was to just get on and do it. She returned to the kitchen, scrambled through the cardboard box marked napkins, snatched up the clipboard for that day's itinerary and carried everything outside to the table in the shade.

For a few moments, she closed her eyes and inhaled the fresh fragrance of the new day; a base note of damp earth as the morning dew evaporated under the sun's rays, the floral top note from the honeysuckle and wisteria entwined around the posts of the pergola. The eternal symphony of cicadas was interrupted only by the occasional cry of a cockerel greeting the day or the whine of a lone Vespa as it strained to make it up the hill to the village. Clearly it must be too early for the Heavy Metal ensemble next door.

When her fourth attempt at napkin-folding looked more like a shipwreck than a swan's neck, she decided to postpone her attempt at mastering the ancient art of origami and spend her time doing something more productive. She grabbed her clipboard and ran her finger down the list to the next item on the agenda that required her attention. She was surprised, and not a little relieved, to see that it was her appointment at *Pasticceria Da Oriana*.

She slotted her file into her duffle bag, scribbled a quick note for Carlotta, jumped onto the back of the Vespa – which had now assumed the role of trusty friend – and trundled down the arboreal tunnel towards the villa's gates and the main road beyond. When she arrived in San Vivaldo the streets were just beginning to wake up and the parking gods were smiling on her because she scooted straight into a space right outside the patisserie.

She paused at the window and feasted her eyes on the cornucopia of assorted *pasticcini* and *biscotti*; from tiny tartlets topped with raspberries, strawberries, kiwis and blackberries to jellied fruits covered in sugar, from gooey slabs of nougat wrapped in cellophane and tied with ribbons to psychedelic pink and yellow bon-bons. The display was worthy of an upmarket jewellery store and Izzie knew which she would rather spend her time inside. She pushed open the door and paused on the doorstep to inhale the bouquet of sugary magnificence that sent happy endorphins rushing through her brain and turned her lips upwards into a smile. Heaven!

'*Buongiorno*,' beamed the proprietor of the sugar palace, brushing her hands on a pristine white apron that had been daintily embroidered with the shop's angel-shaped logo before offering her palm.

'*Buongiorno. Il mio nome è Isabella…*'

'Ah, Isabella Jenkins? From *Villa dei Limoni*?'

'Yes, and you must be Oriana?'

Izzie hoped her relief at the switch from Italian to English didn't show too starkly on her face.

'I am. *Ciao, è un piacere conoscerti, Isabella.* It's great to meet you. I did intend to pop over to the villa yesterday to welcome you, and to see if you needed any help, but I've just this minute put the finishing touches to the wedding cake.'

The creator of the fabulously over-the-top wedding cake in Lucy's photographs was not what she had expected. If Izzie had been working in such a shop, she knew she would be the size of a house. No, the size of a Tuscan farmhouse! The eponymous Oriana possessed the deportment of a runway model and was slender, perhaps a little too slender. But then Izzie had no room to talk about being on the svelte side – having lived off caffeine and toast for the best part of two years, her more truthful friends had told her she was bordering on skinny.

'Would you like to take a peek?' smiled Oriana, displaying a set of perfect white teeth.

'I'd love to!'

'*Vieni.* It's through here.'

Oriana's figure was even more impressive from behind, her glossy mahogany hair brushing her shoulder blades, her cream jeans hugging every contour like a second skin. She even smelled delicious, a cross between oriental spice and sweet jasmine. As soon as Izzie entered the back room she understood why Oriana's figure was so impressive – not only was the rear of the shop being used for the intricate art of sugar craft, she spotted a yoga studio through a pair of glazed French doors.

'Do you teach yoga here, too?'

'Yes. Fancy joining us for a session?'

'Oh, I'm...'

Izzie couldn't remember the last time she had entered a gym; certainly before she and Alex had separated. They'd had a joint membership at the hotel leisure club next to their apartment block and would often meet there for a swim or a workout on the running machine after work, but she'd lost all interest in maintaining her fitness.

'I'd love that, but I'm only here until Saturday. You know, I've always wanted to take up yoga, so I might give it a go when I get back home. I've been very lax in my exercise regime, lately, I'm sorry to say.'

'Sounds like a plan! So, what do you think?'

On the marble-topped bench in the middle of the room stood the most wonderful wedding cake Izzie had ever seen. When she had been shopping for wedding cakes with her sister they had visited several confectioners, enjoying every opportunity to sample the various cakes on offer; from dense fruit cake to lemon drizzle cake, from traditional Victoria sponge to indulgent chocolate cakes. If it had been her choice she would have gone for something simple, but Anna had wanted all three; fruit cake for the top tier which she intended to store to use as a christening cake, the middle tier in Victoria sponge with buttercream and raspberry jam, and the large bottom tier made of rich, gooey chocolate cake that she could slice up and hand out to the children at school. The thought caused tears to spring to her eyes, so she quickly diverted her attention to the masterpiece of culinary artistry in front of her.

'Oh, wow! It's... it's stunning!'

Of course, Izzie had seen the photographs that Oriana had worked from but seeing the cake in all its sugary glory took her breath away. Standing seven tiers tall, it looked more like a piece of Italian sculpture than an edible centrepiece for an intimate Tuscan wedding scene. Each layer was covered in smooth ivory fondant icing and a cascade of pale pink sugar paste roses fell from the top tier to the base. When she looked more closely she saw that interspersed between the roses were tiny ivory butterflies, their wings edged with crystals that glinted in the overhead lights.

'I'm so pleased you like it,' said Oriana, beaming with pleasure as she spun on her stiletto heels and disappeared through a doorway to her left, calling over her shoulder, 'So, that is the *pan di spagna*, the sponge cake, which can be prepared in advance, unlike the *crostata di frutta* and the *millefoglie* which I will bake on the morning of the wedding. We don't want what you English call a soggy bottom, do we?'

Oriana stood in the doorway, her eyebrows raised in question. In one hand she held the most exquisite fruit tart Izzie had ever seen, filled with a mosaic of fresh fruits – raspberries, strawberries, blueberries, kiwi, and mango – all resting on a bed of crème pâtissière and finished off with a sugar glaze. In the other hand she held a chocolate mille-feuille cake, its crispy pastry layers crammed with Chantilly cream, topped with intricately piped lime-coloured icing and finished with pretty curls of lime zest then dusted with cocoa powder. Izzie's taste-bids sprang into action. She loved lime!

'Of course, there'll be the seven graduated tiers of each cake on the day, but I thought you might like a taste test, so I made a sample of both for you to try today. If there is anything you don't think is right, please just say and it can be amended for Friday.'

All Izzie could do was gape at Oriana. She had no idea that there would be *three* seven-tiered wedding cakes, and whilst she had absolutely no objection to a taste test, all that mattered was what they looked like! However, Oriana mistook her confusion for concern.

'Ooops, yes, sorry, I almost forgot.'

And once again she disappeared into the adjacent room, which Izzie realised must be refrigerated, and returned with an ornate silver cake-stand on which a variety of freshly baked cannoli had been artistically stacked; all filled with sweet ricotta and alternately finished with either crushed pistachios or dipped in dark chocolate.

'Go on, try one! I want to know what you think.'

Izzie selected one of the crispy tubes and bit into it, holding out her palm to catch the flakes of buttery pastry that fluttered from her lips. A myriad of flavours crashed through her mouth; the sharp creaminess of the ricotta, the sweetness of the icing sugar and the crunchy nuttiness of the chopped pistachios, a veritable harmony on the tongue.

'Mmm, absolutely delicious.'

'Now taste a slice of the *crostata di frutta*. All the ingredients are fair-trade and organic, and all the fruit is grown within a ten miles radius of San Vivaldo, so there's minimal impact on the environment.'

Izzie watched as Oriana cut into the fruit tart and handed her a fork to sample her creation. As expected, it was mouth-wateringly delicious, light and fresh with just enough cream to compliment the zingy flavours of the fruit. It was the perfect alternative to the wedding cake – but, like the cannoli, it wasn't in the brief.

'Izzie? Is there something wrong?'

The look of anxiety scrawled across Oriana's face brought Izzie to her senses.

'No, no, of course not, everything looks fabulous! It's just…
well, I had no idea about the extra… well, there is rather a lot
of cake? Twenty-eight separate tiers, and apart from the sponge
cake, everything has to be eaten on the day.'

'Well, I've been told to cater for fifty guests and an additional twenty on top of that.'

'Seventy!'

'What? You think there'll be more?'

'No! Why would there be more?'

The conversation was suddenly becoming surreal. Izzie saw
from the creases in Oriana's forehead that she was feeling
exactly the same – baffled, confused and bewildered. Heat
rushed to her cheeks. She knew that Italians loved to indulge
in a kaleidoscope of confectionary treats – hadn't both Carlotta
and Luca been at pains to explain this to her? It was just that
these extra desserts were unlikely to be featured in the scene.
She didn't want to offend Oriana, but equally she didn't want
her to go to all the trouble of preparing the tarts and mille-
feuille unnecessarily, especially as she was clearly interested in
keeping waste to a minimum.

'No, no, it's just…'

'The only dessert I haven't made for you to sample is the
vegan cake. It's an acquired taste but I promise you that it will
look just as amazing as all of these, if not more so! I do have a
vested interest in that one, after all!'

'You're making a vegan cake?' Izzie heard the words come
out of her lips in a mere whisper. 'How many tiers?'

'Seven, but don't worry, I don't expect it'll all get eaten,
but I'm sure there will be a few vegans or vegetarians in the
wedding party, don't you?'

'Yes, maybe, possibly…'

As much as Izzie had enjoyed spending time in the confectionary equivalent of Prada, she experienced a strong urge to

escape, especially when she saw Oriana glancing at her from the corner of her eyes as though she was concerned for her sanity.

'Okay, so everything is just perfect, Oriana, I'm sure Brad will be over-the-moon with what you've done.'

'Brad?' Again, puzzlement floated across Oriana's dark features, but she recovered quickly and laughed. 'Oh, yes, yes, of course, the guy who's organising everything. It's really very generous of him, isn't it?'

'Well, erm, yes, yes it is...'

Izzie averted her gaze, pretending to scramble in her bag for her notebook as her thoughts twisted through a labyrinth of perplexity over Oriana's strange behaviour. Why wouldn't Brad be organising everything? Then it dawned on her, Oriana must be referring to the fact that everyone had been invited to enjoy the food that was being prepared for the reception scene when the filming was over. Nothing would go to waste – although she took issue with Oriana's assessment of the numbers expected. According to her calculations, there would be five people in the bridal group, a handful of supporting actors to stand in as the wedding guests, then the film crew, who Meghan had told her usually consisted of Brad and four or five others.

'You will let me know if there's anything I can do to help, won't you? It's a huge enterprise that you've taken on, at the last minute as well, and I have to say that you are a lot calmer about everything than I would be! This is the most exciting thing to happen in San Vivaldo for a long time. My sister is coming over first thing on Friday morning to help me get dressed and do my hair and make-up, and I've even treated myself to a new pair of shoes.'

'Your... hair and makeup?'

Oh, God, it was worse than she thought. Was Oriana hoping to be part of the filming?

'I know, it's a bit excessive,' she laughed when she saw the look of astonishment on Izzie's face. 'My friends think I'm crazy, but why shouldn't I want to look my best? I might not get another chance to meet a real-life celebrity couple!'

'True...'

'Of course, I can completely understand why there's so much secrecy surrounding the whole thing. I mean, who wants the most important day of their lives interrupted by a horde of fans desperate to score an autograph. It's just that I usually like to meet with the bride and groom before their big day to chat through their likes and dislikes, to get a feel for their personalities, and maybe spend an afternoon with the family doing a taste test. I know Francesca who's supplying the floral arrangements feels the same way. Like me, she's had to deal with everything via email. It's really not the way we Italians like to do our weddings! I mean, what bride doesn't want to choose her bouquet in person?'

Izzie stared at Oriana, confusion swirling around her mind. Why would the actors playing the bride and groom be remotely interested in talking about what were, in essence, the props of a scene?

'Oriana, I think there's been a misunderstanding...'

'What sort of misunderstanding?'

'The wedding at Villa Limoncello isn't a real wedding. It's a film shoot – Brad, the guy who emailed you, he's the director. The bride and groom are actors, they're not *actually* getting married.'

Now it was Oriana's turn to stare at Izzie with bewilderment.

'I don't think so, Izzie. Hang on, I'll show you the email.'

Izzie felt like she was an unsuspecting bystander in an Italian comedy show, and that anytime now a bunch of people dressed in harlequin costumes would leap out of the cupboard and yell 'surprise!'. Except they didn't, and when she read the email Oriana had pulled up on her phone, the surge of shock was so powerful she had to fight to breathe.

'Oh my God! It's a real wedding! Of course it is! What was I thinking? Oh my God!'

Izzie's jaw hung loose and her heart pounded out a staccato of incredulity and disbelief. She was vaguely aware of her new friend taking hold of her arm and gently guiding her towards a huge scarlet bean bag in the yoga studio before offering her a bottle of water. Pressure squeezed her temples in a vice-like grip as the full realisation dawned.

What was the matter with her? Was she so wrapped up in her own little bubble that common sense didn't get a look in? What was she going to do?

If she were honest, all she wanted to do was run for the hills, but that would mean letting everyone down and she couldn't do that. This had been *her* mistake, and Meghan's; no one else had thought the wedding was a film shoot, which, with the benefit of hindsight, had perhaps been a conclusion they shouldn't have jumped to. Indeed, nowhere in the paperwork had there been anything to suggest this was anything other than a wedding – one she only had three days to pull off!

'Why didn't anyone tell me?'

'Didn't you speak to Brad before you came out here?'

'No, he'd already left for a shoot in Bali, and Lucy, his PA, was laid up in hospital and I didn't want to bother her with a list of never-ending questions. I spoke to his wife, Rachel, but she's got so much on her plate with being pregnant and organising the children, as well as trying to sort out all Brad's admin stuff that I suppose we just got our wires crossed. I mean, he's a film director, my friend Meghan's helped him out on shoots plenty of times before. Oh my God, I'm going to kill him!'

'Well, at least you know now,' said Oriana, her eyes filled with sympathy and kindness.

'What about Carlotta, or Gianni, why didn't they say anything?'

'Maybe, like me, they had no idea about the mix-up.'

Izzie thought back to her afternoon with Gianni and realised that Oriana was right. The only hint there had been that perhaps something was amiss was when she had said she was leaving for London as soon as the words 'it's a wrap!' had been declared. No wonder he had looked at her askance. Why hadn't she pressed the subject, but then, why should she have? Then another even more embarrassing thought occurred to her and her face flooded with heat.

'So, are you telling me that everyone in San Vivaldo knows about the wedding?'

'Well, not *everyone*. Only the actual wedding guests and the suppliers like myself, and, as I said before, we've all been told to be discreet until the ceremony and reception are over which is why we don't know who the bride and groom are and our only contact with them is through Brad to ensure their privacy. I'm so sorry, Izzie, I wish I had realised sooner...'

'It's okay, it's not your fault,' smiled Izzie, as her brain reconnected to its modem and the scrambled jigsaw began to reassemble. 'But this makes things so much harder. Set design is sort of what I do for a living – albeit for only a handful of viewers – or it was until recently, and if something isn't perfect the first time around, it can easily be adjusted and filmed again. But that isn't the case with a real wedding, is it? You only get one chance to get it right!'

Nausea began an insidious journey from her stomach, through her chest, and into her throat as she contemplated the challenge ahead. She was no wedding planner, and despite being involved in the arrangements for her sister's wedding to Matt, this was a totally different scenario. The bride, or groom, or both of them, were clearly good friends of Brad's, but they were also celebrities, according to Oriana, although she reminded herself that as their identity was being kept a secret she couldn't know that for sure.

After refusing another glass of water, she waved goodbye to Oriana, and made her way to where she'd left the Vespa, her head spinning with what she'd just learnt. However, as she kicked her leg over the saddle, the strongest emotion swirling through her veins was a concoction of embarrassment and annoyance.

Had Luca realised her error? If he had, then she was upset with him for not telling her. If he hadn't, she had never been so mortified in her life and she would try her absolute best to make sure that their paths never crossed again!

Chapter Ten

The swimming pool next door
Colour: Quintessential turquoise

By the time Izzie arrived back at the villa, it was midday
and the cicadas were building up to an orchestral crescendo.
She wheeled the Vespa into the outhouse and went in search
of Carlotta to confess her mistake, to make sure she had
everything covered now she was aware of the situation, and
then to spend some time amending her 'to do' lists and daily
itineraries. The more she thought about it, the more ridiculous she felt for not realising sooner, but she was able to
comfort herself with the fact that Meghan, too, had thought
she was overseeing the arrangements for a film shoot. She was
desperate to talk to her friend, to have a good giggle over their
misunderstanding, but she needed to speak to Carlotta first.

'Carlotta?'

She poked her head around the kitchen door, but the room
was empty and the note she had left for her that morning
was still on the table. She returned to the terrace, noting
the absence of her bicycle, and a ripple of concern wriggled
through her chest. Where was she? She grabbed her mobile
and scrolled through her contacts for Carlotta's number, but
when she called there was no reply.

She left a voicemail asking if everything was okay, then
took a seat at the table beneath the pergola, relishing the

veil of serenity Villa Limoncello seemed to radiate. Looking across the gardens towards where the wedding would be held, she understood exactly why the venue had been chosen for a couple to exchange their vows. The wedding photographs would be amazing!

She raised her chin, enjoying the warmth of the sun on her face, unconcerned about the reappearance of her freckles, and sighed with pleasure. Again, she wondered who owned the villa and whether they hired it out for other purposes, such as Italian cookery courses (probably not bearing in mind the state of the kitchen), or artists' and writers' retreats, or maybe yoga holidays, or even, dare she add, film shoots? It was a perfect setting for any of these pursuits, as long as Mr Grumpy next door gave up the early morning jackhammering and chainsaw wrangling.

Izzie strained her ears, but no mechanical sound interrupted the peace and a smile spread across her lips as an idea slid into her mind. Could she? No, she'd better not. She really should concentrate on reconfiguring her schedules or becoming proficient in the art of napkin-folding. But the seed of curiosity had been planted. What did the house next door look like? What about the gardens? Did it have a vineyard and olive groves, too? Was there a tennis court, a pond, a *swimming pool*?

Oh, God, the interior designer in her was screaming for her to take a quick peek, and so, with excitement bubbling in her chest, she trotted across the terrace, past the *limonaia* and the wishing well, to where she'd seen a gap in the wall whilst exploring with Gianni the previous day. Well, not a gap as such, more a couple of missing top stones. She glanced over her shoulder to make sure there was no audience to witness her mission – Gianni – and cocked her leg as high as she could, rolling on her stomach over to the other side and landing with an uncomfortable *hurumph*.

She jumped up, dusted herself down and gasped. In front of her stood a completely-renovated villa – smooth antique-gold façade, newly painted shutters, pristine front door – encircled by a perfectly level sandstone terrace. It was a princess of a property compared to its ugly duckling twin sister next door. The owner had clearly spent a fortune on the renovations, and Izzie wondered whether he intended to live there, or rent it out to holidaymakers with cash to burn, or maybe he was intending to open it as a B&B? Really? With the Italian version of Basil Fawlty as the host?

The place was deserted so she felt emboldened to continue her exploration, although others might call it trespass. She had taken only a couple of steps towards the front door, when she paused next to a rose-covered arbour through which was the most wonderful sight of all – a huge, rectangular swimming pool. It was like something from a travel brochure for upmarket Italian holidays; the rolling green hills in the distance, the cypress trees and resplendent rhododendron bushes in the foreground, the honeyed-stone and green shutters of the pool house, all framed by a border of rich yellow roses. If she ignored the discarded tools, the piles of stone flags waiting to be cut to shape, the cement mixers, portable workbenches, stone saws and jackhammers, the image was pure Tuscan paradise.

She made her way along the terrace towards the pool and was surprised to see that it held less than three inches of shimmering aquamarine water. Why wasn't it filled to the top to entice its guests to indulge in a refreshing dip? Nevertheless, the lure was too much to resist. Taking another quick glance over her shoulder, she slipped off her shoes and descended the marble steps into the water.

What an amazing feeling! She kicked her feet in the air with wanton abandon, splashing her arms and face with droplets of water, revelling in the way the sunlight danced on the surface like a sheet of scattered diamonds. She was enjoying herself so much that she completely lost track of time.

Oh, God, if her neighbour saw what she was doing he'd probably have a coronary!

As much as the guy had been a pain in the butt she didn't want his death on her hands, so she clambered back up the steps, grabbed her shoes, and jogged back to the villa. She had just rounded the corner of the *limonaia* when she heard the insistent ring of a house phone. Not sure where to look, she rushed into the kitchen, feeling as though she was six years old again and she and Anna were playing hide-and-seek – a game her sister had excelled at. She eventually located the old-fashioned telephone in the lounge, loitering beneath a pile of newspapers from two thousand and twelve.

'Hello?'

Should she have said *Ciao*? Or *Buongiorno*?

She held her breath, praying that the caller wouldn't launch into a tirade of unintelligible Italian, but relaxed when she heard the dulcet tones of Carlotta. Sadly, her relief didn't last very long.

'Ah, Izzie, at last! I've been calling you for the last hour! I'm so sorry, I won't be able to make it to the villa today.'

'Oh, I…' A myriad of thoughts and questions ricocheted through Izzie's brain. She needed to ask Carlotta about the wedding, to apologise for her mistake, to enquire about the food and the menus, to check exactly how many guests she was catering for, to make sure they were now, at last, on the same page with the arrangements, but she had caught the note of distress in Carlotta's voice. 'Why can't you come? What's happened? Are you okay?'

'It's my friend, Vincenzo. He's had an accident.'

'Oh my God, is he okay?'

'Argh, I tell him every day, he drives like a maniac! Does he listen? No! *Lui è matto!* He's crazy! Like many men his age, he seems to labour under the illusion that the speed of your vehicle is directly proportionate to your masculinity!'

'So where is he…'

'He's in the hospital with a fractured collarbone and he will also have ringing ears to add to his woes when I get to see him, but I really need to be with him, I… well, he needs someone to take care of him.'

Gianni had been right. From Carlotta's reaction it was clear she cared a great deal for Vincenzo, although Izzie wasn't sure she'd admitted it to herself yet. Maybe this incident would be the catalyst to a new beginning? However, did she really believe that every cloud had a silver lining? *Her* own black cloud remained resolutely unlined!

'I'm so sorry, Izzie, I know how much there is still left to do before the wedding on Friday, but when I couldn't get hold of you I spoke to Gianni and he's promised to put his services at your disposal today – just make sure you give him a list of things to keep him busy and away from potential trouble.'

'Oh, erm, thanks…' muttered Izzie, suspecting that Gianni was more likely to *add* to her list of jobs. 'But what about the food, erm, for all the wedding guests? There's no way I can…'

'It's all sorted. Vincenzo and I spent the whole of yesterday afternoon sourcing the non-perishables and checking up on the orders for the fresh food which will be delivered first thing on Friday morning. I'll be with you tomorrow to prepare everything we can in advance, I'm so sorry, Izzie…'

'Please, don't worry, Carlotta, you can leave everything with me and Gianni. Send Vincenzo my love and I hope they discharge him soon.'

'Thank you, Izzie. Good luck.'

Before Izzie had the chance to reassure Carlotta again, the line went dead, and a surge of anxiety threatened to overwhelm her. Even with Gianni's help, there was no way she could handle everything there was left to do. Okay, she had no concerns about the wedding cake and the dessert course, and the venue was almost finished and looked amazing, but there were still the flowers to check up on, the house to clean, the wishing well to paint, the stupid napkins to fold.

Still clutching the telephone receiver, she sank into the folds of the ancient cracked leather sofa, battling the demons that were threatening to poke their heads from their swamp of self-doubt.

Then she gave herself a stern talking to. Of course she could do it! If she could find someone to help Carlotta with the food preparation, all she had to do was concentrate on turning the grounds of Villa Limoncello into the most amazing of venues. Hadn't she spent her life doing just that? Okay, not staging real-life *al fresco* weddings, but she had designed interiors for a great deal of highly discerning clients in her time.

But that was before, challenged the invisible naysayers perched on her shoulder. However, Izzie ignored them – she had her secret weapon, didn't she?

Meghan.

Chapter Eleven

The Garden, Villa Limoncello
Colour: Friendship Gold

'Oh my God,' giggled Meghan, her tinkling laughter easing Izzie's rattled nerves. 'Believe me, I had no idea! I'm so sorry, Izzie, this is totally my fault. When Brad called me on Friday morning, I just assumed that, as usual, he was expecting me to down tools and rush to his rescue like he'd done before. In fact, remember three years ago when I had to fly over to Cyprus to help out with the Jacques Vivian film shoot? That was for a wedding scene and I just thought... well... again, I'm sorry, Izzie. I feel awful for jumping to conclusions when I should have asked for details. So, what did Oriana say when you fessed up?'

'Oh, she was really understanding. You'll like her, Meghan – she's not only a maestro of confectionary heaven, she's also the local yoga buff. She's got a studio and even invited me to join her for a session!'

'Obviously hasn't known you long enough!'

'True! When was the last time you saw me in lycra?'

'Well, it wouldn't do you any harm to take a class, Izz. Yoga is meant to be really good for controlling stress, you know,' said Meghan gently, before swiftly changing tack. 'So, what about everyone else? Didn't any of them realise your mistake?'

'Well, there's only Carlotta and Gianni. Thinking back, they did look at me strangely a couple of times, but I don't think my sanity was in question, just my intelligence. I think they must think I'm a bit flaky that's all, and I'll take that over being an absolute fool for not realising sooner, or not pressing Rachel for more information before I caught the flight over here.'

'Look, Izzie, there's no way you should beat yourself up about this. This is totally my brother's fault. He's staging this wedding – which I admit is very kind of him – but then he went and dumped it all on Lucy. It's easy to make generous gestures when you don't have to follow through on them. He's done it one too many times now and believe me I'm going to have a few stern words with him when I get over there. It just isn't on. If I hadn't had the fashion show, it would have been me dealing with the fallout from another one of his cock-ups! Okay, not a cock-up, but you know what I mean. It's so not fair on Lucy to have to do her job as his assistant and also be expected to singlehandedly organise a wedding for one of his actor friends so they don't have to do it themselves. I know how busy these kind of people are, but it's not on. Brad clearly needs someone else on the payroll – Lucy needs her own assistant… and I have the perfect solution.'

'I thought you loved your job at Harrods…'

'Not me, you idiot! You! You would be perfect, Izzie. You're an ace organiser and a fanatical list-maker. I bet you've got your colour-coded clipboards with you. Together, you and Lucy will have my brother licked into shape in no time at all. And I know I complain about helping him out all the time, but when I do, it's the most exciting gig to be part of, especially with all the exotic locations he films in!'

'I'm not sure I have the skills to be a film set designer…'

'Okay, so maybe a wedding planner, then. Oh, my God, Izzie, I'm so sorry I completely forgot!' cried Meghan, contrition filling her voice. 'Will you forgive me! How could I be so... Are you okay? How do you feel about... well... about organising another wedding after what happened last time? Oh my God, I'm so going to kill my brother. He's really done it this time, he's just so thoughtless. It's always all about him...'

'Meghan, it's okay...'

'No, it's not. He knows about Anna and Matt, he should never have agreed to let you replace me.'

'Meghan, really. I'm okay with it. Well, no, that's not quite true. I'm terrified about getting something wrong when so much depends on everything going according to plan on the actual day, but you know what, I actually think that doing this will help me to move forward.'

'What do you mean?'

'Well, don't get me wrong, every single thing I've handled so far, I've compared to what happened last time. But this wedding is completely different to Anna and Matt's. It's in a foreign country for a start, and there's been no expense spared, and the wedding cakes are just crazy, and I haven't even seen the actual flowers yet, but the photographs are out of this world! Doing this will fill my brain with different kinds of flower arrangements, alternate table designs, other menus and wine lists, other table settings, so that whenever someone mentions a wedding in the future Anna and Matt's won't be the only one that will spring to mind. I'll also have this one – which is absolutely amazing, too. It will help, I'm sure of it.'

'Do you really think so?'

'Yes, I do.'

'Then I'm glad, and I can't wait to get over there and join you to make new memories!'

'I can't wait to do that, too, Meg. I've got so much to show you, so much to tell you about. Anyway, now it's my turn to ask the questions,' Izzie laughed, feeling as though she'd been under a heated spotlight for hours as she confessed her misdemeanour to her friend, yet she knew Meghan only had her interests at heart. Now that she'd admitted what had happened, a weight had lifted from her shoulders. She was relieved that it wasn't just her who had made the crazy assumption. 'How was the Fenella Fratenelli fashion show last night? Tell me everything, leave nothing out.'

'Oh, Izzie, it was absolutely amazing, and I got to be involved in every part of the show! First, I helped Darius set everything up, then Martha showed me how to organise every outfit that was being showcased – along with the matching accessories. I was even allowed to spend thirty minutes with the hair and makeup guys. But meeting Fenella herself was the biggest treat of all. She's a sartorial queen! You should have seen what she was wearing – this gorgeous, mid-calf-length, lemon jumpsuit with a cross-over back and flared trousers, and these cute leopard print pumps in tangerine. She really knows how to work an elegant silhouette. But my absolute favourite piece of the whole show was a turquoise sundress embroidered with tiny daisies – way out of my budget unfortunately.'

'Sounds like you had a fabulous evening. How did the commentary go?'

'Well, Martha opened the show, then she past the baton on to me. I admit, I was *so* nervous I thought I was going to vomit, but as soon as I had the mic in my hands and introduced the first model the nerves flew out of the window and I just went with the flow, let the couture speak for itself. Oh, Izzie, I loved every minute of it. And guess what? Fenella even mentioned to Martha that she thought I was a natural. I hope her endorsement means Martha will let me do the summer show! There were photographers there from the national magazines, too. I'm going to buy every single one of them to see if they mention me. I don't expect they will, but you never know.'

'I'm thrilled for you, darling! I knew you would ace it!'

Izzie's whole body, from the top of her curls to the ends of her toes, relaxed and the lingering nuggets of anxiety over her faux pas began to float away on a stream of gossipy camaraderie with a true friend. Meghan had always been able to do that, had always been there to dish up a portion of that trio of female solace – chocolate, cocktails and a good old chinwag. It was the perfect combination and she would be forever grateful to her best friend for being by her side, through the good times and the worst times.

'Thanks, Meghan,' she said, her voice catching with emotion.

'What for?'

'For everything. You are an amazing friend and I love you. No matter what trauma throws itself in my path, you're always there to pick up the pieces, help me put them back together and then press on. I hope you know how much I appreciate that you are a part of my life.'

'So, what you're saying is that you owe me?' she said with a giggle.

'Well, that…'

'I think you said his name was Gianni? Perhaps you could prepare the ground, so to speak? You know, talk me up as this super-talented, completely gorgeous friend who's in the fashion industry, and loves all things Italian; the couture, the food, the wine, but especially the smouldering good looks of the Italian Stallion? Something like that? I'll leave the details up to you?'

Izzie laughed and the final traces of mortification over her error disappeared. Her spirits soared, her lips curled into a broad grin, and she sent up a missive of gratitude that Meghan would soon be by her side in Tuscany where she would light up the whole valley with her imitable brand of cheerfulness. Gianni wouldn't know what hit him – but he was also the luckiest guy in the world.

'Love you, Meg. See you Thursday.'

'Back atch'a, darling! Now, one last question.'

'What?'

'Do I need to bring a bikini?'

Chapter Twelve

The Pergola, Villa Limoncello
Colour: Dark Espresso

A whoosh of confidence gushed through her and she leapt up from the sofa with a smile. The sooner she got started, the more she'd get done! She took a step towards the kitchen and stopped.

What was that?

She strained her ears and heard it again. The scraping of furniture on a tiled floor. Her heart bounced painfully against her ribcage, her thoughts performing somersaults of alarm as she peered through the gap in the door – but the kitchen was empty.

Had she been hearing things? Was the pressure causing her to hallucinate?

She took another step forward and heard a car door slam. Moments later, a figure appeared on the doorstep, their identity masked by the tall stack of cardboard boxes they were carrying.

Did axe murderers use cardboard boxes as lethal weapons?

'Erm, hello?'

'*Ah, buongiorno!*'

She rushed forward to catch a toppling box from the top of the pile and heaved a sigh of relief when she saw who her visitor was, followed swiftly by a lurch of pleasure, then panic.

She'd hoped to avoid bumping into Luca again so that the whole wedding/film shoot fiasco wouldn't rear its ugly head. She ran her eyes over his attire – smart, powder-blue shirt open at the neck, cuffs rolled back to accentuate his strong forearms, dark blue jeans that looked like they'd been sprayed on. There was an attractive smattering of stubble darkening his jawline, and, as usual, his hair sprang up in random tufts at the nape of his neck. But the best part of having Luca in her kitchen was the aroma of citrusy cologne that swirled through the air, tickling her nostrils and sending her senses into overdrive.

'Have you heard about Vincenzo?' asked Luca, striding to the counter to rustle up an espresso as if he owned the place. Izzie wanted to giggle when she saw his expression as he took that first sip, as if tasting the rich, dark brown elixir for the first time and experiencing ecstasy.

'Yes, Carlotta just rang. Do you know anything about what happened?'

'Apparently, he was on his way to collect Carlotta to give her a lift to the villa with the food they bought yesterday, when a Fiat cut a corner and forced him off the road. I don't think either vehicle will be taking part in a beauty pageant any time soon, but from eye witness accounts – Pani from the Café – both drivers had a lucky escape.'

'Carlotta says he has a fractured collarbone.'

'That's right, but I think they'll discharge him fairly quickly.'

'Poor Vincenzo,' muttered Izzie, shaking her head as she thought of the crazy driving antics she had seen on every corner and every street since arriving in Italy. Her heart filled with sympathy for the pain he must be enduring until her eyes landed on the stack of boxes Luca had brought with him. 'So, what's in the boxes?'

'Well, I thought you might need a hand, so I'm at your disposal. Tuesday is my day off so just tell me what you want me to do and your wish is my command.'

'Anything?'

'Anything,' confirmed Luca, raising his eyebrows suggestively as his lips twisted into a mischievous smile.

Izzie rolled her eyes at him, but a splash of heat radiated through her veins. However, two could play at that game!

'Actually, I do have the perfect job for you.'

'Great. Lead the way.'

Luca shoved back his chair and followed her outside to the pergola.

'Any good at origami?'

'Origami?'

'Yes, these napkins need to be folded into the shape of a swan.'

'You're joking right?'

'No. We have fifty to do. Then there's the table linen to iron, the satin rosettes to make and tie to the back of every chair both in the congregation and in the courtyard, these ribbons to twist around the balustrade...'

Izzie paused, smiling at the scowl on Luca's face as he attempted to make his square of cloth look like a swan rather than a squashed duck. She wanted to laugh, to relax and enjoy the sparks of attraction fizzing through her body at his proximity, but she couldn't whilst her thoughts were fixated on what Oriana had told her. There was only one solution and that was to lance the boil, to say something, suffer the inevitable embarrassment, and then she could relegate her gaffe to the 'dealt with' pile and move on.

'Luca?'

'Mmm...?'

'What do you know about this wedding?'

117

'What do you mean?'

'Well, for a start, did you know that the bride and groom are, well, actors?'

'Yes, of course, that's why we've all be sworn to secrecy. Why?'

She could feel the warmth seeping into her cheeks and she was unable to continue to meet Luca's gaze, preferring instead to finger her folder of papers that was still on the table. After a few seconds she looked back up and saw the realisation dawn on his face.

'You don't mean… you don't mean to tell me that you were under the impression that the wedding was some sort of scene from a movie?'

'Well, I told you that I stepped in at the last minute. All I had to go on was a brief conversation with Brad's harassed wife, and an email forwarded to me by his PA from her hospital bed as she recovered from the after-effects of a severe case of food poisoning. Hardly an in-depth consultation on the requirements for an intimate Italian wedding in the rolling hills of Tuscany. And I would remind you that Brad *is* a film director, the bride and groom *are* actors, and my best friend *has* previously helped him to organise several shoots. We *both* thought it was for a scene from one of his movies!'

Izzie eyed Luca closely, scrutinising his reaction for any hint that he had known of her error and had purposely not told her in order to extract maximum amusement, but she couldn't read his expression until his gaze fell on her purple folder that was open at the page marked Table Accessories.

'What's all this stuff?' Luca reached over and picked up the clipboard with that day's itinerary. 'Is this a timetable?'

'Yes, and you know what, I'm glad I've put so much effort into the organisation. Whilst I might just have been able to stage a location for a film, taking on the role of fully-fledged wedding planner is something completely different. This way, there's a chance the wedding might actually go ahead on schedule. That file contains everything I need for the successful staging of the wedding ceremony, from the layout of the venue and the pre-reception drinks, to how the fabric should be draped around the gazebo, to what food will be served, and the design of the napkins we are folding – all as requested by the director of my humiliation, Brad Knowles, by best friend's crazy brother.'

By the time she had finished her indignant monologue her cheeks were burning, and her breath was coming in spurts as she fought to rein in her rampaging emotions. However, when she met Luca's gaze this time, far from the laughter she had expected to see reflected there, she saw understanding and interest.

'From what you've told me, it was an easy mistake to make – and you're absolutely right. It's much harder to organise a wedding than a film shoot. A scene can be shot a hundred times, if necessary, but you only get one chance to stage the perfect wedding, although I'm sure neither would be a problem with Izzie Jenkins in charge. From what I've seen so far, *Villa dei Limoni* is shaping up to be a fabulous wedding venue.'

Izzie smiled. Well, that had been easier than she'd thought.

'Thanks, Luca, you have no idea how much I needed to hear that. So, what do you think?' she asked, holding up her napkin for inspection, proud that it did actually look like a swan – until the whole thing unravelled and all she was left with was a square of crumpled linen.

Izzie met Luca's dark espresso eyes and saw the corners of his mouth curl upwards, causing the cute dimples to appear. She looked again at the napkin she held in her hand and this time a giggle escaped from her lips, Luca joined in and within seconds they were both howling with laughter. A blissful buoyancy seeped into her body and the concrete block that went everywhere with her melted away on a cascade of contentment.

The sun was shining, she was in one of the most beautiful parts of the world, and she was sitting next to the most handsome of men. What was she doing carrying around such misery when she should be appreciating her good fortune?

'I think it's all in the fold,' said Luca, when they had mastered their merriment and returned to the task in hand. 'Why don't I fetch a few books from the library to press the material into shape?'

After the next two attempts, they got the hang of it and within twenty minutes there was a pile of beautifully folded napkins sandwiched between a pile of books nestled in the cardboard box that Izzie would take out on Friday morning when they set the tables in the courtyard. With Luca's help, she ironed the enormous matching tablecloths and hung them to air on a clothes line he'd discovered in the outhouse where she had found the Vespa, finished all the rosettes that would decorate the chairs, tested the garlands of fairy lights they'd draped around the courtyard, and even brushed the terrace free of leaves.

Dare she hope that things were coming together at last, that she could actually do this?

As she stood back to survey their accomplishments, a sudden flash of guilt burst into her mind – surely Luca had a girlfriend desperate to spend her time with him on his day off? The thought caused perspiration to rush to her temples and she wiped it away with her fingertips.

'Okay, it's getting too hot out here and we deserve a break!' declared Luca, towering over Izzie with his hands on his hips.

Izzie, still deep in the process of formulating an image of what Luca's girlfriend might look like, couldn't meet his gaze for fear he would read her mind. 'Ever made fresh pasta?'

'No. My pasta comes in shiny cellophane bags,' she laughed, emerging quickly from her reverie.

'Come on. I'll give you a tutorial in authentic Italian pasta-making,' Luca grinned, his passion for all things food-related causing his eyes to sparkle with anticipation.

Once in the kitchen, Izzie realised what was in the boxes Luca had brought with him. As he unpacked the ingredients, she inhaled the taste-bud-tickling scent of the fresh, locally sourced produce – crispy loaves of home-baked ciabatta, ripe plum tomatoes, bunches of fragrant basil leaves. Amongst the final items Luca produced from his culinary box of tricks were two striped aprons; he wrapped one around his waist and handed her the other one.

'What? You thought I was going to do all the hard work whilst you sat and watched, then gobbled up the end results?'

'No, no, of course not.'

But she had been intending to do exactly that. Her cheeks coloured, but it was worth it when she saw those cute dimples appear around Luca's lips.

'Then come closer so I can show you what to do!'

She rolled up the sleeves of her T-shirt and took her place next to him, watching carefully as he emptied a mound of flour directly onto the wooden table, added a pinch of salt, and then reached for the eggs.

'Okay, so the first thing to remember is that you should use the freshest eggs available, and they should be at room temperature. Now it's over to you.'

'Already?'

'Just make a well in the flour, crack two eggs into it, and gently incorporate them into the mixture with your fingers until everything is combined.'

With a level of concentration she usually reserved for completing her business accounts, Izzie followed Luca's instructions to the letter, struggling not to flinch whenever their fingers touched and a spasm of electricity shot through her veins. But there was worse to come. In order to demonstrate the correct kneading technique, Luca once again positioned himself behind her, his arms at her waist, directing her in the art of massaging the dough with the palm of his hand. It was like a scene from Ghost except with edible props!

'If you don't knead the dough well, it will be soft when cooked instead of *al dente*. Now we wrap it in clingfilm and allow it to rest whilst we make a simple tomato sauce.'

When they eventually sat down at the kitchen table with a bottle of rich Chianti, Izzie was ravenous and couldn't wait to dig into her plate of steaming fragrant spaghetti. There was something so satisfying about eating a meal that you had prepared yourself from scratch and every mouthful tasted better than the last.

'In Italy, food is about more than filling the body with fuel. It's an expression of love; from sowing and nurturing the ingredients, to harvesting them, to preparing them for the sauce, to sharing the results around a table just like this one. My grandmother always used to say, *A tavola non si invecchia* – it means 'at the table you never get old'. Italians never eat alone, we prefer to be surrounded by our family and our friends, of all generations.'

'So, did you always want to be a chef?'

Luca smiled, but his eyes held a hint of sadness. 'Yes, I always wanted to be a chef. Every aspect of the culinary process fascinates me; the textures, the aromas, the taste, the alchemy

– how the most obscure ingredients can meld together to produce magic on the lips. I used to spend hours with my *nonna*, learning about flavours, listening to her advice, jotting down her recipes in a journal – I still have it and it's my most precious possession. Some of her recipes were handed down from her own grandmother. I'm an only child so she wanted to make sure the Castelotti recipes remain in the family for the next generation. I don't think my father ever forgave her,' he added with a mirthless laugh.

'What do you mean? Forgave her for what?'

Avoiding her eyes, Luca picked up his wine glass and sauntered outside to the terrace, pausing to stare at the view before dropping onto the bench in the shade of the pergola. Izzie sensed the ache of his internal conflict and decided to give him a few moments alone. She collected their plates, washed them in the sink – along with the utensils they had used – and returned everything to their allocated places in the cupboards. When she eventually sat down next to him, it was a while before he spoke.

'I've dreamed of owning my own restaurant since I was ten years old, but when I told my parents they were horrified. My father's a commercial lawyer in Milan and the last thing he wanted was for his only son to work in a kitchen. I won't bore you with the details, the heated arguments, the guilt-filled silences that stretched into weeks, my mother's distress. In the end, I caved in to parental pressure and went off to university in Siena.'

Luca paused, swirling the remains of his red wine in his glass, lost in his memories.

'I graduated three years later with a degree in Economics that landed me a lucrative job in banking which made my parents proud and me miserable. I worked sixteen-hour days; I didn't eat properly, never saw my friends, and my life became one long conveyor belt of work, eat, sleep, repeat. However, the prestigious career did have its compensations – I had a healthy bank balance and could afford to rent a great apartment in Florence and treat myself to the car I'd salivated over for years.'

'The Spider?' Izzie teased him, keen to raise his spirits.

She had never seen Luca look so despondent. Whenever she was with him, he always had a smile on his face, but now his eyes were downcast, his shoulders loose, his thoughts lost in the world he used to inhabit, the one his family had wanted him to pursue. Sympathy nipped at her heart. If there was one thing she knew, it was that living someone else's dream didn't make you happy, whatever the financial advantages. As the shadows from the branches overhead danced on the flagstones and the cicadas continued their hypnotic chorus, a mantle of calmness descended, and Izzie wondered if it was time to share a little of her own history with the man who, for whatever reason, had chosen to reveal a corner of his soul to her.

What if Meghan was right? What if talking about your past to someone who had no pre-conceptions about how she *should* be feeling, would help, even in a small way, to push her towards a place in her life's journey where she could think about moving on?

'I used to be a workaholic, too,' she murmured, keeping her eyes trained on the contents of her wine glass so as not to be distracted by Luca's facial expression when she opened up to a relative stranger for the first time in two years. 'I had my own interior design business with a list of wealthy clients, an ambitious fiancé working his way up the ranks of the legal profession, a fabulous apartment overlooking the Thames, and this really cute sunshine-yellow cinquecento.'

She paused, wondering whether Luca would comment, or encourage her to continue, but he remained motionless, clearly not wanting to break the spell that had woven its tendrils around the pergola to provide a safe haven in which to talk about what had happened. She was grateful for his silence because she could already feel the monsters marching through her veins and into her brain, clambering to be released, to smell and taste the air of freedom, to run wild, and maybe, just maybe, vanish off into the distance.

'My family always complained that they never saw me. It wasn't that I didn't want to see them, I did, but after I graduated from college, I stayed on in London, and Cornwall seemed a world away... well, you know what I mean. But I always, always, always, made time for my sister during school holidays when she was released from her duties as a primary schoolteacher at the local village school where we grew up.'

Her thoughts zoomed back down the memory super-highway to some of the best days of her life when she and Anna had mooched around the capital's cathedrals of consumerism, shopping for paint and fabric supplies; her, for her interior design business, Anna, for her beloved pupils' art projects.

'I can see her now, giggling as we modelled papier mâché masks for Year Three's Halloween party, or the macramé outfits for the Christmas play, or these amazing chiffon hats I wanted to display on bronze busts at an exhibition I was organising with Meghan.'

The clarity of the image of her sister, her head thrown back with laughter, caused Izzie's courage to falter. The pain of her loss seared through her heart, still too raw to vocalise, and she was grateful when Luca relieved her of the conversation baton to give her the space to gather her thoughts.

'I was engaged, too. Sabrina and I met at university, then when I landed my job at the bank we moved in together. She loved the glamorous lifestyle our salaries could afford; the weekend trips to Rome, the foreign holidays to Bali and New

York, skiing in the Alps. I even made an offer on a house which I thought we could renovate together, but when I unveiled the project Sabrina baulked at the prospect – looking back, her reaction should have been my first clue.'

Luca leaned back in his chair and crossed his ankle over his thigh, nursing his empty glass, his eyes fixed on the horizon as though watching those days enfold on a film reel in front of his eyes.

'After two more months of wheeling and dealing, I couldn't stand the high-octane environment a moment longer. I'd completely lost sense of who I was, as if I was living someone else's life. So, I resigned from the bank, took a job in a restaurant washing dishes, and within a week I knew I was exactly where I wanted to be. Of course, my salary nose-dived but I didn't care. I took a couple of roles as an extra in the movies filmed in Florence to make ends meet, but it wasn't enough to maintain our previous lifestyle. Sabrina was horrified and accused me of neglecting her needs in favour of satisfying my schoolboy ambitions.'

'Didn't you talk about your dreams before you got engaged?'

'Every last detail, down to what type of table linen I wanted, which suppliers I would use, what would be on the menu. She listened, but I don't think she really heard what I was saying or if she did, didn't think I'd actually do something as stupid as ditch a lucrative career to work as a general dogsbody in the restaurant trade.'

Izzie wanted to ask where Sabrina was now, but she didn't have to.

'She left me for Claudio – one of my colleagues at the bank who was promoted straight after I left. Sometimes, in darker moments, I wonder whether she actually loved me at all or whether it was the lifestyle my salary bought us. Last

I heard they had just come back from Paris where Claudio proposed at the top of the Eiffel Tower. I'm pleased for her – deep down, I should have known that Sabrina would never have been happy living in a run-down shack in the Tuscan Hills. My *nonna* always used to say *Non tutte le ciambelle riescono col buco* – which, roughly translated, means that not everything turns out as we'd planned. I have my restaurant now and I couldn't be happier.'

At last, Izzie felt she could return to her own story without the threat of tears interrupting their conversation. If she kept the topic to her own childhood dreams, then she should be okay.

'I know exactly how you feel – except the object of *my* affection is fabric, not food. When I was growing up I would devour every TV show that offered even the slightest nod in the direction of interiors – Changing Rooms, House Doctor, Grand Designs – watching every episode over and over until I knew everything there was to know about soft furnishings, flooring, lighting, paint techniques, storage solutions. I had a huge wooden trunk in my bedroom filled with fabric and wallpaper samples, spools of ribbon, cards of buttons, squares of felt. My sister Anna was always the academic one in the family, so when I won my place at RCA my life was complete.'

'And when you left you took the plunge and set up your own business?'

'Yes, it was difficult at first, arranging the funds, building my reputation, but I won an award and after that well… you know, things just snowballed.'

Izzie didn't like mentioning the award. Meghan told her she should shout about it from the rooftops, but she always thought it sounded like boasting.

'So how can you afford the time away from your business to organise this wedding?'

'Oh, erm, well, the company folded eighteen months ago.' Izzie gulped down a lungful of air and switched tact. 'I was lucky, though, I landed a job with a firm of property developers, styling their properties for sale. It pays the rent, or I should say, it did.'

'It did?'

'Yes, my contract was terminated just before I came over here – surplus to requirements.'

She grimaced – her redundancy still stung and reminded her that she needed to make a start on updating her CV so that when she got back to London she could 'hit the ground running' and 'poke a few irons in the fire' – as Darren would have said.

'It's an opportunity to make a fresh start,' said Luca. 'Is your fiancé supportive of your career choices?'

'Oh, no, I mean, yes, he was supportive, but we're no longer together. There was no bust up or anything, we just sort of drifted apart. My fault, I was... well... I was hard to live with for a while when I lost... When I lost my business.'

Despite their mutual soul-baring, she still couldn't bring herself to talk to Luca about her beloved twin sister. Would she ever be ready to just slot what had happened into a normal conversation?

'Well, I'm here to tell you that when one door is slammed in your face, another is stretched wide open! There's no time like the present to shoot for your dreams, Izzie! Why don't you think about getting a job working on film sets? Or events planning? From what I've seen so far, apart from the food side of things, you'd be a natural!'

'You know, that's exactly what Meghan said.'

'Then she's a very astute friend. Are you going to think about it?'

'Maybe, yes, maybe.'

Chapter Thirteen

The Kitchen, Villa Limoncello
Colour: Limoncello Yellow

With only two days to go before the wedding guests were due to descend on the villa's gardens, Izzie needed a lot more ticks on her checklists. She had eventually managed to speak to Brad on the phone, but their conversation had been brief and very one-sided, consisting of him shouting over the noise of what sounded like a jet engine to tell her that he would be flying in on Friday morning and should be with her by nine a.m. at the latest. Keeping her fingers crossed behind her back, she had assured him that everything was on schedule, and that there had been no hiccups. After all, her misunderstanding wasn't Brad fault, she'd made a promise, and the best thing to do was just to get on with it.

She stood on the kitchen doorstep, sipping her coffee, trying to ignore the discordant screech of a still-saw cutting through stone that caused her hair to stand on end. In the distance she could see Gianni steering his ancient tractor between the vines, stopping occasionally to hop off and inspect the leaves for the dreaded disease. She itched to join him, to spend some time learning about the cultivation of the grapes, how the weather affected their taste, and why the soil was peppered with a layer of crushed seashells.

But today was all about the food. Carlotta had arrived half an hour ago with Vincenzo in tow, his arm strapped in a sling, enthusing about his role as culinary guinea pig. She had decided not to mention the unfortunate mix-up about the wedding to either of them, taking her mother's advice that the least said, the soonest mended. If they hadn't known about her blunder in the first place, what was the point in alerting them to her embarrassment now? The same went for Gianni.

Izzie turned back to the kitchen where the rich aroma of oregano and garlic permeated the air, smiling when she saw Vincenzo seated at the head of the table, like a king on a throne, tasting tomato sauce from a ladle being offered by Carlotta. Despite narrowly escaping serious injury only the previous day, he looked surprisingly chirpy, with his panama hat set at a jaunty angle and his eyes dancing with pleasure at being the centre of Carlotta's attention.

She saw the look in Vincenzo's eyes and was struck by a sudden realisation. What he had with Carlotta was much more than friendship – he was in love with her. Like Gianni, Izzie thought they made a perfect couple – both single, both loved good food, and they clearly enjoyed each other's company – and their love story was obvious to anyone apart from the protagonists themselves.

Was Carlotta so caught up in arranging everyone else's love lives that she had overlooked her own? Why hadn't Vincenzo said anything? Carlotta clearly cared for him otherwise she would not have spent the night at the hospital.

However, none of this was any of her business so she grabbed her apron and offered her help. Carlotta's comedic double-take caused Izzie to giggle. 'Not with the cooking, with the washing up!' The look of relief on her new friend's face was priceless.

Three hours later, every item on the menu including the lavender-infused panna cotta had been tested and, whilst Izzie was no expert, everything tasted fabulous – seconded by

Vincenzo who was sipping his coffee with a look of complete satisfaction on his handsome face. Izzie grabbed a mug, filled it to the brim, and took a seat next to him.

'Have you lived in San Vivaldo all your life, Vincenzo?'

'I have – sixty years this year.'

'So you know everything there is to know about the valley?'

'Not everything, but a lot. Why?'

'I was wondering how Villa Limoncello got its name?'

'Actually, the villa will always be known as *Villa dei Limoni* – villa of the lemons – by the people of San Vivaldo, not Villa Limoncello,' said Vincenzo, shaking his head slightly at its recent renaming. 'You've seen the *limonaia*, I take it?'

'Yes, it's an amazing place. Limoncello is a drink, though, isn't it? Did they make it here?'

'They did,' said Carlotta, joining them at the table with a plate of *struffoli* that she drizzled with extra honey. 'Look.'

Izzie cast her eyes across to where an age-flecked picture hung above the mahogany sideboard at the back of the room, its wooden frame chipped, the writing on the scrap of parchment within almost illegible. She scraped back her chair and went over to unhook it.

'Is this their recipe for limoncello?'

'It's the original, I think,' said Carlotta, taking the frame from Izzie and squinting at the faded scrawl. 'Maria's mother grew up on the island of Capri and she was said to have brought the recipe with her when she married into the Rosetti family. Lemons have been grown at the villa for over two hundred years, and some of the species in the *limonaia* are incredibly rare. When Maria Rossetti died three years ago, a professor from the university in Florence came to catalogue the plants and there was a piece in the local paper about it.'

'So what happened to the Rossetti family?'

'It's a sad story,' murmured Carlotta, fingering the frame as she meandered the labyrinth of her memory. 'Although, unfortunately, not an infrequent one. The Rosetti family bought *Villa dei Limoni* over a century ago and it was handed down through the generations, along with its secrets. They managed to survive the First World War relatively unscathed, lost a brother and an uncle, but the Second World War took a dreadful toll on the family. Only Maria survived – she was just fifteen, poor thing.'

Carlotta paused, staring at the recipe in her hand.

'An elderly aunt moved into the villa to take care of her and together they continued to tend the vines to maintain the family's legacy of wine-making in Tuscany, but they also continued to cultivate the lemons to make the limoncello and keep her mother's memory alive.'

'If you want my opinion,' said Vincenzo, running his tongue along his lower lip as if tasting the liqueur, 'Maria Rosetti's limoncello was the best in the whole of Italy because she used only the best ingredients; pure grain alcohol, fresh mountain water they extracted from the well in the garden, and of course the lemons are completely organic, with no toxic extras such as pesticides or chemical fertilisers.'

'Maria never married, and God, in his wisdom, bestowed her with a long life, a life she spent focused on the past, on her memories of her family taken far too soon. When she died, the villa was inherited by a distant second cousin in New York who had no interest in a crumbling old villa in a foreign country. For reasons best known to him, he changed its name to Villa Limoncello, and rented it out for a while, but in the end, he decided to sell it.'

'So, who owns the villa now?' asked Izzie, her curiosity piqued.

'That I don't know. It was bought eighteen months ago, and everyone in the village expected the builders to move in straight away to strip the place of all its character like Riccardo has done next door, but as you can see, nothing's happened.'

'Ah, our grumpy neighbour!'

'You've met him?'

'Yes, I had a run in with him the day I arrived here. I'd inadvertently blocked his access.'

Vincenzo laughed. 'He wouldn't have liked that!'

'No, I can safely say that he wasn't the happiest person I've met since arriving in Tuscany. In fact, he was downright rude.'

'Riccardo has made no secret of the fact that he wants to buy *Villa dei Limoni*. Well, not the villa as such, but its vineyard and olive grove. His property has very little land, only enough space for the swimming pool he's building for the use of his future B&B guests, not to mention the ongoing issues with shared access. Sadly, he's chosen to interpret his lack of progress on identifying the villa's current owner as a personal snub, rather than what it is – no one knows.'

'Except Gianni,' said Izzie, raising her eyebrows at Carlotta.

'Yes, but as he loves his vines more than life itself, he's not likely to disclose the identity of his employer to the man who would deny him the chance of producing the first Rossetti Chianti in over twenty years, is he?'

'No, I don't suppose he is.'

'Anyway, it's not just Riccardo who's interested in buying the villa,' added Vincenzo. 'Gianni told me he's stumbled across at least another three would-be proprietors meandering through the olive groves, drooling at the investment oppor- tunity. He sent them away with a flea in their ears, but it does seem like the villa is being circled by a committee of ravenous vultures!'

Silence spread through the kitchen as each person wondered what the future had in store for the villa and whether Gianni would get the chance to fulfil his dream of reinvigorating the vineyard before it was snapped up by a visiting tourist desperate for their own little slice of Tuscan paradise.

'Hey! Why don't we make a batch of limoncello!' declared Vincenzo, leaping from his seat with surprising agility for one just released from hospital. He grabbed an empty bucket and stared at them expectantly. 'Well? Are you coming?'

'Absolutely!' Izzie grinned, her taste buds already zinging in anticipation.

Following the recipe to the letter, they produced a large bulbous demi-john filled to the top with what would become the first limoncello produced at the villa for a long time. Izzie was proud of their afternoon's work, even if it wasn't an item she could tick from the list. Whilst removing the zest from the lemons they harvested from the lemon house, they chatted about Carlotta's recent matchmaking successes, the progress of Vincenzo's five grandchildren, the dreaded virus attacking Gianni's beloved vines, and speculated about the identity of the bride and groom.

'I wonder what Maria Rossetti would say if she knew that limoncello was being made at the villa again?' said Carlotta, her eyes bright as she clasped her hands to her chest.

'I'm sure she would be thrilled. It's a shame we can't serve it at the wedding on Friday. Are you sure it's absolutely necessary to wait a full four weeks before adding the sugar syrup?'

'If you want the authentic Rosetti limoncello!' laughed Vincenzo. 'But never fear. I will make us all a jug of my speci-ality lemonade with the juice! By the way, where's Gianni? I thought he'd be here in the kitchen offering his services as assistant taste-tester this afternoon?'

'Yes, he did say he'd pop in.'

Izzie made her way to the doorstep and froze.

'Oh my God! Gianni!'

She sprinted to the pergola, but it was too late.

'Don't panic, don't panic! Everything is under control!'

She watched as Gianni deposited a final squirt from the garden hose over the charred remained of the box of napkins she and Luca had spent hours folding the previous day. He turned towards her, his face covered in soot, his eyes and teeth gleaming white.

'What happened?' coughed Izzie, as the toxic stench of smoke hit her lungs.

'Well, I just thought I'd test the barbeque in case we need it on Friday night and, well, the gas canister was a bit fiercer than I imagined and it... well...'

Gianni's face was suffused with such contrition he looked like a naughty schoolboy standing in front of the head teacher pleading his case for leniency. Izzie didn't know whether to laugh or cry, but her heart softened for this clumsy, opera-loving guy who had a heart of gold but who should never be left alone with anything remotely combustible.

By the time the four of them had doused everything down and disposed of the fire-damaged serviettes, the sky was sending ribbons of apricot and violet across the horizon. At last, the drills and jackhammers had fallen silent next door and the cicadas were busy tuning up for a repeat rendition of their more melodious night-time sonata. With a final heartfelt apology, Gianni trundled off down the driveway on his quad bike, followed by Carlotta who wound down the window on the driver's side of Vincenzo's borrowed Jeep.

'Izzie, don't worry about the linen. I know the supplier's mother. Vincenzo and I are on our way over there now and we'll call in a few favours this evening in return for one of my speciality lasagnes. I can't promise the design with be as proficient as yours, but I'm sure they will pass the test.'

Izzie felt a lump form in her throat at the way the whole community pulled together when someone needed help – just as they had in St Ives when the worst had happened to the Jenkins family.

'And Izzie?'

'Mmm?'

'Why don't you take a few hours off tomorrow morning? It would be a shame to come all this way and not pay a visit to Siena or Firenze?'

'Oh, no, I can't do that, there's still so much to do. I have to scrub the bathroom for a start, then I need to cover over the pond, and smarten up the tennis court. I've also still got to go over to see Francesca to check on the flowers...'

'No arguments – it's all sorted,' smiled Carlotta, patting her hand, then crunching the gears and disappearing down the driveway before Izzie could ask what she had meant.

Oh God, surely Carlotta hadn't fixed her up with a tour guide? Or worse, included her in one of her matchmaking schemes!

A wave of exhaustion hit her and instead of making her way back to the kitchen to continue tackling the lists, she decided to take a detour through the herb garden to select a few stems of lavender for the side of her bed. As early dusk tickled the distant hilltops, the whole panorama was suffused with a golden radiance interspersed with twinkling amber lights from the distant village. There was no doubt about it, Villa Limoncello was a truly magical place to get married, in real life or on film, and despite its shabby overcoat, Brad had made an inspired choice as the setting for his friends' nuptials.

She couldn't wait for Meghan to arrive the following day so they could share the experience together. Meghan was such a romantic – even though she was still searching for 'the perfect guy' – and she knew Meghan would be smitten by the Villa Limoncello's charms just as she was. She could easily imagine her friend standing alongside her prince in the wedding gazebo, beaming as she exchanged her vows.

As the light faded, an even more extraordinary realisation dawned. For the first time since she and Alex had separated she could actually envisage herself standing in that gazebo, too. She couldn't prevent a splutter of surprise from escaping her lips, followed by a sharp nip of emotion as tears pricked at her eyes.

Was it really possible that she was contemplating a point in the not too distant future when she would fall in love again and live the life she'd dreamed of before her heart had been blown to smithereens?

Chapter Fourteen

Firenze, Tuscany
Colour: Toasted Terracotta

'Hey, Izzie!'

She shot to her bedroom window, remembering to grab a hoodie before throwing back the shutters and leaning out to see who'd delivered her early wake-up call – at five a.m.!

'What time do you call this?' She laughed, her spirits rising a whole octave when she saw Luca and Gianni's smiling faces staring up at her, holding aloft giant paintbrushes and a menagerie of paint pots.

'Are you going to let us in or what?'

'Down in a minute!'

She pulled on a pair of jeans, her tiredness vanishing as she hurtled down the stairs to open the front door.

'*Buongiorno!*' they chorused.

'What are you doing here?'

'Isn't it obvious? We're rent-a-decorator! You said you needed the bathroom painted and so here we are, at your service.'

With two extra pairs of hands, the bathroom, the pergola, and even the wishing well, were sparkling in the early morning sunlight in no time and the fresh smell of paint – as well as the additional ticks on her list – calmed Izzie's worries about the state of the villa and its ability to feature as the backdrop for a sophisticated Tuscan wedding. As long as everyone stayed outside and avoided the house, then she was confident she could pull it off. The gazebo and the courtyard were staged, the food had been ordered and taste tested, the wedding cakes were sorted, and all that was left on her list was to visit the florist, Francesca, that afternoon to check the table decorations, the bride and bridesmaids' bouquets, the button-holes and the silver urns that would be dotted around the venue to provide additional colour.

'Okay, that's it! I'm done!' announced Gianni, downing his paintbrush and striding towards the kitchen with purpose. 'I deserve a coffee and a slice of that delicious *torte di nonna* I spotted earlier. God knows, I need it – lost another two vines to the dreaded leaf rot yesterday, that's five this month alone.'

'Any idea what's causing it?' asked Luca, his eyes filled with concern.

'None. I've tried everything. I think it might be time to call in the experts. Anyway, I'll catch you two later.'

'What do you mean you'll catch us later?' Izzie smiled, wondering what new weird and wonderful plan he had brewing in his brain – until she saw Luca staring at her, hesitating. 'What?'

'I have something planned.'

'What sort of thing?'

'A trip.'

'Where to?'

A coil of unease began to wind its way from deep in her stomach towards her chest.

'To the most beautiful city in the world.'

As soon as the words floated from Luca's lips, Izzie's anxiety tightened into a helix of alarm, squeezing the air from her lungs and making her feel lightheaded.

'Oh, well... thanks, Luca. That's really kind of you, but I can't leave the villa today. I've still got so much to sort out before tomorrow.'

She tried to smile to indicate her apology at having to turn down such a fabulous offer, but the strangled pitch of her voice gave her away.

'I've taken the liberty of sneaking a peek at that clipboard of yours, and it looks like, apart from the flowers, everything else is in hand. And Carlotta agrees with me, too. You need a break from all the organising. It'll help you see the bigger picture instead of focusing in on the insignificant details like what colour the loo rolls are. It's a couple of hours, that's all.'

'Yes, but my appointment with Francesca is at...'

'At four o'clock, I've checked, and I give you my solemn word to deliver you back in plenty of time.' Luca placed his hand over his heart and repeated, 'Promise!'

Izzie swallowed down on the rampaging emotions that had escaped their tethers, trying to formulate the right response to show her gratitude for his kind offer, but also her regret that she couldn't take him up on it. However, eloquence had hung up its shoes and deserted her so she went with a simple, clear refusal.

'Sorry, Luca, I can't go to Florence with you. I just can't.'

She saw the disappointment float across his face, but thoughts and images of 'what should have been' ricocheted around her brain, and her demons circled their prey so vehemently that she struggled to focus on Luca's response.

'I understand. You have memories? I can see them in your face.'

But Luca didn't understand. How could he? He had obviously misinterpreted her reluctance to join him as an unwillingness to spoil a previous 'special' visit and that wasn't the case at all. In fact, it was the complete opposite.

'I'm sorry, Luca.'

'No problem.'

Yet, ever since she had stepped from the aircraft steps onto Italian soil, somewhere deep inside she had known she would have to face her fears about visiting the city she and her sister had spent months preparing to visit. They had even started a scrapbook containing photographs, recipes, timetables, skip-the-line tips, menus; all snipped from various holiday brochures, magazines and cookery books. The scrapbook had been Anna's idea of course; it was the schoolteacher in her – always thinking of ways she could share her special experiences with her pupils. They had intended to add little things like bus tickets, serviettes, postcards and more photographs and recipes, but of course that had never happened and the unfinished album had been wrapped in tissue paper and stored in a trunk alongside other trunks that held similarly painful memories, none more heart-breaking than the one Izzie had upholstered in ivory satin containing Anna's unworn wedding dress, veil and tiara.

With difficulty she managed to drag herself back to the present and saw that Luca was watching her closely, as if he could see her reminiscences reflected in her eyes, a question on the tip of his tongue but melting away on a reluctance to pry. His expression of complete dejection caused something deep inside her to shift, allowing a shaft of sunlight to penetrate the hard block of dread that had festered in her chest since Meghan had suggested the trip to Florence. Then a question burst into her head.

What would Anna do if she were standing in her shoes?

Izzie didn't have to wait for the answer. Her sister had greeted every day with a smile in her heart and a spring in her step. Her motto had always been yesterday was gone and tomorrow would never come so why not enjoy today!

Why not enjoy today!

She felt as though Anna was standing in front of her, her hands on her hips, her flowery skirt ballooning in the breeze, cajoling her on like she would one of her pupils, telling her to grab her courage and take a leap of faith, because until you tried something how did you know whether you liked it or not?

Go on, Izzie! Say yes!

She could hear those words, spoken in her sister's musical voice, and tears pricked at her eyes. So, as instructed, she inhaled a deep breath, plastered a smile on her face, met Luca's dark eyes, and said, 'I'd love to visit Florence with you. Thanks, Luca.'

Her spirits edged up a notch when genuine delight spread across his face, right up until they walked round the side of the house and she saw his Spider parked in the driveway. She rolled her eyes at him and he smiled.

'Izzie, I'm sorry about running you off the road. I can assure you that under normal circumstances I'm a very safe and responsible driver.' This time it was Luca's turn to engage in an inner squirm. 'It's just that I didn't expect to see... well, I'd had a bit of a shock, but that's no excuse. I apologise unreservedly and promise to make it up to you by driving like a Sunday afternoon gentleman.'

Izzie giggled. 'It's okay. Actually, it's the donkey you should be apologising to.'

'The donkey? What donkey?'

She laughed and jumped into the passenger seat, enjoying the exhilaration that whipped through her body when Luca fired up the engine and they roared away down the driveway and through the gate posts. Zipping through the Tuscan countryside in an open-topped Spider, along the winding lanes, bordered by olive groves and fields filled with ripening vines, with her hair flying high into the slipstream, instilled a sense of lightness in her that she hadn't experienced for a long time. She relaxed as Luca kept up a stream of conversation, telling her about his favourite places; some she and Anna had included on their list of Must See's, others that were new to her.

When they arrived in Florence, or *Firenze* as Luca called it, they scooted straight into a parking space and entered the city on foot through a soaring Etruscan archway into a cobbled piazza surrounded by four-storey villas with façades the colour of pale caramel, paint-blistered shutters and Juliette balconies. At ground level, every building boasted either a trattoria or a cafe, their tables and chairs spilling out onto the pavements and occupied by a mixture of tourists and local residents, the latter clutching their pet poodles whilst partaking in a tiny cup of rich, fragrant espresso to kick-start the morning.

Beyond the square, Izzie found herself in a labyrinth of narrow streets and shady alleyways bordered by independent family-run stores selling lingerie, handbags, shoes, confectionery, pizza slices, postcards, original artwork – there was not a multinational behemoth in sight and she loved it! Every corner revealed something new – shops selling beautifully carved wooden toys and hand-painted ceramics, market stalls crammed with a kaleidoscope of leather goods, a violinist entertaining the crowds – until she came to an abrupt standstill, her jaw dangling loose as she contemplated the awesome sight before her that no picture or photograph could have prepared her for.

'Wow!'

It was the only word that came to mind but was completely inadequate to describe the exquisite artistry of the famous *Cattedrale di Santa Maria del Fiore* and its adjacent bell tower. Its façade, dressed in an intricate mosaic of white, pink and green marble, sparkled in the mid-morning sun, and the engineering masterpiece that was Filippo Brunelleschi's terracotta copula stood out like a crown on a particularly ornate wedding cake.

'It's fabulous, isn't it? *Il Duomo* is my second favourite place in the whole city!'

Awed by its elegance, a cauldron of emotions churned through Izzie; appreciation of the creative genius towering above her, fellowship with the myriad groups of tourists who, like herself, stood speechless with their heads tipped backwards in amazement, and searing pain as she was reminded that she was gaping at the city's most famous architectural wonder without her beloved Anna by her side. Tears gathered along her lower lashes, but she brushed them away with her thumb.

'Hey, are you okay?'

She felt Luca's hand on her arm, his breath on her cheek, and she tried to smile, but knew her lips had twisted in something more akin to a grimace.

'Sorry.'

'No apology necessary.'

Luca produced a huge white handkerchief and waited for her to dry her eyes.

'Come.'

She allowed Luca to lead her to a quiet café where he ordered two iced lemonades in rapid Italian. To the backing track of Italian opera, her turmoil eased and her spirits brightened, as if she had broken the seal on her carefully controlled memories and the resultant fizz had dissipated the bottled-up emotions leaving a more serene sensation. As the sugar-fix seeped into her veins, her mood improved further. Now that she had faced the worst – that first sight of the iconic Duomo, the place that screamed Florence – from here on in things could only get better.

'Florence's beauty inspires a variety of reactions in its visitors, but I suspect that the city means much more to you, Izzie, than a first-class example of Renaissance Italian architecture. Am I right?'

She nodded, fiddling with her glass, wondering if she had the courage to talk to Luca about Anna and what they had planned.

'Then it is I who should be apologising. If I had any idea that the trip would cause you such sorrow, I would never have insisted on bringing you here. I assumed, wrongly, that you were employing your workaholic tendencies and I wanted to show you that life is about more than just work. It's about love, passion, creativity, art, culture, and delicious lemonade!'

She smiled, and Luca smiled back.

'Okay, so shall we terminate the tour and head back to the villa?'

Izzie took another sip of the freshly squeezed lemonade, taking her time to savour the acidic tang of lemon juice as it glided across her taste buds whilst she considered his offer. Meghan had told her that her trip to Italy would be good for her because no one knew her story there and she could avoid having difficult conversations about her past. Conversely, far from allowing her to hide from her trauma, Italy had stirred up an avalanche of emotions and introduced her to people who could read her sadness easily, despite her attempts to disguise it. Luca might know nothing about what had happened to cause her to morph from the happy, contented owner of her own colour-filled interior design studio into a dull shadow of her former self where magnolia and vanilla were her go-to preferences, but he knew something was wrong and his empathy introduced a blast of faith in the future.

'No.'

'No, what?'

'No, I don't want to go back to the villa. We're here now and I want to make the most of it.'

'Really?'

She loved the way Luca's eyes lit up at her response.

'Great! Come! There's something you have to see!'

Chapter Fifteen

The Boboli Gardens, Pitti Palace, Firenze
Colour: Enchanted Emerald

Izzie laughed as Luca dragged her out of her chair, slotting his palm into hers and adding yet another emotion to the mix – excitement. As the sun beat down from directly overhead, scorching the roofs and the pavements and casting a veil of sparkling diamonds over the River Arno, Luca slipped into his tour guide role, pointing out details, favourite sights, little nooks and crannies that only a local would know.

They meandered through the maze of cobbled streets, past the emporiums of high-end fashion, soaking up the pantomime of daily life. They giggled at a group of Americans dutifully taking selfies on the Ponte Vecchio before following a striped umbrella to photograph the next magical sight on their itinerary. After drooling over the expensive jewellery shops on the bridge, they grabbed a gelato – Izzie's strawberry, Luca's saffron – and climbed the hill to the gardens at the rear of the *Palazzo Pitti* where they settled on a vacant wooden bench to gaze at the magnificent view spread out in front of them.

'Now *this* is my favourite place in Firenze.'

Izzie had to agree with him. Every attraction the city of Florence had to offer was displayed before her and she feasted her eyes, fixing the panorama in her memory so that, at a later date, she could take it out and examine it at her leisure. It was so beautiful; the ancient honey-hued stonework, the higgledy-piggledy terracotta roofs, the battalions of marble statues, the way the dappled sunlight danced in the branches overhead, and once again her sorrow poked its head above the parapet causing a tear to trickle down her cheek.

How Anna would have loved to be there, sitting on that bench, jotting her thoughts down in her journal, snapping photographs and selfies, maybe collecting one of the fallen leaves as a memento or as part of a presentation for her class.

'If you want to talk…' began Luca, his voice a mere murmur as he reached out to lace his fingers between hers in a gesture of support. 'If you don't, then that's good, too.'

Could she?

Could she really contemplate baring her soul to someone she'd just met when she hadn't been able to talk to those she loved the most? Could she tell Luca about the soaring peaks of pain that punctuated every day since Anna had disappeared from her life? Okay, Meghan and Jonti knew the facts about what had happened. Meghan had listened, offered sympathy and a shoulder to cry on more times than she could remember, but Izzie had never been able to truly express the deep-seated feeling of guilt that inhabited her heart. Or to explain about the immovable burden she carried with her every day, like a turtle carries its shell, the weight dulling her senses, creating the lethargy in her bones that stole her creativity and stifled her life – all because she was still alive, still functioning, when her sister, her mirror-half, wasn't.

She snuck a quick glance at Luca from beneath her lashes. He wasn't sitting there looking expectantly at her, waiting for her to launch into an explanation. He was gazing at his most cherished view, lost in his own thoughts, maybe wrestling with a few demons of his own; the loss of his fiancée or the fact that her love had turned out to be only as deep as his bank balance.

'I lost my sister, Anna, two years ago.'

There, she'd said it and the world hadn't come tumbling down on her; the sun was still shining, the leaves were still rattling in the breeze, and the birds continued with their infinite concerto of joy.

'She wasn't just my sister, though, she was my twin sister, and my best friend.'

She stopped, inhaled a strengthening breath, desperate to get her narrative in order so she could make Luca understand what had happened as succinctly as possible in order to cut down on the possibility of being faced with a barrage of questions she would struggle to answer.

But Luca simply nodded and remained silent.

It suddenly occurred to her that everyone had a story to tell, whether it be happy, sad or indifferent. If she looked around the pretty manicured gardens of the Pitti Palace, there were lots of people enjoying the view just like they were. What sacrifices had they made to get there? What sorrows did *they* carry in their hearts? Maybe they were making this special trip in a loved one's honour?

Those last three words reverberated in her brain.

Why hadn't she looked at this trip in those terms? That she was there, in Florence, in Anna's honour; to pay tribute to all those wonderful times they had spent together researching and gossiping and planning every detail of the trip.

'Anna was a reception class teacher at our local village school in St Ives where we grew up. Everyone loved her and she loved every single one of them back, even the most challenging children – no, scratch that, especially those children. She was the most popular teacher in the school – you should have seen the piles of home-made cards and presents that landed on her desk at the end of each term… and when she and Matt got engaged.'

She allowed herself to smile as she recalled the artwork the children had created to celebrate Anna's engagement to Matt; an enormous collage of doily hearts and red tissue-paper flowers, buttons, sequins and ribbons, with the letters A and M interwoven in embroidered felt. Anna had loved it so much that she'd had it framed and it hung above the fireplace in the tiny cottage she and Matt lived in on the outskirts of the village.

'We agreed on most things, it's a twin thing, I think, and one of the things we definitely shared was a passion for all-things Italian; the food, the wine, the architecture, the culture, the history, the art, the language, its people. Anyway, we decided to plan a girlie trip to Florence as a sort of hen weekend a couple of weeks before she and Matt were due to get married. Spent hours scrolling through the museums websites, booking tickets, looking at menus and recipes, shopping for clothes, reading guide books, watching films, we even enrolled on a language course.'

She paused, swallowing down the resurgence of the urge to succumb to more tears. Now she had started, she wanted to get every last painful morsel out into the open before she crumbled. Anyway, she couldn't stop even if she wanted to – the genie was out of the bottle.

'Then, one sun-filled spring morning, May twelfth to be precise, Anna was cycling to school, just as she had done every morning for the previous five years, probably humming a tune from the end of term school play she had singlehandedly written, choreographed and directed. She was… she was found two hours later by a passing motorist, lying by the side of the road. Much later, the doctors told us that she had died from a brain aneurism – apparently it can happen to anyone, anytime, and she wouldn't have suffered at all. But that was no consolation. The whole village went into mourning, everyone devastated by the loss of an adored schoolteacher, a community champion, a best friend, a fiancée, a daughter, a… a sister. The light in my life was extinguished like that!'

She was unable to continue – the pain of loss had bared its teeth and her breath had caught in her chest, causing her tears to flow unchecked, dripping from the end of her chin. Silently, Luca withdrew his handkerchief and passed it to her, before guiding her head to his chest where she remained for a long time.

'I'm sorry for your loss, Izzie.'

Then she said it, said the sentence she had never uttered to a soul before, but which had played on a never-ending loop through her exhausted brain every day for two years.

'Why wasn't it me?'

'What do you mean?'

'We're twins. We have the same genetic make-up. Why wasn't it me? If it had been me, the pupils would still have their much-loved teacher, the marginalised children would have their vociferous champion, the wedding of the decade would have gone ahead the following month, and our parents would probably have a couple of longed for grandchildren by now.'

'Do you really think life would have continued as normal if it had been you?'

'Well, no, of course not, but things would have been better than they are now, that's for sure.'

Her tears had dried, and the relief at having spoken the words that had stalked her for a long time was beginning to seep into her veins and soothe her ragged emotions.

'Things would have been different, yes, but not better – that's crazy. Your parents, your sister, and did you say your partner was called Alex? They would all have suffered *exactly the same* trauma if they had lost you and not Anna. You have to know that!'

'I suppose…'

Her brain told her Luca was right, of course. Her brain had screamed that same argument at her many times, but her demons were always there ready to douse any hint of optimism with cold water, pointing their accusatory fingers at her for living when her sister hadn't. How could she explain that what she had experienced since that fateful summer day when the sun had gone from her life wasn't just sorrow at the loss of her sister but the insidious scorch of guilt? Guilt that the Director of Fate had chosen to take Anna; the most cheerful, the most creative, the most loving person you could possibly wish to meet. Why hadn't it been her who had been struck down on that late spring morning as she cycled to work?

Luca was watching her closely, his eyes filled with compassion.

'Izzie, have you been carrying this guilt around with you ever since… well, ever since your sister's passing?'

'Yes, I…'

'And what did your friends say when you spoke to them about how you felt?'

'I haven't, I mean, I didn't…'

Luca's jaw sagged in disbelief. 'This is the first time you've spoken about it?'

She nodded, staring at her fingertips. When Luca put it like that it did sound ridiculous.

'But why?'

'I just, well, I thought I was…'

'Grief sends a kaleidoscope of emotions, some easier to deal with than others; some vanish as soon as they appear, others stick around. There's no pattern, it's different for everyone and we all deal with it in different ways. However, there is one thing that helps everyone and that's talking about how we feel. Why didn't you talk to your parents about it?'

'Because they're grieving, too. I didn't want to burden them with any more pain. They had enough to deal with without adding me to their list of worries. They had the funeral to organise, and Matt – poor Matt – he had all the wedding arrangements to cancel. Can you imagine how hard that must have been for him and his family?'

'No, I can't.'

'Me, neither.'

'So, is that why your business folded?'

'Yes, and why Alex moved on. He tried *really* hard, but I couldn't go back to a normal life. How could I? Our relationship just fizzled out, and so did my creativity. How could I create designs filled with vibrant colours, edged with panache and flair when I had died inside? The only colours I wanted to work with were black, grey, taupe, pewter – would you believe me if I said I hated the sight of crimson, or cerise, or lemon chiffon? I lost most of my clients, apart from Grace Hambleton, my ex-boss's wife who, it turned out, had also lost her sister – in a car crash – and when she found out I was looking for work, she practically ordered her husband to offer me a job with his building company staging houses – until his son took over the business and I lost that job, too.'

Luca nodded as she spoke, clearly working on formulating his next sentence, taking care to get it right.

'Your sister sounds like you, Izzie. An amazing person who loved her family and her friends and was there for everyone who needed her friendship and support. Can I ask you a question?'

'Sure.'

'Knowing her as well as you do, would Anna have wanted you to stop living just because she had? Would she have wanted

155

to see her beloved twin sister using her grief as an excuse for retreating from life?'

'It's not an excuse...'

However, Luca was right. The loss of her sister had been the catalyst for the mundane, drab, yes, excuse of a life she now pursued. Despite strenuous attempts to maintain her equilibrium, she had moved through the days and weeks that followed Anna's passing like an automaton – a ghost going through the motions from dawn until dusk when she could embrace the oblivion that sleep offered. She had lost interest in everything; the gym, the cinema, the theatre, the interior magazines she loved, the travel memoirs she used to devour as she and Anna dreamed of their next girlie holiday.

'Don't you think she's sitting up there... on that cloud,' Luca pointed to a fluffy white Simpsonesque cloud that had paused in its eternal travels around the world, 'cheering you on, urging you to squeeze every ounce of happiness from what life throws at you? Just like she did by organising plays for the schoolchildren she taught, arranging her wedding, and spending time shopping and dreaming of trips with her sister – she was living life to the full, pursuing her dreams with passion and conviction.'

Izzie stared at Luca, his expression filled with earnest persuasion. As she replayed his words, and considered their meaning, she knew what he had said was true, and another chunk of stone was fell away from the granite block that had taken up residence in her chest.

Chapter Sixteen

Fioraio Francesca, San Vivaldo
Colour: Fuchsia Cascade

True to his word, Luca got Izzie back to the Villa Limoncello by four o'clock just as the sunflowers were turning their faces towards the west and the cicadas' song was at its most vibrant. After opening her heart and talking about her guilt surrounding Anna's death, she felt lighter, more buoyant than she had in a long while and a smile tugged at her lips – despite the lists she could see waiting for her on the patio table. She turned in her seat and this time it was no surprise when a frisson of attraction shot through her body. Luca was extraordinarily handsome, especially when his dark brown eyes met hers, those liquorice lashes caressing his cheeks.

'Thank you, Luca. You've given me more than a tour of your favourite city, you've given me an insight into how to move on, a glimmer of hope that instead of standing still and looking over my shoulder to the past, I can fix my eyes on the future.'

'*Niente*,' smiled Luca, holding her gaze for longer than necessary.

She sensed a shift, a few millimetres only, but it was enough to tell her what was in Luca's mind. Her lips tingled in anticipation and a flutter of desire tickled at her abdomen, yet it was tempered by a generous dose of uncertainty and her reflexes forced her to pull back, causing her heart to scream 'coward'.

But what was the point in taking their friendship to another level – she couldn't afford to add an extra dimension to the feelings of loss that would inevitably surface when she left Tuscany in two days' time. After the progress she had made that morning, after the surge of optimism that still smouldered in her heart, she didn't want to risk introducing anything that could destroy the fragility of hope. She jumped from the car, smiling, hoping he couldn't see the rush of emotion that had risen to the surface and tightened her vocal chords.

'Okay, thanks again, Luca. *Ciao!*'

Izzie stood beneath the pergola, waving as the Spider crunched its way past the pink rhododendron blooms basking in the afternoon heat, their petals floating on the breeze like confetti, before disappearing through the gates and towards the village to prepare for his shift at the restaurant. She glanced at her watch and realised that if she didn't grab the Vespa and follow in his wake she would be late for her meeting with Francesca.

As she zipped along the twisting roads towards San Vivaldo, memories flooded her thoughts of the times when she and Anna had frequented their local florist's shop in St Ives to select a bouquet for their mother on her birthday. Anna had adored roses, peonies and tulips, in any shade as long as it was pink, the colour she had chosen for her bridal bouquet, whilst Izzie preferred flowers that were a little more quirky, like sunflowers and hydrangeas. Those days had been happy occasions, proving the old adage that it was just as joyful to give gifts as to receive them.

Another emotion tumbled through the mix too – that of gratitude. Spending time with Luca that morning had made her realise how fortunate she was for having had her wonderful sister in her life for a whole twenty-seven years. After all, some people didn't even get that long! She cast her eyes skywards, fixing her gaze on a pretty cloud in the shape of a heart, and imagined Anna sitting there, her legs crossed, a smile stretching her lips, silently urging her to enjoy every moment she had left in their favourite country.

Fortunately, just as she thought her head would burst with her constant reflections, she spotted *Fioraio Francesca* squashed between a *gelateria* and a *fruttivendolo*. Unlike Oriana's *pasticceria*, the window display did not cause an instant bout of drooling, but as soon as she stepped over the threshold her nostrils filled with the rich fragrance of jasmine, lilies, and crushed pine. It was a few moments before her eyes adjusted from the bright sunshine of outside and she noticed the young woman perched on a high stool at the wooden counter fiddling with her mobile.

'*Ciao*, I'm Izzie Jenkins.'

'*Ciao*, Izzie, I'm Francesca Caruso. Are you here to talk about the wedding flowers for *Villa dei Limoni* on Friday?'

'Yes, I am.'

Izzie heaved a silent sigh of relief that not only did Francesca speak English, but she spoke it with a broad West country accent. Francesca grinned as if reading her thoughts.

'My mother's English, my father's Italian,' she explained, jumping down from her seat and clearing a space on the counter for Izzie to open her folder. 'They met when Mum was inter-railing back in the eighties. I've been looking forward to meeting you – I can't wait to show you what I've created.'

Izzie connected with Francesca immediately. She reminded her of Meghan – with her ivory chiffon top offering a peek of her lacy bra, her cropped trousers and ballet flats, not to mention her raspberry tipped fringe. But it was her cheerful personality, the laughter lines around her lips and her eyes, and constant stream of chatter that really sealed it, and when Francesca pulled open the door to the room at the back of the shop Izzie stopped in her tracks.

'Wow!'

There was no other way to describe the cornucopia of floral art lined up ready for inspection on the huge battered oak table. A cloud of heady perfume lingered in the air like a Parisian lady's boudoir – or Jonti's bedroom before a Saturday night out on the town. Shelves ran around the perimeter of the room, crammed with everything a busy florist could possibly ask for and more; blocks of green oasis, floristry twine, spools of ribbons, baskets, vases, storm lanterns, skeletal ironmongery.

'Would you like me to talk you through what I've done? I've stuck to the brief as much as I could, apart from the ivory *zantedeshia* which were a problem. So, these are the table decorations,' said Francesca, indicating three elegant arrangements of white roses and pale and fuchsia-pink peonies interspersed with baby's breath and surrounded by glossy green foliage.

'They are gorgeous!'

Izzie could picture the floral masterpieces in pride of place on each of the three long tables they'd set up in the courtyard against the backdrop of the starched white linen cloths and the crystal candlesticks, silver cutlery and white bone china crockery.

'And there'll be a single rose, like this one, placed on each napkin. These are the buttonholes; one for each guest and I've made a few extra just in case. And this, here… is the bride's headpiece. What do you think?'

'It's perfect,' sighed Izzie, feasting her eyes on the circlet of exquisite white roses that would be woven through the bride's hair on the morning of the ceremony. 'And are these the bouquets?'

'Yes, that's for the bride, and these are the posies for the two bridesmaids.'

'They are really beautiful and will look amazing in the photographs!'

'Thank you, I have to admit that I'm more nervous than usual. I keep telling myself that it's just another wedding, but it's not, is it? These people are celebrities, the photographs could be seen by thousands of people and I want to make doubly sure that everything is perfect. Okay, so these are the arrangements that will be placed at intervals along the red carpet, on the steps of the gazebo, and in the stone urns that guard the entrance to the venue.'

'Oh, Francesca, everything is amazing! In fact, this whole room looks like something from a Monet painting!'

Francesca beamed. 'And you haven't seen the chandelier yet!'

'The chandelier?'

Izzie was confused – there definitely wasn't a chandelier on the list.

'Yes, I got a call a couple of weeks ago from Brad Knowles himself, asking if I could design something spectacular to hang over the reception tables. What do you think?'

Francesca was clearly enjoying her 'Ta dah' moment.

'It's absolutely stunning! A work of genius!'

Hanging from the rafters in an adjacent room was a white wrought-iron chandelier entwined with fresh flowers to match the bouquets and buttonholes, so large and elaborate that it could have done justice to a hallway in Versailles.

'Wait.'

Francesca stooped to flick a switch and a twinkling ribbon of lights that had been woven through the flowers sprang into life transforming the workshop into a fairy grotto. Izzie's heart ballooned. With Francesca on board, the venue would not only conform to the brief, but would be filled with a romantic ambience.

'Thank you so much,' smiled Izzie, beginning to feel a little light-headed from the feast of floral fantasy and the almost overpowering scent of so many different fragrances.

They returned to the workshop where the air was fresher, and Izzie's eye snagged on a rustic wicker basket filled with brown paper cones slotted into a wire mesh.

'What are these?'

'I'm going to fill them with rose petals for the guests to use as confetti when the bride and groom walk back down the aisle as husband and wife. They're not on the list, but it won't be an authentic Italian wedding without confetti. I hope that's okay?'

'It's perfect, thank you.'

'So how are the arrangements going? I heard you stepped into the breach at the last minute. You're very brave... or should that be crazy!'

Francesca laughed, a warm, infectious sound that drew Izzie even more to the young woman, especially when she offered her an ice-cold bottle of water. She met her new friend's gaze to thank her and she could have been looking into Meghan's mischief-filled eyes, even her fingers sported a selection of silver rings, just as Meghan's did. Once again, Izzie was flooded with gratitude for those people who started off as strangers but, within the blink of an eye, became friends.

'It's been a bit stressful, to say the least, but so far things are on schedule.' She paused to take a long draught of water, wiping her lips with the back of her hand, and instantly felt better. 'Your designs are amazing – how long have you been a florist?'

'Ten years, but I've adored anything to do with horticulture for as long as I can remember. One of my earliest memories is running through the wildflower fields alongside my cousins, with daisies and poppies twisted through our hair, pretending to be princesses. I love everything about flowers – the infinite variety of colours, of shapes or scents, but I also love the folklore, too.'

'The folklore?'

'Yes. For instance, did you know that there's a reason why brides choose white flowers for their bouquets?'

'No?'

'It's because they signify pureness, whilst red flowers mean passion and love, and yellow mean jealousy. Also, roses are never given in even numbers, except at weddings where the number twelve means the couple with have a long and healthy marriage.'

'Gosh, it sounds like a minefield!' laughed Izzie.

'It's fascinating. So, is there anything I've missed? Or would you like me to change any of the designs? When I accept a commission to supply the flowers for a wedding, I usually have a long consultation with the couple, get a feel for their personalities, their likes and dislikes, that sort of thing, but this time all I've had to go on is a few photographs. And there's so much secrecy surrounding the whole thing, I've had to do everything myself! My sister Gabriella usually helps me when I have a big order, but she's the biggest gossip in the whole of Tuscany, so I've had to forego our fun prosecco-fuelled nights. I can't wait to tell her when it's all over, though. She's going to be *so* jealous!'

Izzie wasn't sure whether it was the talk of sisterly camaraderie or the sight of the blousy pink peonies that reminded her of the bouquets Anna had chosen for her own wedding – and had then been featured in abundance at her funeral – but she was suddenly ambushed by a wave of emotion and she couldn't prevent a single tear from escaping down her cheek.

'Oh, gosh, are you okay?' asked Francesca, sliding down from her stool to place her arm around Izzie's shaking shoulders.

'I'm fine, thanks. Sorry.'

Izzie brushed the tear away, annoyed at herself for succumbing to her emotions. But that day she had spent more time talking about Anna than she had in the whole of the last twelve months and her presence was strong, sending her senses into overdrive. However, she felt Francesca deserved an explanation for her tears.

'It's just... peonies were my sister's favourite flowers. She'd chosen exactly that shade of pink for her wedding bouquet before she... before she... passed away.'

'Oh, no, Izzie, I'm so sorry. How terrible.' Francesca squeezed Izzie's hand and gave her the space she needed to stem the tears before asking 'What was your sister's name?'

'Anna. Annabel.'

Francesca nodded. Then, as Izzie watched on in mute fascination, Francesca began browsing through the medley of flowers in the shop, eventually selecting one stem from the last bucket, adding a branch of foliage and wrapping it in cellophane.

'Many roses are named after loved ones. My father named one for my mother for their thirtieth wedding anniversary last year. This rose is called Annabelle.'

Francesca presented the rose to Izzie and the gesture caused her tears to return.

'Thank you,' she managed to mutter, bringing the red/orange rose to her nose and inhaling the sweet, floral perfume. 'It's gorgeous.'

'Like your sister,' smiled Francesca.

'Yes.'

Izzie dried her tears and the two women sat in companionable silence for a few moments.

'Okay, I need to get back to the villa. There's still lots to do, and my friend Meghan is due to arrive from the airport at six!'

She thanked Francesca for her kindness and understanding and told her she would see her first thing the following morning to help stage the floral artwork before the wedding entourage descended. On the doorstep, Francesca drew Izzie into a warm hug before depositing kisses on her cheeks, and her heart filled with joy at finding another new friend in Tuscany.

With the reverence it deserved, she slotted the rose gently into her duffle bag and took her time navigating the winding roads back to the villa, memories of her beloved sister tumbling through her thoughts until she drew to a halt at the villa's front steps, exhausted from all the emotional turmoil.

And yet she felt freer than she had done for a long time, as though by talking about her sister, including her in her conversations with others, made things *less* painful and not more.

It was time to change, she knew that, and she needed some time alone to think through what she had learned that day. However, it wasn't to be because as she stepped from the Vespa all hell broke loose.

Chapter Seventeen

Riccardo's B&B, San Vivaldo
Colour: Electric Blue

'Oh, Izzie, thank God! Where've you been? We've been trying to contact you!' cried Carlotta running from the back door to greet her, her arms flying in the air, her hair bouncing around her cheeks like silver angel's wings.

'Why? What's happened?'

She saw Carlotta roll her eyes in the familiar way before embarking on a tirade of high-speed Italian, the only words of which Izzie could catch were *imbecile* and *Gianni* and her heart sank. What had he done now? She placed her hand on Carlotta's arm to calm her down.

'Where is he?'

Carlotta pointed to the far end of the terrace and together they made their way to where Gianni and Vincenzo were standing, their heads bent, hands on hips as they surveyed the results of the current catastrophe.

'What happened?' asked Izzie, surprising herself at the calmness in her voice.

'I'm so sorry, Izzie, I had no idea...'

Instead of launching into a complicated explanation, Gianni simply pointed to a large hole in the ground alongside his wheelbarrow, a bay tree he'd been in the process of planting, and his discarded spade.

'He's lucky to be alive,' mused Vincenzo, rubbing his thumb and forefinger across his moustache as he contemplated how much worse the incident could have been.

'What do you mean?'

'Take a look.'

Izzie squinted into the trench Gianni had been working on and shot backward, managing to stand on Vincenzo's toes in her haste to escape.

'What is it? A snake? Are they poisonous?'

Vincenzo grinned.

'It's much worse than a snake, Izzie. That's an electricity cable.'

'Thank goodness,' sighed Izzie, until she realised that Carlotta, Vincenzo and Gianni were staring at her, waiting with bated breath for the penny to drop. The clogs in her brain clanked and clanged until realisation eventually dawned.

'Oh, no, surely you're not telling me...'

'Yes, I'm afraid so,' nodded Vincenzo, glancing at Gianni who remained mute whilst running his fingers through his curls until he actually did look like he'd endured an electric shock.

'How bad is it?'

Izzie's stomach performed a flip-flop of panic and she sent up a quick prayer to the director of fate – please, please, please don't let it be the main cable into the house.

'It's the main cable into the house.'

She groaned. How much worse can it get!

'I'm so sorry,' muttered Gianni, his dark brown eyes filled with contrition. He looked like a spaniel who'd been caught sneaking a treat from the cookie jar, and Izzie couldn't be angry with him. Irritated, yes, but it wasn't as if he'd selected the cable and purposely attacked it with his spade only hours before the wedding of the decade.

'How long before we can get it repaired?'

'Could be today, could be tomorrow, but it could be next week.'

'Oh, God!'

Now it was Izzie's turn to run her fingers through her hair whilst the four of them stood staring morosely at the hole in the ground like a congregation of mourners, each hoping that if they concentrated hard enough the severed cable might just miraculously reconnect.

'I have a cousin who's an electrician,' offered Vincenzo. 'Why don't I give him a call to see if he can do a temporary repair?'

Izzie forced a smile on her lips.

'Thanks, Vincenzo, that would be great. Okay, let's grab a coffee. I take it there's still water and gas?'

'Of course,' said Carlotta, reaching up to pinch Gianni's cheeks.

Gianni raised his head, nodding at Carlotta's gesture of forgiveness, and seeking out Izzie's eyes for the first time. She smiled at him, linked her arm through his, and together they followed Carlotta and Vincenzo into the kitchen to ponder the disaster over an espresso and one of Carlotta's cannoli, to try to come up with a solution. As the ancient cooker ran on bottled gas, the culinary side of things would be okay – it was mainly the lights and an idea began to worm its way around her crevices of her brain.

'It's not as bad as it seems. We'll use candles, and I'll ask Francesca if we can borrow her storm lanterns which will add to the lighting and the romance.'

Suddenly the air was filled with a cacophony of drilling, exuberant hammering and the continuous buzz of a cement mixer. Carlotta rolled her eyes.

'Do you think Riccardo's tuning up his architectural orchestra for a Friday Morning performance?'

'Oh, God, I hope not!'

But what if Carlotta was right? That would be her worst nightmare – the bride and groom poised to deliver the most heart-felt lines of their lives accompanied by Riccardo on the cement mixer and his fellow workmen on the jackhammer and the circular saw. She needed to have a word with him, to appeal to his softer side, if he had one, which she feared he might not.

'Okay, Gianni, Vincenzo, why don't you see if you can source a couple of generators while I pay our friend next door a visit?'

Vincenzo looked at her askance.

'Is that wise?'

'What's the worst that can happen?'

Vincenzo exchanged a worried glance with Carlotta, ready to vocalise his opinion on the reasons why she shouldn't seek the impromptu advice of their bad-tempered neighbour who lived alone in luxurious splendour with one eye coveting the land next door.

'Well, my cousin, Umberto, had a run-in with him over some parking issue outside his café a few weeks ago. Apparently, there was a great deal of shouting and fist-shaking. I don't think you should go round there by yourself.'

'Do you want me to come with you?' asked Gianni, pushing himself out of his chair, his jaw clenched, his expression stony, looking altogether too keen to confront his nemesis.

'No…' Izzie just managed to stop herself from saying 'no way' and changed it to, 'No, thanks. I think the softly-softly approach might work better. I'll take him a peace offering and ask him in the nicest possible way if he could refrain from his musical artistry just for one day. It's not a lot to ask, is it?'

With a show of confidence she didn't feel, she grabbed a bottle of their home-made-but-not-yet-ready limoncello, and trotted through the garden towards the crumbled part of the wall which separated the two properties, stopping briefly to toss a silver coin in the wishing well and make a wish.

Was it too much to ask the wishing well gods to deliver free-flowing electricity?

It was after six o'clock, but the air was stifling, and clouds of dust ballooned from the building activities Riccardo and his men had resumed to put the final touches to the poolside terrace. It was several minutes before anyone noticed her presence and their drills and hammers fell silent. Riccardo was the last to see her and she couldn't mistake the look of irritation that floated across his expression. He issued a brusque order to the workmen who didn't need to be asked twice, abandoning their tools quickly and strolling towards the house for a cool refreshment.

'Hi, I was wondering if I could have a word?'

'What about?'

Impatience oozed from Riccardo's pores, mingled with a generous dose of exasperation at her interruption. Instead of launching straight in with her plea for help, Izzie decided to take a different approach and dress her request in a cloak of flattery.

'The pool house looks amazing.'

Riccardo dragged his piercing blue eyes away from hers to scan the stone structure with its neat terracotta roof and shutters painted the same colour green as those on the main house. Although new, the building had clearly been designed to blend sympathetically into its surroundings.

'Pretty pointless having a pool house without a pool, don't you think?'

'What do you mean?' Izzie frowned, glancing at the handsomely proportioned, albeit still empty pool.

Riccardo rolled his eyes as though talking to an imbecile. 'No water.'

Izzie heard him sigh, then his eyes caught on the bottle in her hands.

'Oh, yes, this is for you. Made by my own fair hands,' she offered the bottle to him, recognising the hint of pride in her voice.

'What do you want?'

God, why did the guy have to be so grumpy? What was the matter with him? But she swallowed her own irritation, forced a smile onto her lips and prepared to launch into her request for peace in both senses of the word. Would he agree to cease the construction cacophony for just twelve hours whilst they held the wedding? But before she could utter a word, her brain marched off on another tangent, speeding away down the superhighway of strategic negotiations.

'Why haven't you got any water?'

'Some sort of bureaucratic mix-up with the water company,' he growled, sticking his hands in his pockets so as not to bunch them up into fists. 'Morons!'

'Ah, so no water, no pool?'

'On the nail.'

'And when were you hoping to open your B&B?'

'Next weekend.'

'Will the issue be sorted by them?'

'Your guess is as good as mine.'

Izzie paused as her brain finished joining the dots.

'I could help.'

'How?'

172

Izzie decided to overlook the expression of deep scepticism that she was even capable of turning on a tap, never mind filling up a large swimming pool with gallons of water.

'You could use the water from Villa Limoncello's well which is just a few feet away over that wall.'

Riccardo opened his mouth to utter a derisory riposte, but stopped, clearly not expecting the offer.

'You have a well?'

'Yes.'

Izzie couldn't keep the smirk from her lips as the tables had very clearly turned.

'And you'd do this because…?'

'Well, yes, there is something I would like in return.'

'Thought so. What is it?'

'Actually, it's two things.'

'Two things?'

Riccardo raised his bushy eyebrows, but she could see a slight twist at the corners of his mouth and a glint of wry amusement had appeared in his eyes.

'Well, I don't know if you are aware, but we are…' Now, should she tell him that the wedding involved a couple of high-profile Italian actors, or should she continue the embargo on its disclosure. After all, she had no idea whether Riccardo was a celebrity stalker in his spare time. Unlikely, yes, but not impossible. 'We are hosting a wedding at the villa tomorrow, so I wonder if you could postpone your work on the pool, just for the day? Just so the bride and groom and their guests can hear what's going on at the ceremony and can enjoy listening to Puccini at their reception without the accompaniment of a chain saw concerto?'

'And the second thing?'

Izzie could feel her cheeks flood with warmth, but she ignored her discomfort at having to admit their disaster and cement this man's opinion of her as a clumsy, disorganised scatterbrain. This was not about her, it was about saving the wedding.

'I wonder if we could hook up to your electricity supply?'

Whatever Riccardo had been expecting, it wasn't this and to her amazement, he burst out laughing, shaking his head in disbelief, opening his mouth to say something, then being overcome by another bout of hilarity.

'Well, it's not that funny!'

'Oh, it is, it really is. What happened?'

Izzie considered concocting an elaborate story, but her mother had always told her that honesty was the best policy, no matter how embarrassing. And anyway, since recovering from his episode of maniacal laughter, Riccardo's shoulders had relaxed and his features had taken on a less confrontational attitude.

'Gianni cut through the main cable to the house.'

'Got nine lives that guy! So, are you telling me that you have no electricity for the wedding of the decade? Are the rumours flying around the village true? That the bride and groom are some kind of celebrities, desperate to preserve their tenuous grip on their privacy?'

Izzie saw Riccardo had curled his upper lip in disdain.

'They might be,' she hedged. 'So, what do you say? My water for your electricity? I'd say it's a fair exchange, wouldn't you?'

Riccardo held her eyes for what seemed like a long time, but Izzie felt something between them shift, and not for the first time she noticed the kernel of sadness lodged deep in his eyes and knew there was more to his grouchy behaviour than simple moodiness. She realised that she knew nothing about him. Why did he live alone in such a large property? Where were his family? Was he really planning to run a B&B

by himself? Basil Fawlty sprang to mind again – maybe he was going to offer an alternate twist on holidaying in the glorious Tuscan countryside.

'Maybe you'll permit me to ask a question of my own first, Miss…?'

'Jenkins, but please, call me Izzie. What's your question?'

'Who's paying your fee?'

Izzie gawped at Riccardo, stunned that he had asked such a personal question, before realising that he clearly thought she was working for the owner of the villa.

'Oh, if you want to know the identity of the villa's absent owner then I'm afraid you're asking the wrong person. I genuinely have no idea. Sorry. So, what do you say about my proposal that we help each other out?'

Riccardo eyed her for several beats whilst he weighed up his options.

'I might live to regret this, but okay, you have a deal.'

Riccardo offered Izzie his palm and she took it, unsurprised at the strength of his grip.

'Thank you.'

She spun on her heels to return the way she came when she caught a glimpse of what she thought was a brightly coloured painting hanging on the back wall of the pool house. She took a couple of steps towards it, but Riccardo stepped into her path, taking her arm and guiding her back towards the path.

'Goodbye, Isabella.'

His dismissal brooked no argument but piqued Izzie's curiosity. For a man who had queried the bridal couple's desire for privacy, he certainly had secrets of his own to keep.

Chapter Eighteen

The Terrace, Villa Limoncello
Colour: Raspberry Ripple

So, what was Riccardo hiding? What was in the pool house he didn't want her to see? And what had happened to cause such deep-seated pain to linger in his eyes?

However, Izzie's internal reverie came to an abrupt end when she rounded the corner of the villa and her gaze fell on the terrace. For there, with her pink tipped hair flowing in the breeze like a mermaid stepping from the ocean for her first foray onto dry land, was Meghan, a wide smile stretching her lips.

'Izzie!'

'Meghan!'

Within seconds she had covered the space between them and flung her arms around Meghan, inhaling the delicious whiff of floral scent that would forever remind her of her best friend. Her heart ballooned with delight and she wasn't surprised to find tears prickling at her eyes as her emotions surged.

'Welcome to Villa Limoncello, darling. I'm so happy you're here at last.'

'Me, too! Wow, what an amazing place! I knew it would be stunning, but it's even more beautiful in real life. It just so…'

Izzie waited for Meghan to continue, but her litany of superlatives had frozen on her lips because her gaze had fixed on a point just over Izzie's shoulder. At first Izzie assumed it was the breath-taking view of the vineyards or the terracotta roofs of San Vivaldo nestled on the hillside to her right, but she should have known better because Meghan was almost drooling.

Izzie giggled. 'That's Gianni, and yes, as far as I know, he's single.'

'What's the matter with the women around here?' declared Meghan, flicking her hair over her shoulder and straightening her luminous orange T-shirt that she'd accessorised herself with gold-appliqué butterflies. 'He's leading man material, if you ask me! Are you absolutely sure this isn't a film shoot and he's not playing the role of dashingly handsome groom?'

And in pure Meghan style, forgetting the fact that she had just arrived and had promised to spend every minute of her time helping Izzie with the wedding arrangements, she skipped off down the garden steps on a mission to introduce herself to the new man in her life – even though Gianni didn't know it yet.

'Hey! You've just arrived!' Izzie called after her, amusement in her voice. 'Have you even unpacked?'

'Sure,' Meghan shouted over her shoulder. 'Carlotta has put me in the pink room! Bit like my aunt Lydia's boudoir. Who puts rose-covered wallpaper on the walls *and* the ceiling?'

'I...'

But Meghan was already out of earshot and was introducing herself to a bewildered Gianni who was in the process of rehoming the bay tree in a huge ceramic pot and had no idea of the maelstrom of attention that was about to hit him. She briefly wondered if Carlotta's matchmaking skills had woven their magic spell and caused this swift introduction. Could she have pointed Meghan in the direction of their intrepid estate manager when she was settling Meghan into her suite?

Izzie shook her head but was happy Meghan had arrived at Villa Limoncello bringing with her a whirlwind of carefree positivity and jubilation. She decided that Gianni was old enough to look after himself and continued her journey to the kitchen to report on her breakthrough with Riccardo to a very relieved Carlotta and Vincenzo.

'I don't understand why he has to be so grouchy,' muttered Izzie as she rinsed the last of that day's cups and saucers and returned them to the designated place in the cupboards, ticking off the final item on that day's agenda with a sigh of relief.

It had been a very long day, filled with a cornucopia of emotions. It was only seven thirty, her shoulders ached and exhaustion swirled, yet despite this her spirits were flying high. Not only had her conversation with Luca freed some of her demons from their cage, but now that Meghan had arrived to adorn Villa Limoncello with her effusive cheerfulness, she knew that with her help she'd be able to stage the wedding according to Brad's carefully crafted plan, especially after the deal she'd struck with the enigmatic Riccardo. Her brain snagged once again on that wisp of turmoil deep in his eyes that only someone who had experienced something similar themselves might notice. She wondered what had caused it and if anyone had the answer it was Carlotta.

'How long has Riccardo lived next door?'

'Not long,' said Vincenzo, slotting the mop he'd been using to wash the tiled floor back into the cleaning cupboard before coming to sit down at the table. 'He and his wife bought the place around the same time as *Villa dei Limoni* was sold by the American. It was a real wreck, even worse than the villa, and to give him his due, he's spent time, effort and a great deal of money renovating it. Do you know him?'

Izzie paused in her task of restacking the white china plates in order of size on the sideboard and stared at Vincenzo.

'Know him?'

'He's English.'

A bolt of surprise hit her between the eyes, then realisation dawned when she realised that Riccardo had spoken with no accent whatsoever, but then a lot of Italians did. Even so, was Vincenzo really suggesting that she would know everyone who lived in Tuscany with a link to the UK?

Carlotta saw her confusion and smiled.

'I think Vincenzo means do you know his work?'

'His work?'

'Yes, he's a writer? Quite well-known, I'm told, although I've never read any of his books. Richard Clarke?'

'Richard Clarke!'

It took Izzie's brain a few moments to recover from the shock. She had actually read a couple of his crime novels, a good five years ago though, when she enjoyed reading that sort of fiction. After she'd lost Anna she just couldn't bear to go near such stories and restricted herself to light-hearted, uplifting reads.

'I had no idea… I…'

'Sadly, his wife passed away rather suddenly twelve months ago whilst they were in the throes of renovating the house,' explained Carlotta, removing her apron and hanging it on the back of the door and joining Vincenzo at the table with a mug of coffee.

Izzie slumped down at the table in the middle of the kitchen like a puppet clipped of its strings, a myriad of thoughts racing through her brain. Now she understood that haunted, guarded look she had seen buried just beneath the surface. Although they were different people in many respects, the trauma they had experienced was very similar; both struggling to deal with that one devastating event that had defined them and turned them into a mere shadow of what they had been before. She had glimpsed in Riccardo the immensity of the daily struggle and put his demeanour down to impatience, grumpiness, the physical exertion needed to renovate a crumbling old building.

Did people meeting her for the first time feel the same way about her? Did they not bother to pursue their initial contact into a tentative friendship because she gave out such negative vibes which they interpreted as grouchiness and rudeness, when actually she was simply shooting up barriers to protect herself from the anguish of more loss?

The clarity of that insight into her personality over the last two years shocked her. Before Anna had passed away she had been a cheerful, confident, sociable, optimistic and open person who made connections easily and indeed had a wide circle of friends. Now, a mere twenty four months later, only a few hardy souls had stuck by her, loved her for what she now was, mainly because they understood as they were dealing with issues of their own; Jonti with his father's attitude towards his chosen lifestyle; Meghan who refused to face the issue of her family's desire for her to take over the reins of their business – literally – at their stud farm.

Gratitude for their friendship spread over her like a warm shower and a window of self-knowledge opened up allowing her to peer inside. It was a light bulb moment and she resolved to make more of an effort to forge a new path through life that wasn't based on her grief. Yes, she would still think of her sister every day, carry her memory with her in everything she did – she was still her twin after all – but now she understood that she had a responsibility to take on the world for both of them, to live enough for two!

Gosh, she had her work cut out, but she was enthused and ready to give it a go.

When she met Carlotta's gaze, her friend reached over to pat her hand in a gesture of understanding, as though she had been following everything that had spun through her mind. How did she do that? How had she become so intuitive, so aware of people's emotions, their secret dreams, even before they were? No wonder she was a formidable matchmaker if she could read people so well.

A giggle erupted from her lips. Would Carlotta turn her attention to her? And if she did, how would she react? She had no need to ponder this question too long as a fully formed image of Luca floated across her vision and sent a delicious shiver down her spine.

'Okay, it's time Vincenzo and I left you,' smiled Carlotta, flashing Vincenzo a look that said let's go as he looked like he was settling in for the evening.

'Thanks for everything you've done today, both of you. This wedding would never be happening without your help.'

'*Non è niente!*'

Izzie hugged Carlotta and Vincenzo goodbye, promising to have an early night and to be up and raring to go the following morning at six a.m. She waved them off from the terrace, then took a bottle of Chianti out to the pergola in the hope that Meghan might return to indulge in a girly gossip before she succumbed to the delicious lure of her bed. She was shattered but keen to catch up with what was happening at home.

As she sipped the rich red wine the region was famous for, she watched the sky send streaks of apricot across the horizon, drenching the whole valley with a soft coppery light. The cicadas added their interminable backing track, their musical narrative never changing, reassuring the listener that whatever happened time marched on regardless. For some unknown reason, an image of Darren Hambleton drifted into her mind. She was surprised to find that she had thought very little about her dismissal from Hambleton Homes since leaving London, but then every spare minute had been taken up with sorting out the wedding arrangements. The assignment had landed on her lap with perfect timing and was something else she had Meghan to thank for. Again, her friend had known what she had needed most.

Dusk now tickled the regimented line of cypress trees edging the driveway and the temperature dropped from sticky to comfortable. A tinkle of laughter floated on the early evening air from the direction of the wedding gazebo and, a couple of beats later, Meghan appeared with a beaming Gianni in tow. Izzie couldn't stop herself from rolling her eyes, but she poured another two glasses of wine and handed one to each of them.

'To Villa Limoncello.'

'Cheers, darling!'

'*Salute!*'

'So, has everything been completed in accordance with my darling brother's meticulous requirements? You know, I tried to call him five times before I left London and once when I landed in Florence to get an update on when he might get here, and he still hasn't had the decency to call me back. Rachel says it's because he's in editing hell with the new film he's working on, apparently the deadline's midnight tonight. Crazy time for a deadline, but that's Brad all over. I have no idea how Lucy puts up with him; I would have throttled him ages ago!'

Meghan shook her head in disgust but Izzie knew she didn't mean it. Meghan adored her brother with the same ferocity Izzie had loved her sister and would defend him with staunch indignation to anyone who had the audacity to write a subpar review of any of his work. Her loyalty to her family and friends was legendary, as long as it didn't include anything to do with horses.

'I assume you've managed to talk to him, Izzie?'

'Yes, but only for about two minutes.'

'God, the selfish…'

'It's okay. I've had Lucy's emails and the lists and itineraries I drafted on the flight over here. And, apart from a couple of unavoidable events,' she cast a surreptitious glance in Gianni's direction, 'I'm pleased to report that we're on schedule to hold the most spectacular wedding San Vivaldo had ever seen.'

She quickly filled Gianni in on the deal she had struck with Riccardo to share his electricity and suggested that he start work on the reconnection first thing the next day. She saw the relief float across his face and was touched when he slid his hand across the table to give her fingers a quick squeeze before excusing himself to make a few calls.

'So, how are things back home?'

'Yes, I should have told you as soon as I arrived, but well, I got a little distracted.'

Both Izzie and Meghan glanced over to where Gianni was standing with his back to them, his melodic voice drifting towards them as he finished up his call and began serenading his precious vines whilst combing his unruly locks away from his forehead. For a fleeting moment the statue of David standing proud in the Accademia sprang into Izzie's mind and she had to supress a giggle.

'What should you have told me?'

'That I had a visitor at the flat last night.'

'Who?'

'Dastardly Darren.'

Izzie groaned and took a gulp of her wine to prepare herself for what was coming.

'Actually, he came bearing gifts.'

'What sort of gifts? My P45?'

'Champagne and flowers.'

'Pardon?'

'And a letter that I had to promise to deliver to you in person. Here.'

Meghan scrambled in her fuchsia-coloured satchel and withdrew a crumpled envelope with Izzie's name scribbled across the front. Izzie recognised the handwriting – it wasn't Darren's but Harry's bold scrawl. Her heart gave a sharp nip of concern.

'Oh, I...'

'Open it!'

Meghan hated waiting for anything. Although Izzie knew she would stop short of steaming open the envelope, she also knew that her friend was probably chomping at the bit to contain her curiosity.

She inhaled a deep breath, ran her fingertip along the flap and withdrew a sheet of paper that had obviously been torn from an invoice book. She smiled when she saw a smudged fingerprint of dirt in one of the corners. It was good to see that Harry was still hands-on when it came to his love of building projects and had clearly been in the middle of something when he put pen to paper – an old-fashioned way of dealing with business matters, maybe, but that was Harry Hambleton's style.

> *Isabella,*
>
> *Sincere apologies for my son's poor management skills. I've read him the riot act which didn't include any of that corporate bullshit he loves! Your services are indispensable to Hambleton Homes and I hope to see you back at work first thing on Monday morning where*

I will offer you my personal apology along with a twenty percent pay rise.
    Harry.

Izzie held the missive in her hand for several minutes as she re-read the straight-to-the-point message from her former boss.

'Well? Is it good news? Do you have your job back?'

'Yes, apparently Harry is livid with Darren. He's apologised and has even offered me a raise!'

'Phew, thank God for that!'

Meghan held up her glass in a gesture of congratulations, but confusion filled her eyes when Izzie didn't respond to her toast.

'What's the matter?'

'I'm not sure. I know I should be over the moon, but to be honest the thought of going back to staging houses for resale just doesn't fill me with any enthusiasm. Look around you – look at the vibrancy of the colours, listen to the song of the crickets, feel the warmth of the sunshine, inhale the perfume of the flowers, and wait until you taste the kaleidoscope of dishes that'll be on offer at the wedding – all home-made from the freshest of ingredients. It's a world away from the beige, bland, monochrome life I've been living in London for the last two years. Do I really want to go back to that?'

'Hooray! Now that *is* something worth celebrating!' beamed Meghan, putting her glass down on the table and reaching over to gather Izzie in her arms. 'That's the most positive thing I've heard you say in a long time. If this is what a week in Tuscany has done for you, then imagine what spending a month here would do. I can see in your eyes how much you love it here, but as someone who knows you better than you know yourself, I also know that it's not just the gorgeous views, the exceptional wine and the delicious pasta that's causing that glint of joy in your eyes.'

'Meghan…'

'Okay, so Gianni did happen to mention a certain Italian chef who's been 'showing you the sights'. Come on, Izzie, spill the juicy details. Jonti was so jealous he couldn't come over with me that he made me promise to squeeze every ounce of gossip out of you. He even suggested I upload a video diary to my YouTube channel – but I'm not going to do that. So, who's this secret tour guide?'

'There's no need to look at me like that,' laughed Izzie, aware that her cheeks had coloured and therefore she'd completely given the game away on her true feelings. 'Yes, I've made a few friends since I arrived. Carlotta and Gianni, whom you've met, a couple of women from the village, Oriana who makes the most amazing cakes and is also a professional yoga teacher too, and Francesca who…'

'Izzie…'

'Who's a really talented florist. Did you know…'

'Izzie!'

'And there's Luca, the chef at the local trattoria in San Vivaldo, Antonio's.'

'So, was it love at first sight?'

Izzie rolled her eyes, but she was used to fielding these questions from Meghan so she rallied well.

'No, it was fury!'

'Fury? What do you mean?'

'He was the guy I told you about, the one who ran me off the road causing me to end up sprawled in a field of sunflowers, staring into the dark, quizzical eyes of a very bemused donkey.'

Meghan giggled and was about to press Izzie for further details when Gianni returned to the table.

'Any wine left in that bottle?'

'No,' said Izzie, 'but I'll fetch another one from the kitchen.'

'Make it two; Luca's on his way over.'

Izzie couldn't help the corners of her lips from curling upwards. Ignoring the look of satisfaction on Meghan's face, she made her way to the kitchen to collect another couple of bottles of Chianti, some fresh glasses and a few candles, relishing the swirl of excitement spinning through her veins.

That day had been the best day she'd had for a very long time – and it was not over yet.

Chapter Nineteen

The Terrace, Villa Limoncello
Colour: Sparkling Sapphire

'Hey!'

Luca greeted Gianni with a fist bump and a manly hug before depositing the customary kisses on Izzie's glowing cheeks. Over his shoulder she could see the smirk on Meghan's face as her friend pushed herself out of her chair to experience the same greeting, her eyes sparkling with interest.

'Luca, this is my best friend, Meghan Knowles, Megan this is Luca Castelotti.'

'Hi Luca.'

'Hi, Meghan, good to meet you. I've heard a lot about you already. So, is everything ready for tomorrow?'

'Almost,' said Izzie, glancing at Gianni as she poured everyone a generous glass of red wine before sitting back down at the table, revelling in the relaxed ambience on Villa Limoncello's wonderful terrace now suffused with the golden glow of candlelight. 'We had a bit of a hiccup this afternoon...'

'Ah, yes, Gianni told me all about that. How on earth did you persuade Riccardo to agree to set you up with an electricity cable? He's not the easiest man to deal with.'

'Quid pro quo,' said Izzie smiling.

'Well, whatever it was, I could do with a slice of your diplomacy at the restaurant when customers complain about the service. Would you believe that some visitors expect their meal on the table within five minutes of ordering? I'm weary of explaining that everything we serve at Antonio's is freshly prepared and does not come in a shrink-wrapped container. And if I'm asked for "salad dressing on the side" again, or for a sprinkle of bacon bits...'

Izzie watched Luca run his palm over the stubble on his jawline, noting the tiredness beneath his eyes. It seemed Gianni had seen it too.

'Okay, we all have a very early start in the morning with a very long day ahead, so I vote we call it a night. Meghan, have you discovered the reason the villa got its name yet?'

'Not yet.'

'You'll love the *limonaia*! Come, I'll show you. Did you know that the lemons that are grown here are the most...'

Izzie watched the two new friends disappear from the end of the terrace, their voices melting away into the dark night and her heart gave a nip of pleasure at the happiness they had both found in each other's company. Luca, too, stared after them, his lips curled into a smile as he tasted his wine.

'The place looks amazing, Izzie. You've obviously worked hard to pull this off, especially after the initial... misunderstanding. Why don't you consider staying on? I heard that the owner has plans to hold more weddings here, and maybe even offer courses if everything goes according to plan. Maybe you could be just the right person they're looking for to organise them?'

'Oh, I...'

Izzie couldn't help her eyes straying to the letter from Harry that was still lying on the table.

'What's that?'

'It's a letter Meghan brought with her from the UK.'

'And...'

She heaved a sigh. She hadn't had time to think about what Harry's offer meant. Should she stick with the comfort offered by familiarity, or perhaps think about resurrecting her interior design business, albeit on a smaller scale? Or did she have the courage to explore Luca's suggestion? Until that afternoon she had never for one minute contemplated the possibility of staying on in Tuscany. That was a crazy idea, wasn't it?

'It's an apology from my boss for the way his son handled my redundancy. He wants me to go back. Offered me a raise.'

Luca remained silent as the scant breeze played with the candle's flame, sending shadows dancing across the terrace. All around them, the villa's nocturnal residents prepared to reclaim their habitat from their daytime predators and a pleasant aura of calm descended.

'And how do you feel about that?'

'To be honest, I'm not sure.'

When she met Luca's gaze to explain, she thought he was going to say something first; to remind her that she had blossomed under the Tuscan sun and that she was crazy to even contemplate a return to the same old drab existence that had been her life before she arrived at Villa Limoncello. But he didn't.

'Come on.'

Luca stood up and held out his hand to pull her to her feet. When their fingers touched, her nerve endings thrummed with sparkles of desire and she smiled. Luca tucked her arm through his and guided her towards the path leading to the wedding gazebo, nestled in its clearing like a majestic Roman monument beneath the sparkling sapphire of the starlit sky. Together, they climbed the three steps that lead to the raised dais where the bride and groom would exchange their vows the following day and Izzie surveyed the surrounding scene from the elevated vantage point.

The venue, the location, the backdrop, whatever term Brad used in his professional life, was perfect and a frisson of pride sped through her chest at what she had managed to accomplish in such a short space of time. Whether for a film shoot or a real Italian wedding, the setting was magical and very romantic. She inhaled the delicious lemony tang of Luca's cologne, and, with her heart hammering against her ribcage, she raised her eyes to meet his, every sense zinging with anticipation. Warmth radiated from his body, and the whisper of his breath on her ear lobe sent delicious ripples cascading down her spine, but just as her lips were millimetres from his, something caused him to pull back.

'Okay, Signorina Jenkins, I think it's time for bed.' Luca must have seen the surprise on her face because he grinned at her mischievously and she chastised herself for jumping to conclusions when he continued, 'I don't want to be responsible for any mistakes tomorrow due to sleep deprivation!'

Before she could register what had just happened, Luca had guided her from the gazebo to the terrace, pecked her chastely on the cheek and jumped into his Spider, waving cheerily from the window. Silently, her emotions churning in confusion, she watched him race down the driveway in a cloud of dust before disappearing through the gateposts.

Chapter Twenty

The Wedding Day, Villa Limoncello
Colour: Pearly Chiffon

Despite the tumultuous events of the previous day, Izzie slept better than she had for years. When her alarm woke her at five thirty, a trickle of dread invaded her chest. How on earth was she going to get through the day without succumbing to an avalanche of painful memories of a wedding day that had never happened? How would she be able to stop herself from comparing the bride's dress with the simple ivory silk column that Anna had chosen, or the way she had decided to style her hair, or the music she had chosen?

A fully-formed image of her beloved sister appeared before her, her eyes smiling softly, her auburn curls held away from her face, as familiar as her own, with a pretty white Alice band. To her surprise, Izzie's heart was not filled with sadness for Anna's absence, but with joy that her sister was there with her, in her bedroom, in Villa Limoncello, silently urging her to discard the painful memories and to enjoy her last full day in Tuscany.

And Anna was right! There was no point dwelling on what might have been. And hadn't she made a promise to live life for the both of them? She had no intention of reneging on the pledge she had made when she and Luca had been sitting on the bench in Boboli Gardens, so she shoved any thought of the past into the deep, dark crevices of her mind, leapt out of bed, with a smile on her face and a song in her heart, filled with determination to make sure the wedding went without a hitch.

She showered and dressed quickly before giving Meghan a knock with the promise of coffee and warm croissants if she was downstairs in the next five minutes. After setting the kettle to boil, she checked her mobile and a squirm of delight meandered through her chest when she saw she had three missed calls from Luca already! She dialled his number, her spirits climbing even higher, but surprisingly the call went to voicemail. She left a quick message to say she was sorry she'd missed his calls and to text her when he got a moment.

Feeling as though she was walking on cloud nine, she grabbed her trusty arch-lever file and opened it at the page headed The Big Day where every task was itemised right up to the minute the bride set foot on the red carpet. Of course, she realised that the situation was different to when she had drafted her list what seemed like eons ago, and that as soon as Brad turned up he would assume control of every detail, but until then, it was up to her to make tweaks and changes as necessary.

Could some of her old self-reliance be returning? Was that possible? A swoop of confidence raced through her veins as she relished revisiting the skills she had learned from running her own business and the feeling of empowerment heightened her excitement. Was it really so different, staging someone's home to staging a wedding venue?

'*Ciao*, Carlotta,' she trilled, causing Carlotta to peer over her glasses with suspicion.

'*Boungiorno*, Isabella. Where's Meghan?'

Izzie glanced out of the window and giggled. 'There.'

Carlotta put down her bread knife and joined Izzie at the window just in time to see the two lovebirds disappear behind the pergola. She didn't need a degree in Quantum Mechanics to work out what was going on.

'I think it might be just the two of us this morning!'

'And Vincenzo,' added Carlotta, her cheeks colouring slightly.

Feel-good endorphins zoomed through Izzie. Love was certainly in the air that day! Meghan and Gianni, now Carlotta and Vincenzo. Would she be adding Isabella and Luca to that list before the day was through? She checked her mobile, disappointed to see that there was no text from him, but she knew there was a lot to do at the restaurant to prepare for a day's service. Maybe he would just appear at the villa, a smile lighting up those dark sexy eyes, dimples bracketing his soft lips…

God, what was the matter with her? Get a grip, Izzie!

With synchronised efficiency, Izzie worked alongside Carlotta to add the finishing touches to the reception menu until the first delivery of the day arrived at seven thirty.

'Hey, Izzie, where do you want these?' called Francesca from the doorstep, weighed down by a huge white cardboard box containing the bridal bouquet and the two bridesmaids' posies, their perfume adding a different dimension to the leg of lamb roasting in the oven.

'Could you put them, and the table decorations, in the dining room, please. It's the coolest place until we can start dressing the tables. Need any help erecting the floral chandelier?'

'Actually, I already have that sorted.'

'Gianni?'

'Yes, I bumped into him when I was unloading the van and he offered his services.'

'Great, another item I can tick off the list.'

'I noticed someone rigging up a generator over by the wishing well. Do you have a problem with your electricity?'

'Not anymore,' smiled Izzie, resolving to make a point of thanking Riccardo for his contribution by ensuring that his swimming pool was filled to the brim before she left for the airport the next day.

The next half hour flew by with Francesca staying on to help out in the kitchen, chattering in high speed Italian with Carlotta and Vincenzo as they prepared the antipasto on six long wooden boards that would sit in the middle of the tables. There was food from every part of the colour spectrum; orange cantaloupe melon wrapped in prosciutto, green and black olives, sliced mozzarella and plump tomatoes, salami and fresh figs cut in half, pickled artichokes and mushrooms, a selection of sliced local cheeses, and fresh bread that was baking in the oven and sending wafts of mouth-watering smells into the kitchen.

When Oriana arrived with the first of the seven-tiered wedding cakes, everyone stopped what they were doing to oooh, and ahhh in admiration. By ten forty-five, the photographer and his assistant had arrived to set up their equipment – surprisingly a lot more than Izzie had imagined – the harpist had settled into her allocated spot next to the gazebo steps, and a minivan had disgorged all thirty guests dressed in their wedding finery with professionally coiffed hair and make-up. Everything was ready for Brad's final inspection, whenever he decided to arrive.

Wherever Izzie looked, people were chattering, laughing, or being berated by Carlotta for touching the food. She closed her eyes, enjoying the way the sun's rays wrapped her body in a warm embrace, until her brief daydream was interrupted by the squeal of an engine struggling to master the gradient of the hill. Within seconds, a giant SUV with dark tinted windows swung through the entrance and crunched towards the front door.

From her vantage point she watched two men, dressed in identical black suits and crisp white shirts, alight from the vehicle, their matching mirrored sunglasses completing the impression that Villa Limoncello was getting a visit from the local Italian mafia. It was only when Meghan appeared from behind the pergola and flung her arms around the tallest man's neck that Izzie realised that one of the men was Brad.

For all Meghan's gripes about her brother's fortuitous escape from the weight of family obligations at the stud farm, and his continual requests for last minute support at his film shoots, it was clear that she loved him with a ferocity that was heart-warming to see. Standing next to each other, even the least observant of onlookers would immediately guess that they were brother and sister, with their matching ski-slope noses, their blue-green eyes, and their habit of flicking their blonde hair behind their ears only for it to fall back into their faces immediately. However, there was one huge difference; Meghan sparkled, and Brad looked like he hadn't slept for a week.

'Hi Izzie,' he smiled, leaning forward to deposit a kiss on her cheek and give her a friendly squeeze. 'Great to see you, and thanks for everything you've done to pull this off. I admit there were moments when I thought it wasn't going to happen and I would never have been able to live with myself. I can't apologise enough for the initial mix-up, and for being incommunicado for the last few days – first filming, then editing – but from what I've seen it looks like you've got everything under control. In fact, the villa's even more picturesque than I had hoped – and, wow, that floral chandelier over there is an absolute showstopper. Right, if you'll excuse me, there's a few last-minute changes to sort out before we can get this show on the road.'

And that was it. The sum total of three minutes with the man whom Izzie credited with changing the whole direction of her life – even though he didn't know it. Nevertheless, she resolved to find the time to thank him properly when all the mayhem was over.

'Don't worry, Izz, he's always like that,' laughed Meghan, seeing her disappointment. 'Total focus is his mantra when it's work, total chaos when it's not! Perhaps it's for the best that he seems to have categorised the wedding ceremony as work, otherwise who knows what would have happened! Come on, let's do our own final check of the gazebo and the courtyard. Got a pen?'

Izzie nodded, removed the last of the checklists from her file and ran her eyes down the items that should be in place before the wedding guests took their seats for the ceremony, after which she would just have to leave everything in the capable hands of the gods of matrimonial harmony. Gianni joined them to help tie the last of the floral wreaths to the shutters and watching him flirt with Meghan made Izzie wish Luca could have been there to witness what they had achieved in the space of a few days.

And what an amazing achievement it was.

Villa Limoncello had been transformed from a dusty old duchess into a sparkling princess. Its front door and paint-blistered shutters were still shabby but that only added to the charm of the rustic Tuscan farmhouse. The shady courtyard had been transformed into a banqueting area with three long trestle tables covered in pristine white linen, set with silver cutlery and crystal glasses all presided over by that magnificent floral chandelier. The gazebo was both dreamy and romantic, the only sound floating in the air was soft classical music, and when Izzie ticked off the last item on the last list she turned to Meghan with tears in her eyes.

But there was no time to indulge in sentiment. Brad had taken control of the event and was already directing the arriving guests towards the gazebo and orchestrating the seating arrangements with competence and aplomb. She realised with a stab of regret that her part in the organisation was over and it was time to hand over the reins to the man whose vision this was. Difficult though it was, she had to bow out gracefully and allow him to bask in the glory of a project delivered on time and on brief.

Izzie loitered on the edge of the action, chastising herself for feeling like a spare part, asking herself what she had expected to happen when Brad arrived. Then another bolt of surprise hit her. She wasn't needed anymore; she wasn't a guest at the wedding, merely the hired help who should now blend seamlessly into the background so that the main players could take centre stage.

She suddenly craved a few moments of solitude to reflect on everything she had learnt from her experience of staging a wedding at Villa Limoncello, as well as the strides she had taken along the path of self-discovery and acceptance of the way her life was now. She had come to terms with a great deal over the last week and it was time to take stock and decide how to thank those who had supported her on that journey.

'I think I'll go and see if Carlotta and Vincenzo need any help,' said Meghan, giving Izzie's arm a gentle squeeze, clearly sensing her change of mood.

'Thanks, Meghan. Catch you in a few minutes.'

Izzie watched Meghan trot off towards the kitchen, then swivelled on her heels and made her way through the gardens towards Gianni's beloved vineyard, a world away from the hectic gathering of wedding guests. She took her time, sauntering several metres down the first row of vines, smiling at the scattered seashells under foot, before pausing to relish the ambient calm and drink in the wonderful view.

She would never grow tired of Tuscany's natural beauty, of how every time she raised her eyes there was something new to appreciate. Her gaze fell on the village of San Vivaldo, its buildings clinging to the hillside with ancient tenacity, and although she couldn't see Antonio's, she thought of Luca busily serving lunch to diners at the trattoria and wondered why he hadn't taken a break to pop down to the villa, just for a few minutes, to wish everyone luck.

She closed her eyes and exhaled a long, low breath, only to catch it again when she heard a rustle in the vines over to her right, followed by the unmistakeable crunch of swiftly retreating footsteps.

'Hello?'

Izzie stood up onto her tiptoes, but apart from the ripple of leaves, she could see nothing. Curiosity heightened to anxiety, sending goose bumps across her forearms and her senses skywards, until she gave herself a swift talking to. Whoever's slumber she'd disturbed, it was probably more frightened of her than she should be of it. She was about to spin around and return to the villa when a splash of red on the periphery of her vision caught her attention.

What was that?

She strode towards the object, crouching down to invest-igate what turned out to be a plastic bottle with a red spray nozzle, filled with a clear liquid, that had been part-hidden underneath one of the grapevines. When her gaze fell on a section of crumbling brown leaves further down the row, real-isation and indignation exploded simultaneously. This wasn't some naturally occurring disease as Gianni had thought –

someone was sabotaging the vineyard – and whoever it was had just narrowly escaped being unveiled by her!

Her stomach performed a somersault of trepidation. Warily, she picked up the bottle and sniffed the nozzle, reeling backwards as the odour assaulted her nostrils. She knew immediately what it was; her mother had always insisted that her father made his own organic weed-killer by using a mixture of commercial-strength vinegar and lemon juice. Sprayed on the vine leaves, they would wither and die, particularly in high temperatures.

Who would do such a thing?

A myriad of other questions began to ricochet around her brain, but she knew she had to stay calm, gather her thoughts, and make a plan about what to do next, particularly who she should confide in. There was only one place she wanted to be to do that – the *limonaia*.

She took a couple of photographs of her find on her phone, slid it back into her pocket, and made her way back towards the villa, heaving a sigh of relief when the glasshouse appeared in front of her, its presence as impressive as ever, radiating an aura of eternal serenity and calm. As she pushed open the door, her nostrils primed to inhale the soothing aroma of the lemon trees, she heard voices. Someone was already in there, probably with the same idea as she'd had earlier, grabbing a moment to gather their thoughts before the wedding frenzy began. Uncertain what to do, she was about to retrace her steps when she heard Luca's voice.

Izzie smiled. Thank God! If anyone would know what to do, it was Luca!

She had taken only a couple of steps across the chequerboard floor when she caught a glimpse of him, partially concealed behind the tallest of the lemon trees. Why was he wearing a tuxedo? And was that one of Francesca's button-holes?

Before Izzie had the chance to dissect that piece of inform-ation, a high-pitched female voice replied to Luca's question in rapid staccato Italian and she froze. Leaning slowly to her right, she could just about make out the silhouette of a woman, her hair the colour of melted chocolate and threaded with fresh lilies. However, it was what she was wearing that sent a thunderbolt of pain through her heart: a diaphanous white gown that floated like a waterfall around her slender body, as well as the fact that Luca had his hand resting on the woman's shoulder, his lips inches from hers as he stared into her eyes. She felt as though she'd inadvertently stumbled on the climax of a Hollywood romcom!

Who was this woman? Why was she dressed like that? And why was Luca whispering with her in the *limonaia*?

Izzie's stomach lurched, and, in a bubble of confusion and disbelief, she managed to swivel noiselessly on her heels and walk away from the devastating scene, back towards the villa, completely oblivious to the continuing chaos around her. Her brain felt like it was crammed with cotton wool as she tried and failed to slot the image imprinted in her mind's eye into an explanation that did not involve the fact that Luca and this mystery woman were a couple. A couple who, for the few brief seconds she had watched them together, seemed so totally at ease in each other's company that it was obvious they knew each other well.

Fighting a surge of rising panic, she made it as far as the pergola, willing herself to hold it together until after the wedding and she could melt away into the ether. Somewhere on the edge of her senses she heard Brad's distinctive voice above all others and tuned in to what he was saying.

'Where the hell's Luca disappeared to? I assume he's with Sabrina. Can someone find them please and tell them that we're all waiting!'

Sabrina?

Had she heard right?

Oh my God! The dark-haired woman Luca was with in the *limonaia* was Sabrina, his ex!

As the rusty cogs turned in her head the truth finally dawned, and she had to grab onto the wooden post of the pergola to keep her legs from crumbling beneath her as realisation exploded like a firework in her brain, clouding her judgement and causing all common sense to fly out of the window.

This was their wedding!

Sabrina was wearing a bridal gown, Luca was wearing a wedding suit! Was Sabrina the celebrity part of the couple who was anxious to maintain her privacy? She had to get away; there was no way she could stand around and watch Luca and Sabrina exchange vows. She just couldn't. Now she understood why he'd backed off from kissing her the previous evening in the gazebo, and why he'd not responded to her calls and texts that morning.

All thought of her discovery in the vineyard vanished from her mind and the flight instinct took over. Settling her face into what she hoped was a neutral expression, and with as much dignity as she could muster, she made her way to the kitchen.

'Is everything in hand with the food, Carlotta?' she croaked, her throat constricted and dry.

'*Tutto bene*,' smiled Carlotta, her cheerful face morphing into surprise when Izzie dragged her into a hug.

'*Grazie. Carlotta.* You and Vincenzo have been amazing.'

Ignoring Vincenzo's astonishment, she rushed from the room, raced upstairs to her sunflower-bedecked bedroom, and began tossing random items of toiletries and clothes into her duffle bag. She was just about to leave when she paused, grabbed a pen and scribbled a note for Meghan.

> *Sorry, Meghan, I had to get away. By the time you read this, you'll know why. If you get the chance, please pass on my congratulations to Luca and Sabrina and tell Brad that I needed to catch a flight back to London so I can return to my job at HH on Monday. I'll call you tonight about the rest of my things and the hire car.*
> *Thanks, Izzie. x*

She dashed across the hallway and left the note for her friend to find when she inevitably came looking for her, by which time she hoped she'd be long gone. In a stealth-like manner that she would have found comical if she had been in a better frame of mind, she crept down the staircase and detoured to the front door so as not to alert Carlotta and Vincenzo to her earlier than scheduled departure.

With her heart hammering out a painful concerto against her ribcage, she made it to the outhouse unseen. She grabbed the little pink Vespa and wheeled it as silently as she could to the driveway, grateful that she had managed to co-ordinate her escape whilst everyone's attention was focused over by the wedding gazebo where the harpist was in the throes of playing the wedding march.

At the end of the driveway, unable to look back for a final glimpse of the villa, she cocked her leg over the seat and started the engine, her cheeks glowing with embarrassment at her mistake, but it was the cracks in her heart that hurt the most.

Chapter Twenty One

The Wedding Gazebo, Villa Limoncello
Colour: Paprika Panic

'Has anyone seen Izzie?'

'I thought she was with you?'

'No, I've not seen her for a while. I thought she was in here helping with the food?'

Carlotta cast a worried glance across at Vincenzo who, with his arm still strapped, was attempting to assemble a sumptuous cheese board using only his good hand, then back at Meghan.

'She popped in about fifteen minutes ago, gave us both a hug – which we did think was a bit strange – then disappeared upstairs. It's all been a bit manic since your brother arrived so maybe she's grabbing a few minutes to herself whilst the ceremony is under way.'

'Thanks.'

Meghan took the stairs two at a time, her anxiety mounting. She knew Izzie better than anyone and there was no way she would take a break until she had made double-sure every last detail had been checked and rechecked and the project – whether it was a Hambleton Homes house-staging or a glamorous Tuscan wedding – had been delivered in accordance with her brief. Also, she had been stalking her brother for the last twenty minutes, trying to catch him on his own so she could blast him personally for the brevity of his thank you speech for everything Izzie had done, but he'd been completely surrounded by arriving guests and she didn't want to embarrass him.

God, he was *so* irritating. It was obvious he'd grabbed the organiser's baton from Izzie's capable hands and Meghan wondered, knowing her obsession with minutiae, how she was coping with this sudden change in dynamic.

'Izzie? Are you in there? Izzie?'

She pushed open the door to Izzie's room, but it was clear she wasn't there. She decided to pop into her own room to run a comb through her hair and retouch her lipstick before the reception got under way. She knew she had to stay in the background, it was one of the orders Brad had barked at her when he'd seen her loitering, but she still wanted to look decent, especially if the opportunity presented itself to get Gianni on his own whilst the wedding party were stuffing their faces.

She sat down on the flowery dressing table stool, and immediately another, much more likely scenario, burst into her mind and she chastised herself for not thinking about it sooner. This was the first wedding Izzie had been involved in since she'd lost Anna only weeks before her sister was due to exchange her vows with Matt. No wonder she'd disappeared before the wedding got under way; Meghan couldn't begin to understand how Izzie must be feeling.

She sprang from her seat and had taken only a couple of steps towards the door when her eye snagged the note lying on her bed. She snatched it up and scanned the contents, her stomach performing a summersault of dismay and confusion.

'What the…?'

She grabbed her mobile and scrawled through her contacts for Izzie's number, but, as she had suspected, there was no answer. What did Izzie mean, 'pass on my congratulations to Luca and Sabrina'?

'Oh my God! No! No! No!'

What was Luca playing at? Anger bubbled up inside her. Why hadn't Gianni said anything to her? Or Brad? No, scratch that, she wasn't surprised her stupid brother had kept her out of the loop. He never told her the details – just ordered her around like one of his crew, expecting her to second-guess what he needed. She knew he didn't do it on purpose, that his brain twisted so many different themes, plots, storylines together it was at risk of exploding and she didn't want to add to the strain. And she could hardly expect Gianni to confide something like that – Luca was his best friend and she had only known him for a few hours.

How dare Luca do this!

Her indignation on her friend's behalf clouded her rationality. She was determined to give Luca a piece of her mind – but only if she could get him alone. She had no wish to upset Sabrina, although really, she should be warned what a snake he was.

Meghan hurtled down the stairs, Izzie's note crumpled in her fist. She checked the terrace, then the *limonaia*, but there was no sign of Luca, or Gianni for that matter. Her suspicions mounted and, as she dashed towards the gazebo, she saw that the guests had been seated and every eye of the congregation was on Brad as he performed the final tweaks – but there was no sign of Luca standing in the gazebo waiting for his bride to arrive, nor of his best man proudly bearing the ring.

Then the realisation hit her with such force she gasped.

Of course! If Luca was the groom, then Gianni was his best man!

God, what kind of arrogance made them think they could get away with this?

But before she could come up with an answer she spotted Luca, pacing backwards and forwards next to the wishing well, his head bent, his hands in his pockets as he muttered to himself – and even better, he was alone. She sprinted towards him, along the overgrown path where weeds sprouted from the cracks like a giant's nasal hair, and scooted to a halt in front of him, her eyes narrowed with fury.

'Luca!'

'Meghan, hi. Sorry, do you mind? I just need to...'

Luca continued to pace, his whole demeanour exuding nervous tension, as he rehearsed a repetitive monologue of Italian which Meghan took to be his vows.

'You complete and utter bastard!'

She was pleased to see her greeting caused Luca to stop in his tracks and stare at her, his jaw loose, his eyes filled with incredulity.

'What...'

'I don't know how you thought this was going to pan out, but what you've done is despicable, so... so absolutely heartless, especially after Izzie confided in you about Anna and Matt. How could you? How could you inflict such hurt on someone who thought you were her friend? Don't you think she's suffered enough? Don't you think...'

'Hey, hey, hang on a minute.' Luca stepped forward and grabbed Meghan's shoulders, forcing her to look into his eyes where she saw only bewilderment and concern. 'What are you rambling on about?'

'Don't pretend you don't know. She saw you – with... with Sabrina.'

'She saw me with...'

'Yes, Sabrina, except she's not your *ex*-fiancée, is she?'

'I can assure you that Sabrina is not any kind of fiancée! What gave you that idea? What's all this about? Ahh...'

'Oh, so the penny drops at last, does it?'

'Izzie saw us in the *limonaia*, I take it?'

'Yes, that's what I said… canoodling with the bride…'

'Oh my God! Sabrina isn't the bride, she's the bridesmaid. And, as of midnight last night, I'm the best man!'

'Oh, well, that's alright then,' said Meghan sarcastically, her head starting to spin from the surreal path the conversation with Luca was following. 'Thanks for clarifying that. But it still doesn't excuse the fact that you're in a relationship when you led Izzie, and me, to believe you were single.'

'I am single! Oh God! Where is she? I think it's time to stop all this ridiculous secrecy! Your brother has a lot to answer for, Meghan!'

'Hey, Brad has many faults, but you can't blame him for your skulduggery. And Izzie isn't here. She's gone.'

'What do you mean gone?'

'I mean Brad's in charge of the wedding now. Izzie has delivered everything on the brief, magnificently I would add, and now she's gone home to London. She didn't want to stick around to watch you get married.'

'I'm not getting married!' shouted Luca, throwing his hands into the air in a typical Italian gesture that would have caused Meghan to giggle had the circumstances been different. He resumed his pacing, frantically checking his watch, fighting indecision before he stopped abruptly and grabbed Meghan's arm.

'Ow!'

'Sorry, sorry, but will you call Izzie, please? Stop her. Ask her, beg her, to meet me at Antonio's and I'll get there as soon as the ceremony is over. Okay? And Meghan, I insist you have a conversation with Brad. You have to tell him to explain to you what's going on here. You know, I did actually think he would have told you who the groom was – you're his sister,

209

right? – but I'm a man of my word and I won't breach the confidentiality clause he asked us all to sign.'

'Confidentiality clause? What confidentiality clause?'

'Call her!'

'Luca…'

But Luca was already racing towards the gazebo leaving Meghan reeling from their conversation. She believed him when he said he wasn't involved with Sabrina, that they weren't the wedding couple but the best man and the bridesmaid. Yet, looking at Luca in his elegant morning suit and fancy pink tie and matching buttonhole, she could equally understand how Izzie had jumped to the conclusion she had. She grabbed her phone and tried Izzie's number again, but again it went to voicemail, so she left a message.

'Hi Izzie, darling. I've read your note and there's been a complete misunderstanding. I've spoken to Luca and he is not, I repeat, *not* getting married – he's actually the best man, and a last-minute replacement at that – and the person you saw him with is a bridesmaid. And they are *not* a couple. I don't know what's going on, my head's spinning to be honest – I need to speak to my idiot of a brother – so whatever you do you have to give Luca a chance to explain. He's genuinely upset about what's happened, but the wedding's about to start so he can't come and find you. Please, please, please, wherever you are, you need to wait for him at Antonio's so he can talk to you.'

Meghan disconnected and replaced the phone in the pocket of her jeans, her heart pounding so hard in her chest that she thought it would burst through her ribcage and canter away through the vines.

'Okay, right,' she muttered to herself, inhaling several steadying breaths before she pushed back her shoulders and tilted her chin in the air. 'You'd better have a good explanation for all this, Brad Knowles!'

When Meghan emerged from the foliage, the wedding guests were all in their seats, their expressions filled with happy expectation, and Luca had taken his place in the gazebo next to the groom. With chiselled good looks, brilliant blue eyes and elegantly tousled dark hair, she had to admit that the guy about to take his vows oozed super-charged sex appeal and she recognised him as Stefano Rossellini, the actor who had won a Nastro D'Argento award for *Attore Non Protagonista* in one of her brother's most successful films. Whilst he could probably walk down the street in London without a second glance, he most certainly couldn't do the same in Italy.

Within seconds the music started, and she completely forgot her annoyance at her brother as she watched the bride and her two bridesmaids make their way down the red carpet. Stefano's wife-to-be looked stunning in an off-the-shoulder, floor-length gown in ivory silk that enhanced her willowy figure perfectly. She carried the most amazing bouquet, as did her bridesmaids, her dark hair was threaded with fresh flowers and the smile on her face told its own story. Meghan glanced back to the groom and when she saw the depth of love reflected in his eyes her heart performed a somersault of joy.

Why shouldn't this couple be afforded the privacy they craved on their wedding day? No wonder her brother had gone to such lengths to keep the whole thing under wraps – not everyone wanted their wedding day splashed across the front page of a daily newspaper.

The ceremony was the most beautifully orchestrated, visually stunning, occasion she'd ever had the pleasure of attending, and yet the whole thing was marred by the fact that the person the bride and groom should really be thanking for pulling the whole thing off without a hitch, was not there to enjoy her triumph.

Where was Izzie? Had she got her message? Would she be waiting at Antonio's to give Luca a chance to explain? And how did Luca know Stefano? Why had he been asked to step in as best man at the last minute? What had happened to the original best man? And how soon could she grab her brother and give him a piece of her mind, because all this was totally his fault! If he had only trusted her, and Izzie, to start with, none of this would have happened.

Chapter Twenty Two

Antonio's Trattoria, San Vivaldo
Colour: Romance Red

Izzie fingered her phone, contemplating the voicemail Meghan had left and wondering why she hadn't answered straight away when she'd rang her back. Then she checked her watch and realised that she was probably, at that precise moment, witnessing the bride and groom exchange their vows.

Okay, so she'd made a mistake about thinking Luca and the bridesmaid were a couple about to become man and wife, and she was embarrassed about that. But when she had seen them together in the *limonaia*, their heads bent towards each other, the intimacy of the gesture told her there was clearly more than friendship between them.

She sat on the Vespa, surrounded by the same sunflowers she had crashed into when Luca had driven her off the road the previous week, which seemed like a lifetime ago. So, Luca had asked her to wait for him at Antonio's to give him a chance to explain, but did she really want him to? Was there any point? He didn't owe her anything – they had been friends for only a short time. He wasn't to know how much that had meant to her, how much his kindness had helped her to cast off the cloak of misery she had worn around her shoulders for too long.

Wouldn't it be better to just make her way to the airport and fly back to London a day early, to use the time to prepare for a new start at Hambleton Homes on Monday morning? But then, no matter what he had done in the *limonaia*, she would always be grateful to him for what he had given her and surely that deserved a chance to explain?

She scrolled through her contacts in her phone and selected a number, then paused trying to work out what to say before deciding just to keep it simple. That way there could be no misunderstandings.

'See you at Antonio's.'

She had no idea how long it would take Luca to get away. She suspected Italian weddings could go on for hours and the fact that Luca was best man would mean he'd have to deliver a speech at the reception afterwards. She sighed, resigned to the fact that she could be indulging in more than the permitted one cup of the thick, dark espresso she had grown to love, along with a myriad of other tasty treats that were as far away from her coffee-and-toast routine as you could get.

She pushed the Vespa out of the field and back onto the road, replaced her helmet and took a moment to absorb the scenery. Despite the trauma of the last hour, her spirits edged up a notch as her previously sluggish creativity tore away from its tethers and a kaleidoscope of new ideas and design concepts burst into her brain, all featuring the spectacular colour palette that was spread out before her. She started to mentally catalogue how she could weave them into her next commission; the dark emeralds and silver-greens of the foliage, the saffron yellow of the sunflowers, the rich terracottas of the roof tiles, the honey-gold façades of the buildings, the infinite blues of the sky dotted with random puffs of cotton wool.

A kernel of intense excitement popped like corn in her chest and a feeling of complete elation whipped through her veins as the ideas came thick and fast, like a technicoloured tsunami. She thought of the bedroom in her flat, of what she could do to transform the space from drab functionality to a place she wanted to spend her time nurturing fresh designs, textures, fabrics, paints, wallpapers. Maybe she could persuade Jonti to let her loose on his room, or approach a couple of her old clients who might be ready for a change of scenery?

She paused, allowing the thoughts ricocheting around her head to calm to a canter. Did all the enthusiasm mean she had made the decision not to return to Hambleton Homes?

Yes!

She smiled at the momentous decision she had just made, euphoria whooshing through her like a revitalising breeze. She grabbed her phone, searching for the number she had dialled more often than any other down the years. When she found it she stopped and a dart of intense pain scorched through her whole body causing her to gasp at its ferocity.

In that moment of unbridled joy, she had forgotten that Anna wasn't simply at the other end of a phone, that she would never again hear her sister's sweet, cheerful voice encouraging her, supporting her, championing every idea she had. Sadness and loss threatened to overwhelm her and she could do nothing to prevent tears from trickling down her cheeks and landing with a splosh on the dusty earth at her feet.

Yet, she brushed them away, raising her eyes to the clouds as they raced towards their uncertain destination. Anna wouldn't want to see her cry! She would encourage her to rush headlong into a new chapter of her life, to squeeze every bit of happiness from every situation. And anyway, she may not be on the end of a phone, but Izzie could feel Anna's uplifting presence right there next to her, accompanying her every single day, urging her to be the best she could be – her beloved sister was her own personal guardian angel.

With a surge of optimism, she mounted the little pink Vespa, contemplating the possibility of investing in one when she got back to London – it would certainly solve her parking problems. As she navigated the twists and turns of the road leading to San Vivaldo, another thought niggled at her brain.

If she wasn't going back to Hambleton Homes, could she perhaps reconsider Luca's suggestion to speak to the owner of Villa Limoncello about their plans to host courses there? She realised with a start that she never had found out who owned the villa and made a mental note that she would get their details from Luca before she left – just in case.

By the time she arrived in San Vivaldo, her stomach was complaining vociferously that she hadn't eaten since the previous evening. That was another thing that had changed since she'd arrived in Tuscany. Breakfast was a new concept to her, but she loved it! All those warm, flaky buttery croissants and cannoli oozing with cream. On impulse, she decided to call in at Oriana's bakery, ordering a frothy cappuccino from a smiling teenager before taking a seat at the bistro table outside to savour every mouthful.

It had taken her a while to realise it, but food, and patisserie in particular, was one of the good things in life and the injection of sugar and caffeine sent her spirits skywards. She had only been in Italy for a few days and already she found that her clothes were actually starting to fit her instead of hanging from her frame as if she were a human coat hanger.

She glanced across the cobbled piazza to Francesca's flower shop where her sister Gabriella was holding the fort for the day, then on to the *fruttivendolo* where a medley of exotic fruits had been displayed with the artistry of a grandmaster. Local residents were going about their daily business, their shopping expeditions bathed in golden sunlight, with smiles on their faces and all the time in the world to stop for a few words with their neighbours. This sense of community was something Izzie had never experienced in London. In fact, it was quite the opposite, with the early morning rush of time-starved commuters, their heads down so as not to risk inadvertent eye-contact, their shoulders hunched against the drizzle and the burden of making it to work on time.

What would it be like to stay in San Vivaldo? Could she perhaps take a sabbatical before starting up her business again? She still had most of her redundancy money left, and when she received her fee from Brad for organising the wedding she should be able to eke out a couple of months there.

As she sat back in her chair, relishing the warmth on her face, she experienced an overwhelming surge of positivity and she knew for certain that Anna was looking down on her and smiling, nodding her head in agreement and shouting 'go for it'.

Could she?

However, before she could plan any further, she had to talk to Luca. The clock on the church tower struck three o'clock. Where had the time gone? She gathered her duffle bag and wheeled the Vespa down a narrow alleyway towards Antonio's Trattoria with a smile on her face and a plan forming in her mind.

'Hey! Izzie! Thank God, I thought I'd missed you!'

Her first glimpse of Luca running towards her from the veranda of Antonio's, his hair flapping at his forehead, his dark eyes filled with anxiety, told her everything she needed to know. He had changed out of his morning suit into his preferred uniform of black jeans and matching T-shirt, for which she was grateful, and greeted her with a broad smile before depositing the usual kisses on her cheeks.

Strangely, the power of coherent speech seemed to have deserted her, but she smiled back and followed him into the trattoria where he guided her to a table in the corner. At that time of the day there were only a couple of patrons, both perched on bar stools next to the bar, staring morosely into their cups as if hoping that the meaning of life would be lurking somewhere in the dregs at the bottom.

Izzie slid into a chair and Luca brought over a couple of glasses of iced lemonade.

'Izzie…'

'It's okay, Luca, Meghan's told me what happened.'

Luca held her gaze, clearly struggling with where to start. Izzie wanted to make it easy for him, but that meant admitting the fact that the reason she had jumped to a very embarrassing conclusion was that she had feelings for him.

But so what? It wasn't the worst thing that had happened to her.

'When I saw you in the *limonaia*, I thought you and Sabrina… well, I made a mistake, but you seemed very… erm, close and I just thought… Anyway, it's fine…'

'No, it's not fine. When you told me about your misunderstanding over the film shoot, I tried to contact Brad to talk to him about it, to insist he brought you up to speed or I would, but I couldn't get hold of him. Let me assure you, I've wanted to explain what's been going on all week, but everyone involved – the guests, the suppliers, the waiting staff – we were all asked to sign a confidentiality agreement preventing us from revealing any details whatsoever about the wedding, so if I'd said anything, well…'

'It's okay, Luca, I completely understand.'

'No, you don't.'

Luca heaved a long sigh, took a gulp of his lemonade and placed the glass down on the table before meeting her gaze head on.

'Will you just listen? Let me finish before asking questions?'

'Luca, it's okay…'

'Please? It's too complicated to deliver in short bursts.'

'Okay, but there is something really important I need to talk to you about, too.'

'Want to go first?'

'No, you can go first.'

'Sure?'

Izzie nodded, intuition warning her that if she told Luca about her discovery in the vineyard before he'd had a chance to get his explanation off his chest he might just explode. The vines weren't going anywhere, and she suspected that the culprit wouldn't risk returning that day.

'Okay. So, Meghan told you I was the best man, right?'

'Right.'

'And that Sabrina was one of the bridesmaids, right?'

'Yes.'

'Well, up until last night, I was happily anticipating performing the role of usher at an old university friend's wedding. Stefano and I did our degree together in Siena and we've been friends ever since, although I don't get to see him as often as I would like now that he's a major film star!'

'He's a *major* film star?'

'Well, he is in Italy, and he gets a lot of attention wherever he goes. However, there was no way he was going to risk a coterie of exuberant fans causing mayhem on his wedding day or the paparazzi taking photographs and splashing them all over social media. That was why Brad offered to organise the whole thing, so that Stefano and Louisa wouldn't have to talk to anyone about the arrangements, and it would be less likely to get out. Of course, they've planned a fabulously excessive party in Venice next weekend with everyone who's anyone invited, but for the actual ceremony they just wanted an intimate declaration of love in front of family and a few close friends and a fabulous Italian feast afterwards.'

'Okay, but…'

'Anyway, after leaving you last night, I got a call from Stefano in a complete panic, asking if I would step in as best man because Alessandro's mother had been rushed into hospital in Naples with a suspected heart attack and wasn't expected to survive the night. Of course, I agreed, but it also meant I didn't have a best man's speech prepared for the reception. Alessandro emailed me his. I've been an extra in a few films before, so I tried to think of it as just another role, but I admit I was terrified and wasn't thinking straight when Sabrina offered to help and dragged me off to the *limonaia* to "rehearse my lines".'

'But when I saw you…' Heat flooded her face and she couldn't meet his eyes.

'When you saw me I was in the middle of telling Sabrina that there was no way I wanted to resume our relationship. As well as reminding her that she was newly engaged to Claudio, I also had to tell her that I no longer had feelings for her and that the best thing we could do was forget the conversation had even happened.'

Izzie's brain felt like it had been crammed with cotton wool as she tried to connect the dots and come up with a realistic picture after all the twists and turns of the last few days. It was so surreal, she actually felt like she could be in a film!

She swallowed half her lemonade in one go, wishing Luca had added a shot of vodka. Everything was slowly falling into place, and instead of annoyance at being kept in the dark, or embarrassment over running away from the villa, a surge of hilarity bubbled through her chest. She burst into laughter, laughter she couldn't control until tears ran down her cheeks and she had to wipe them away with her sleeve as Luca watched on, bemused, uncertain how to react to her sudden hysterics.

'I'm sorry, Izzie.'

'You don't need to apologise – none of this is your fault. I'm sorry, too. Sorry for jumping to conclusions about you and Sabrina. Sorry for running away when I should have stayed and given you the chance to explain. We'll call it evens, shall we?'

'What do you mean?'

'Well, I'll always be grateful to Brad for asking me to come over here, no matter what his intentions. If I hadn't come to Villa Limoncello, I would never have met you and I wouldn't have realised that hiding from the past is never a catalyst to meaningful change.'

Luca smiled, producing those dimples that caused her heart to squeeze. 'Come here.'

Izzie stood up and it was the most natural thing in the world to move into Luca's arms. His eyes sought hers, a question floating in their depths, and instead of saying anything, she raised onto to her tiptoes and, ignoring the patrons' curious audience, kissed him until she was breathless. She could have stayed there all day, exploring the way Luca's body moulded so perfectly to hers, enjoying the ripples of pleasure that cascaded through her veins when his fingers glided around to the nape of her neck to pull her closer, inhaling the intoxicating scent of his citrussy cologne, but Luca hadn't forgotten that she too had something to talk about.

'So, what was it you wanted to tell me?'

'Ah, yes, I think we should sit down for this.'

'Why? What's going on?'

Luca held out a chair for Izzie and she collapsed into the seat, the muscles in her stomach tightening as she contemplated Luca's reaction to what she had uncovered.

'Izzie?'

'Before I… before I stumbled on you and Sabrina in the *limonaia*, I took a stroll down to the vineyard. I just needed a few quiet minutes to myself away from all the hustle and bustle of the wedding, but when I got there someone else was there.'

'Who?'

'I don't know, but they left something behind.'

'What?'

'A bottle of weed-killer.'

'A bottle of what?'

Luca leaned towards Izzie, his forearms on his thighs, his eyes fixed on hers, his forehead creased in confusion and concern.

'The person I disturbed was in the process of spraying Gianni's vines with a concentrated solution of vinegar and lemon juice. It's an organic weed-killer, but it wasn't being used to get rid of weeds. I suspect it's the cause of the recent spurt of dried, crumbling leaves that's been upsetting him so much.'

Luca stared at Izzie whilst he assimilated what she had just told him.

'Sabotage?'

'It looks that way.'

'I don't know whether to be angry or relieved!'

'I agree. Now we know what's causing the problem, Gianni can take the appropriate action, but who do you think would do such a thing?'

'I know exactly who would do such a thing!' growled Luca, springing from his seat and grabbing his car keys. 'Come on! We need to get back to the villa.'

Chapter Twenty Three

The Driveway, Villa Limoncello
Colour: Livid Purple

Luca swung the steering wheel of the Spider to the left and drove through the wide welcoming stone pillars of Villa Limoncello. Izzie was surprised that, despite her apprehension over what Luca intended to do, a warm feeling of home-coming surged through her body until they came to an abrupt halt only yards past the gate, their progress blocked by a plethora of expensive cars and dark-windowed SUVs. Never-theless, the traffic chaos did not detract from the grandeur of the entrance to the house.

'I love this driveway,' sighed Izzie, feasting her eyes on the avenue of arboreal magnificence; the arrow-straight cypress trees lining the route to the front door, the splash of cerise from the azaleas, the glossy foliage of the magnolia bushes.

She opened the car door and inhaled a long breath, savouring the fragrance of baked earth, of crushed pine needles and the herby, peppery aroma of lavender. Her ears buzzed with the sound of the cicadas striving to out-do the soft melody of Italian classical music coming from the direction of the terrace.

'I wish…'

She stopped mid-sentence when she realised that Luca had remained in the driver's seat, his arms wrapped around the steering wheel, staring through the windscreen at the villa.

'What's the matter?'

Deep creases ran the width of his forehead and her heart gave a nip of concern when she saw his attention was miles away, focused on the far horizon where the dusty hillside met the azure of the sky. Luca must have sensed her scrutiny because he quickly reconnected with the present and jumped out of the car to join her, his hands shoved deep into the pockets of his jeans and his shoulders stiffened with repressed anger.

'Luca? Are you going to tell me what's going on?'

'Not until I'm absolutely sure.'

However, it wasn't long before Izzie guessed exactly who Luca suspected was responsible for the damage to Gianni's precious vines. Instead of walking towards the villa, he grabbed Izzie's hand and guided her in the direction of the half-concealed entrance to Riccardo's B&B. With impressive agility, he vaulted over the gate and, a little more clumsily, Izzie followed suit.

'Luca, I don't think we should…'

'Shhh…'

Izzie shook her head, her heart flaying her ribcage as she oscillated between wanting to support Luca and ditching her investigative deerstalker to high-tail it back to the safety of the villa where she knew the champagne would be flowing and she could share the details of her reconciliation with Luca with Meghan. However, her curiosity won out in the end, even though her self-confidence demons had raised their ugly heads above the parapet once again. She lifted her chin, squared her shoulders, and inhaled a deep breath.

What was the worst that could happen? Riccardo would either bawl them out, or call the police and have them escorted from the premises, but if Luca was right and he was to blame for the sabotage, then he wasn't going to do that, was he?

'Looks like he's given his workmen the day off,' whispered Luca, peering around the corner of the house to the swimming pool where a regiment of building equipment and DIY tools had been abandoned in situ.

'Actually, I asked him to do that.'

'You did? And he agreed?'

'Well, it was part of the deal we struck. Look, Luca, maybe we should talk to Gianni about this before we start casting about accusations. I didn't see who left that spray in the vineyard – it could have been anyone.'

'Everyone in the village knows how keen Riccardo is to buy the vineyard – he's made no secret about it. When you spoke to him about the electricity, did he ask you if you knew who the owner of the villa was?'

'Yes, he did but… Luca? Luca? Where are you going?'

Izzie jogged in his wake, catching up with him on the front steps of the B&B and reaching for his hand just in time to stop him from hammering on the door.

'Hang on a minute – I really think we should wait until we've thought this through a bit more. We don't have any evidence that Riccardo is to blame – none whatsoever.'

She held Luca's gaze, surprised at the level of distress scrawled across his expression. But then, it wasn't just Gianni's job that was at risk if the saboteur had succeeded, it was his dream to reinvigorate the vineyard and produce the first batch of Rosetti wine for over two decades. If Riccardo *had* been spraying the vines with home-made weed-killer, it was a very serious matter, but they needed more than mere suspicion before they said anything to him.

'Sorry, Izzie, you're absolutely right, and I shouldn't have involved you in this. Let's go back to the villa and enjoy what's left of the wedding celebrations. I'll have a chat to Gianni and Vincenzo later when everyone's left, and we'll have a look at that spray you found before deciding what to do. Thank you for injecting a dose of sanity into the situation.'

Luca smiled at Izzie, his eyes crinkling attractively at the corners as he linked her arm, and her heart ballooned with pleasure. She wanted to kiss him there and then, but the sooner they left the B&B the better.

'This way, I know a shortcut.'

Izzie lead Luca through the rose-covered arbour, across the terrace next to the swimming pool, and towards the gap in the wall between the properties she had used before, behind Villa Limoncello's wishing well. Just like they had been on her previous visit, her eyes were drawn to the pool house and what she had thought was a multi-coloured painting on its rear wall.

'Hang on a minute.'

She dashed to the window and peered in, a spasm of alarm whipping through her body like an electric shock. No wonder Riccardo had steered her away from the pool house the last time she was there, because displayed on a shelf running the width of the building were a brigade of exactly the same spray bottles as the one she had found in the vineyard, each containing a different colour liquid, ranging from pale pink, to inky blue and transparent.

'What are you looking at?' asked Luca, coming to stand next to her, curling his palm around his eyes as he squinted into the building. 'What are those?'

'I think some of them contain chemicals for the swimming pool, but I recognise the bottles with the red nozzles. Look.'

Izzie fished out her phone and showed Luca the images she had captured of the spray she had found in the vineyard. It was identical to those lining the shelves, same size, same red nozzle.

'So, I was right? We have our culprit?'

'It looks like it.'

Luca extracted his own phone from the pocket of his jeans and spent a few minutes taking photographs of their discovery, before turning to Izzie, relief spreading across his face.

'Okay, the mystery is solved and Riccardo isn't going anywhere. I think I can predict how Gianni's going to react when we tell him, so what do you say we keep what we've discovered to ourselves for the time being? Just so we can enjoy your last night in Tuscany without having to spend it explaining everything that's just happened in minute detail?'

'Sound like the best idea you've had all day!'

Chapter Twenty Four

The Courtyard, Villa Limoncello
Colour: Caramel Symphony

Luca plastered a smile on his face, grabbed Izzie's hand and together they made their way back to Villa Limoncello, pausing on the terrace where there were a few guests still enjoying the fruits of Carlotta's culinary expertise and Vincenzo's generous servings of Chianti.

'Hey, Izzie, Luca! Where've you been?' cried Carlotta, rushing forward to greet them with kisses and cheeks squeezes. 'I've been worried about you, Izzie. Meghan said you'd left for home already.'

'Just went for a spin on the Vespa, that's all,' said Izzie, knowing her smile hadn't fooled Carlotta in the slightest. She expected a grilling later.

'And Luca?'

'Oh, I bumped into Izzie on my way over to San Vivaldo to check up on the restaurant. Everything's cool, Carlotta. Hey, isn't that Vincenzo calling you?'

All three of them turned to see Vincenzo waving vigorously with his left hand, a smile lighting up his handsome face. The music had bumped up a notch, and now that the meal was officially over, the bridal couple had taken to the floor to start the dancing.

'I expect to see you two on the dance floor, too!' laughed Carlotta, waving her finger at Luca and Izzie before accepting Vincenzo's arm and joining him for a surprisingly accomplished waltz around the courtyard to the delight of the audience.

'They make a handsome couple, don't you think?' mused Luca, resting his hand casually on Izzie's shoulder, a gesture that sent ripples of pleasure through her veins.

'Perhaps someone else should grasp the matchmaker's baton? What do you think? Turn the tables?' suggested Izzie, a glint of mischief in her eyes.

'Another accolade to add to your many accomplishments!'

'Hey, what's Meghan doing?'

Unusually, Meghan hadn't spotted their arrival. Her oversight wasn't because they were hidden from view by the vine-covered pergola, but because she only had eyes for Gianni who was standing on the edge of the makeshift dance floor watching Carlotta and Vincenzo dance.

'I'm not sure…'

As Izzie and Luca watched on, Meghan grinned at Gianni, but he shook his head fervently, reaching across to grasp her arm, but she wriggled from his clutch, and continued her path towards her brother, her long hair flying behind her like an earth-bound mermaid as she whispered in his ear. Brad looked over Meghan's shoulder to where Gianni stood, his face flooded with colour, but Gianni gave an imperceptible nod and Brad strode off to speak to the band. Beaming, Meghan skipped back to usher Gianni towards the steps of the terrace where he was handed a microphone and stood trembling like a puppy on his first visit to Crufts.

'Oh my God, Meghan's persuaded him to sing!' gasped Izzie, delight sweeping through her like a warm summer shower.

When Gianni launched into an accomplished rendition of *Maria, Mari*, his voice as smooth as liquid caramel, Izzie could see that Luca was choked with emotion. All that singing to his vines had given Gianni all the practice he needed to hone his considerable talent and Izzie had to fight to hang on to her own tears. He had a deep, mellow voice perfect for an outdoor performance, and he certainly looked the part. With his dark suit and white shirt open at the neck to reveal a smattering of chest hair, he could easily have graced the stage of La Scala – and would be the most handsome tenor in the ensemble!

As soon as the final elongated note faded into the late afternoon air, rapturous applause broke out from an appreciative, if somewhat biased audience. Luca dashed forwards to hug his best friend, then stepped back to allow Gianni to enjoy the onslaught of congratulations. Izzie's heart ballooned when she saw how his eyes shined with pleasure.

'Hey, Izzie! Thank goodness Luca found you!' said Meghan, joining them on the terrace steps. 'Have you ironed out the misunderstanding?'

'We have!' beamed Izzie.

'Well, you can also rest assured that I've given Brad a piece of my mind. He's under no illusion that he owes you big time for everything you've done to pull this off – but I have to say I don't hold out much hope of him changing his modus operandi anytime soon! I love and loathe my amazingly talented brother in equal measure at the moment. I'm highly offended that he couldn't trust his own sister not to divulge the details of Stefano and Louisa's wedding location! As if I would go around blabbing about one of Italy's most famous film stars getting married at Villa Limoncello! What does he take me for?'

Meghan's sulk was comical, but it was also misplaced, and Izzie laughed. 'Meghan, I love you. You are the best friend a girl could wish for, but you have to admit that you are the biggest gossip this side of the Mediterranean.'

Meghan placed her hands on her hips, preparing to make her argument to the contrary when she giggled instead.

'I am, aren't I? Oh, well, if you can forgive him, then I suppose I can. You *have* forgiven Brad, haven't you, Izzie?'

'Of course. Luca has explained what happened about the confidentiality clause, about him being a last-minute stand-in, everything.'

'Everything?' asked Meghan, her eyebrows raised in the direction of Luca.

'Yes…'

Izzie glanced at Luca and her heart sank when she saw his reluctance to meet her eyes. Oh, God, what now?

'Right,' said Meghan, giving Luca a meaningful look. 'There's a future opera star waiting for me over there. *Ciao*, darlings!'

Playing for time, Izzie watched Meghan wriggled her way through the crowd until she reached Gianni, slid her arm through his and guided him away from the courtyard towards the gazebo where she knew they would find some privacy and she could congratulate him in her own imitable way.

'Luca? What did Meghan mean, have you told me everything?'

'Ah, Izzie, I'm glad I've caught up with you at last,' said Brad, appearing from behind the pergola with a bottle of Chianti in one hand and two glasses in the other. 'I believe an apology is in order, as well as a massive dose of gratitude. To be honest, I thought you knew about the wedding. I admit I didn't confide in Meghan because she's the least discreet person I know, but I thought Lucy or Rachel would have filled you in when they spoke to you about the brief. I had no idea you were under the impression that this wasn't the real deal. I'm sorry.'

'Brad, it's okay, really.'

'Well, if it's any consolation, what you've pulled off here is a triumph. The villa looks amazing, better than I dared to dream when I was searching for the right venue to hold Stefano and Louisa's wedding. You really do have a flair for dressing a set, Izzie, but then, if I'd taken the time to stop and think about it, I should have known that. I've seen your work before you... well, when you had your own interior design business. Is it true what Meghan said? Has that moron Darren Hambleton dispensed with your services?'

'Well, no, actually, his father...'

'If you're interested, I might have a job for you in the production company. I've been left in no doubt by my sister that she does not intend to drop everything to come to my aid again, and the next shoot is in July down in Sorrento. Are you free?'

Izzie stared at Brad. It was the last thing she had expected him to say and her brain felt scrambled.

'That would be... that would be...'

She struggled to find the right word. Not because the thought didn't excite her, it did, but because she had no idea what she wanted to do next and needed time to think things through. She glanced across to Luca, who had been listening intently to Brad's proposition, hoping for inspiration.

'Ah, sorry, Luca.' Brad slapped Luca on the back as though they were old friends, and Izzie stared at the two men in confusion. 'Were you thinking of offering Izzie something here at the villa? Wouldn't blame you!'

'Offering me something at the villa?'

Brad's jaw dropped, and his face flooded with contrition at his faux pas.

'So, if you'll excuse me, I need to get this show wrapped up or the wine bill will blow the budget. *Ciao!*'

She watched Brad stride towards Vincenzo, just to give her a few moments to gather her thoughts before turning to meet Luca's eyes, seeing immediately his discomfort.

'Luca? What did Brad mean?'

'Actually, I was about to tell you…'

'Tell me what?'

Oh, God, not another secret. She didn't think her heart could cope!

Chapter Twenty Five

The Wishing Well, Villa Limoncello
Colour: Sunshine Yellow

'Luca?'

'Come on.'

He reached for her hand and instead of leading her towards the courtyard that was filled with increasingly loud merriment and chatter, clinking glasses and the scraping of chairs, Luca led her towards the garden, coming to a standstill next to the wishing well. To her surprise, he delved into his pocket, produced a silver coin and handed it to her.

'Want to make a wish?'

'Erm, yes, sure.'

Confusion swirled, but she gave him a smile, took the coin and without a moment of hesitation she tossed it down the well into oblivion.

'Did your wish have anything to do with *Villa dei Limoni*?'

'I can't tell you that – there's a superstition in the UK that if you tell someone what you wish for, the wish won't come true.'

Not that it mattered, thought Izzie. It was unlikely she would get the chance to come back to the villa again, even for a holiday. She laughed, hoping to lighten the mood, but Luca had started to shuffle from one foot to the other, clearly uncomfortable, his thoughts far away from the villa's gardens.

'Luca, if there's something you want to say, then just say it.'

'I'm sorry, Izzie. I haven't been entirely honest with you.'

Her stomach gave a good impression of following the coin down the well before bouncing back to lodge somewhere in her chest like a poker-hot ember.

'What do you mean?'

But whatever it was she wished he would just get it over with. All the tension that had been mounting since they pulled onto the driveway was making her feel nauseous.

'It's about Villa Limoncello.'

Again, Luca paused, struggling to formulate his words.

'What about it?'

'Oh, and the Vespa.'

'The pink Vespa?'

'Yes.'

'The one I was riding when you ran me off the road?' Izzie grinned, hoping to lighten the mood.

'I'm sorry, Izzie. I do actually have a very good explanation for that.'

'Apart from your pretensions of becoming a Formula One driver?'

'Yes. And I wasn't driving too fast. I'd had a huge shock.'

'What kind of shock?'

'I had just seen someone riding a pink Vespa. My pink Vespa. I know I ran you off the road, but I also very nearly wrote off the Spider.'

'*Your* pink Vespa?'

What was going on? Since when did the Italian driver of a scarlet Alfa Romeo cabriolet invest in a pink Vespa? For those weekends when he visited his pet unicorn? And she'd stumbled on the Vespa in the outhouse at Villa Limoncello – that veritable menagerie of random objects. If it belonged to Luca, what was it doing there?

'Yes. I'd bought it for Sabrina. I was going to present it to her before she dropped the bombshell and ran off with Claudio. I nearly had a coronary when I saw you riding it towards San Vivaldo that morning. For a moment I thought it was Sabrina, or maybe a ghost, or perhaps I'd just been working too many hours in the restaurant and was hallucinating! I had to have a couple of stiff brandies when I arrived at the trattoria and I fully intended to go back out to look for you, but, as you'll recall, you came to me.'

'Ah, so that explains the Vespa, but it doesn't explain what Brad was talking about.'

Izzie braced herself for another twist in the saga. What next? She didn't think she could take any more revelations. It was all beginning to feel a little surreal. Could this all be a dream? She surreptitiously gave herself a pinch, relieved to see that she didn't wake up in her bed at home in London but was still standing next to the wishing well in front of the most handsome man she had ever met, even though his eyes were clouded with guilt.

'Ah, yes, about that…'

'What did Brad mean when he said you might be thinking of offering me something at the villa?'

'*Villa dei Limoni* – it's mine. I own it.'

'You own it?'

'Yes.'

Her brain disconnected from its modem and all cogent thought froze in an instant. It was a few seconds before she thought of something to say about this final confession.

'You own Villa Limoncello? But… why? Why didn't you say anything?'

'I bought it eighteen months ago. I told you I wanted to leave the city, that I'd bought a rundown place in the Tuscan countryside that Sabrina refused to even consider living in.

When she ended our relationship, I couldn't bear to live here alone, so I moved into the flat above Antonio's, and, like the villa's previous American owner, I left the house to fade into its current shabby glory. In fact, until Monday when I came to see you to apologise for running you off the road, I'd never been back. It was the hardest thing I have ever done.'

'You stayed away for eighteen months? But why didn't Carlotta or Vincenzo tell me?'

'Very few people know I own it. It was my decision to keep it quiet, otherwise I would have been bombarded with questions, or offers to take it off my hands. Look at Riccardo – so desperate to buy the land that he was prepared to resort to sabotage to persuade the elusive owner to cut their losses and run! Anyway, I just couldn't face dealing with any of it to be honest. The only person who knew the villa was mine, apart from my parents and Sabrina, was Gianni who agreed to take on the role of guardian of the vineyard and the olive groves until I decided what to do with the place. He's done an amazing job and he's going to absolutely freak out when we tell him about what Riccardo has done to his beloved vines.'

'And who can blame him!'

'I'm furious too, but I hope I can persuade him that this outcome is better than what he *had* feared – that the vines had succumbed to some untreatable disease which would have put paid to his ambitions to produce the best wine Tuscany has ever seen. That's if he doesn't get snapped up for a stint at La Scala before then.'

Luca laughed, but he still hadn't met Izzie's eyes and her heart blossomed for this man who had kept such a heart-breaking story to himself for so long. She understood how much loosing Sabrina to one of his friends must have affected him, and how, like her, he'd been struggling to come to terms with his past and to move on.

'So how did you get involved with Brad?'

'It was Stefano who made the first contact. Apparently, Brad wanted him to take the lead role in his next movie, but Stefano had to turn him down because of his wedding plans. So, Brad offered to host, and pay for, the whole wedding if they agreed to bring the date forward by six months to accommodate the filming schedule. Stefano was reluctant, but Louisa didn't have a problem with that as long as they could find somewhere amazing to hold it. As Sabrina's best friend, Louisa knew about the villa and urged Stefano to ask if it was available.'

'Well, it *is* the perfect setting for a wedding...'

'The gardens are, but, as you know, the interior won't be winning any awards! I wasn't keen at first, I just wanted to brush the whole embarrassing saga of 'buying a quaint house in the countryside' under the carpet, but Stefano, and Gianni, persuaded me to go for it and to use the hire fee to start renovating the place. I took some convincing, but they won out in the end – with the proviso that I wouldn't have to have anything to do with it.'

'So you never met Brad?'

'No, everything was dealt with via Lucy who was adamant that the whole thing had to be wrapped up in secrecy, which was easy really as no one had shown any interest in the old place for years. Stefano and Louisa engaged Carlotta, Francesca and Oriana, and liaised with them through Lucy who requested everyone to sign a non-disclosure agreement. I didn't have a problem with that because I had every intention of keeping as far away from all the festivities as possible – until Stefano asked me to be one of his ushers!'

Luca ran his palm over the stubble on his jaw, his eyes focused on a point in the far distance where the rolling hills met the darkening sky.

'If I could have found a way of refusing, then I would have. It was one thing agreeing to the use of the villa for a friend's wedding, quite another to be part of the bridal party when your ex-fiancée is the chief bridesmaid and the wedding venue was the place where you'd hoped to live together! Of course, I couldn't let them down, so I agreed, but I warned Stefano that I didn't want any part of the organisation, especially when Brad dumped the whole thing on Lucy, which I realise is not an unusual occurrence.'

'No, it's not,' smiled Izzie, thinking of all the hard work Lucy had put into preparing for the wedding and not even getting to see the end result. She would most certainly be making sure that she sent a whole swathe of photographs to her when she got back to London.

'You know, I thought I'd got away with it until you burst on the scene.'

'What do you mean?'

'If I hadn't nearly killed you that morning, I would never have rustled up the courage to come over to the villa to apologise. When I brought the furniture across on Monday afternoon, it was the first time I'd set foot in the place since I found out about Sabrina, and it wasn't as bad as I had anticipated – I don't suppose anything is. We build these things up to be huge, terrible challenges requiring every ounce of our willpower simply to take the first step, when actually the obstacles are all in our minds. Once we realise that, we can relegate the trauma to its rightful place – just a moment in our past – and face the future with fresh eyes. Thank you for helping me to realise this, Izzie.'

Izzie stared at Luca, happiness flooding her heart, delighted that she had been able to return the favour. After all, she knew that it was because of him that she intended to pursue her dreams with renewed vigour, not only for Anna, but also for herself.

'I think we should call it evens, don't you?'

'Sounds like a great idea.'

Luca's gaze held hers with such intensity she felt her insides turn to jelly. There was no mistaking the emotions churning through her veins and when he took a step closer, his breath caressing her cheek, she almost lost her train of thought as she meandered through the labyrinth of sexual attraction. Could she really leave Villa Limoncello the next day, never to set eyes on this man again, the man who had dispersed the grey raincloud that had hovered over her head like a comic book character and replaced it with an endless sun-filled landscape?

'So, are you going back to your old job?' Luca whispered softly, gently moving her hair from her forehead, his lips inches from hers as he waited for her to reply.

'No, that much I do know.'

She had come such a long way in the last week that she was not going to risk that progress by returning to her previous sombre existence where she inhabited a dull, drab, magnolia world and lived on an uninspiring diet of coffee and toast. She wanted her world to be filled with every colour of the spectrum, vibrant oranges, vivid blues, zinging yellows, luscious green, but most of all the chocolate brown of the eyes that were holding hers, searching for an answer to the question of what she intended to do now.

'I'm thinking of starting my interior design business up again, but I don't want to rush into anything. I need to spend some time doing some research, to continue to replenish the coffers of creativity after they've been empty for so long. I want to investigate new fabrics, fresh paint effects, stencilling, sculpting techniques, visit a few more art galleries, museums, gardens…'

'And there's no better place to do that than here in Tuscany!' declared Luca, wrapping his arm around her waist and pulling her close, so close that she could see the desire reflected in the depth of his eyes.

'Will you teach me some more of your recipes?' she asked, laughing.

'I'll do more than that.'

'What do you mean?'

'Well, if you really are planning to stay on here at Villa Limoncello, then I have a proposal for you.'

'A proposal?'

Izzie gulped, enjoying the electricity sparkling between them as they planned to spend more time together. A week ago, she would have been shocked if Meghan or Jonti had told her that she would be contemplating a fresh start in a new country with a dark-haired Adonis with a sharp line in Italian pastries, but she had never been more certain of anything in her life. She wanted to stay a little longer at Villa Limoncello, wanted to experience more of its calming aura, but more than anything else she wanted to spend time with Luca, a man who had shown her how to discard the mantle of sadness and confront the world with her face turned towards the sun.

'Well, Brad got there first, but I've been thinking about running courses here – painting courses, yoga courses, creative writing courses, Italian cookery courses – and I need someone with amazing organisational skills to host them and make sure they run smoothly. I don't know anyone more qualified than you, Izzie. What do you say?'

Izzie didn't have to think about it. It was perfect!

'I say yes! Yes, please! I'd love to do that!'

'Fantastic! And I think there's only one way to seal the deal, don't you?'

Izzie grinned but before she could utter another word, Luca's lips were on hers, gently at first, his fingers curling round her neck to guide her closer. Ripples of desire spread from deep within her abdomen, sending sparkles to her finger-tips as she responded to his kiss, relishing the way his muscular arms held her, inhaling the fragrance of his cologne, and finally enjoying the whoosh of vibrant emotions she had once thought she would never experience again.

Tuscany had been even more amazing than she and Anna could have hoped and, as she pulled away from Luca to catch her breath, she glanced upwards, fixed her gaze on a particularly fluffy white cloud, and sent up a missive of gratitude to her sister, whom she knew was watching the epilogue unfold from her celestial perch and nodding her approval.

Villa Limoncello's Limoncello

Limoncello can easily be made at home and is delicious served as an after-dinner *digestivo*, drizzled over ice cream, or added to a home-made panna cotta.

Ingredients

9 unwaxed lemons (organic if possible)
1 litre of grain alcohol (or you can use vodka)
1.5 litres of water
700g of white sugar

Directions

1. Wash, then peel the lemons, making sure you only take the zest and not the white pith underneath which will make your limoncello taste bitter. Put the peel into a large, sterilised jar, pour in the alcohol and seal it. Leave the mixture in a cool, dark place to marinate for 20 days.

2. Bring the water to the boil in a saucepan, add the sugar and simmer until syrupy. Allow to cool completely, then add to the lemony liquid, stirring well. Leave for a further 10 days.

3. Strain into decorative bottles, placing one in the freezer for a couple of hours before use, and storing the others in a cool place for later.

Enjoy responsibly.

Acknowledgements

A huge thank you to my wonderful editor, Laura McCallen, for all her support and guidance.

And a *Grazie Mille* to Trevor and Mariangela Williams for checking the authenticity of my Italian phrases. I owe you both a frothy cappuccino and a generous serving of Luca's lemon & pistachio cannoli!

Tuscan Dreams

Wedding Bells at Villa Limoncello
Summer Dreams at Villa Limoncello
Christmas Secrets at Villa Limoncello